Coming Back

£5-

Coming Back

Diary of a mission to Afghanistan

Edoardo Albinati

Translated by Howard Curtis

ET REMOTISSIMA PROPE

The royalties of this book will be donated to help provide housing and water to
Afghan refugees returning to their home villages destroyed by years of conflict.

If you wish to make a donation, you can transfer funds directly to UNHCR's bank
account number: 343-140 (UNHCR), Citibank (Switzerland), Zurich, Switzerland.
You can also send a cheque to UNHCR, Public Information Section, CP 2500,
1211 Genève 2 Dépôt, Switzerland. Alternatively, you can make an online donation
from UNHCR's website: www.unhcr.ch

Views expressed in this publication are those of the author and are not necessarily
the opinion of the United Nations High Commissioner for Refugees.

Published by Hesperus Press Ltd
4 Rickett Street, London SW6 1RU
www.hesperuspress.com

Coming Back first published in Italian as *Il ritorno* in 2002
Il ritorno © Arnoldo Mondadori Editore S.p.A., 2002
First published by Hesperus Press Ltd, 2003
English language translation © Howard Curtis, 2003

Designed and typeset by Fraser Muggeridge
Printed in the United Arab Emirates by Oriental Press

ISBN: 1-84391-904-4

Contents

Preface   vii
Abbreviations   xii

Coming Back
April   3
May   71
June   131
July   183

Notes   233

Preface

I spent the period from 7th April to 31st July 2002 in Kabul working as a United Nations Volunteer (UNV) for the United Nations High Commissioner for Refugees (UNHCR). My job title was Community Services Officer.

I had been thinking about working with the UNHCR in Afghanistan since the beginning of 2001. That was well before the events that everybody knows about.

'Why do you want to go to Afghanistan?' From the many contradictory answers that I gave when I was asked this question, I realised that there wasn't only one reason. In the end, I preferred not to answer at all. I would just shrug my shoulders and give a little smile. A vague but strong desire to do something that was not just for myself; a sense of weariness, a lack of interest in European affairs, which I had started to feel were comfortable but smug; a longing for the practical, for simplicity, for physical action; a need to be with people different from myself, as different as possible, and at the same time to put myself to the test (Who am I? What am I good for? How far can I go?); an attraction to regions afflicted with the curse of violence.

Reasons which were not so different from those that had led me in 1994 to work in a prison.

In this respect, I do not think I am all that different from many people who feel dissatisfied with life as it is. I am thinking not of my personal life as much as of the life we all lead in this part of the planet in which freedom from want is more or less a given.

Coming Back makes no claims to explain the current situation in Afghanistan, let alone the even more complex history of the last thirty years. Nor does it make any attempt – even if that were possible – to give a comprehensive picture of the work of the UNHCR and other aid organisations in Afghanistan during the repatriation. It is only a diary, the diary of someone doing demanding work in the middle of a major emergency, and trying to record the events happening in front of his eyes.

Yes, it was work. The position of a simple observer is a privileged one, but it has its dangers. I was genuinely not interested in going to Afghanistan to 'do a reportage'. There are journalists and writers who have performed this task very well, and indeed their books were useful in preparing me a little before I went. Only a little, mind you, because I wanted to arrive in Kabul without preconceptions. What I was looking for was commitment: human, profound, total, and far-reaching. I can honestly say that I found it.

My diary records fragments of what happened in Afghanistan: the stories of individuals, purely personal observations, the small amount of news I was able to gather as I went about my daily business.

I know there are aid workers who are more serious, more efficient and more determined than I was. I know it because I have met them (and I must say, with a sense of team pride, that many of them work for the UNHCR). I offer them my apologies if they have difficulty identifying with the questionable character – whining, childish, hotheaded – who is designated in these pages by the pronoun 'I', and I think they are perfectly within their rights not to recognise themselves in his desires and his weaknesses. The only reason I recount certain surreal bits of 'private life' is that I was amused by these attempts to recreate a normal existence while imprisoned by security regulations, curfews and the misery which was our daily bread. I would liken these attempts to taking a shower and never getting clean.

What was my assignment in Afghanistan? In my work as a Community Services Officer I was mainly concerned with three things:
  – repatriation and related social problems in the city of Kabul;

– setting up an aid programme for the so-called Extremely Vulnerable Individuals (EVIs), in other words the weakest categories among the refugees: widows, orphans, families with chronically ill members;

– conducting a survey into the plight of the Kuchis, the nomads who have lost their grazing land and flocks through drought, and are now camped in inhospitable areas.

To carry out these tasks, my experience of working in an Italian prison, the most significant precedent in my CV, gave me a solid base and provided me with a viable working method. Nine years in Rebibbia had taught me to be cautious, to judge people not by their words but by their actions, and to try and stay calm in the most appalling situations. Apart from specific professional skills, my mission to Afghanistan convinced me that what aid workers need above all to help them confront the most difficult situations are such ordinary talents (or what we consider ordinary talents) as common sense and patience.

But there are aid workers who have something else: an inner light – I can't really describe it – a kind of radiance...

The source of this light is probably the determination never to give up, and it goes hand in hand with the most clear-sighted, the most merciless realism. Yet it is able to see beyond the limitations. As for what it sees, I cannot say. But I do admire that light.

In the course of my work I had to familiarise myself with the structures of the UNHCR and with the division of roles within it. I will limit myself here to summarising those functions with which I came into contact and which appear in the book. The section called 'Protection', for instance, is concerned, broadly speaking, with human rights, legal assistance, defence of minorities, etc. The 'Programme Officers' are responsible for contracts with partners for the supply of services, materials and machinery, and the realisation of projects. 'Reintegration' deals with ensuring the basic necessities of life, above all housing, water and sanitation, and 'Repatriation' with the organisation of the reception centres, the registration of refugees, transport, food distribution, and so on. Many of the specific details of repatriation, especially in small towns and remote areas, are handled by 'Field Officers'. There are also, of course, experts in information and logistics, telecom engineers, and administrators. And then there are the leaders, who perform the political and institutional work about which little or nothing is said in this book, but on which so much depends: the major decisions that are taken, the agreements with governments and between states, and ultimately the destinies of tens or hundreds of thousands of refugees.

Last but not least, there are the drivers, with whom I fraternised a lot while I was in Afghanistan.

I hope the reader will not be too irritated by how disordered my notes may appear, especially those made in the first few weeks. My impressions after arriving in Kabul were too vivid to be set down in a calm and collected manner. I was confused and anxious to understand, but I had no time to stop. There are many pages in this book I should have tidied up later, for the sake of consistency: I have left them as they are, dictated by the breathless urgency of the situation.

(One could compare it to playing a match and having to give a running commentary on it at the same time.)

Rereading the text, I became aware of a curious paradox, which is that sometimes the most important or dramatic events are narrated only in passing, because of the immediate need to deal with them, whereas less lurid episodes are recounted at greater length, precisely because I had time to do so: a spare moment here, an unexpected slack period there. Even in such cases I have refrained from making changes in the cold light of day and have avoided literary devices. The spirit blows where it will, as the Gospel says. And there is more than one kind of battle, including the one you wage with a dripping tap that keeps you awake all night…

Sometimes, thinking about little things helps us not to be overwhelmed by the big things: things that are so big they cannot be described. The conditions in which very large numbers of the Afghan people live are such that I feel ashamed at the idea of being able to render them adequately through words.

A final technical point. Ninety percent of aid work is conducted in English: a bastardised, standardised English, full of abbreviations and numbers, contaminated and at the same time enriched by the various nationalities. Reports are written in English, as are work notes. Conversations with Afghans, and most of the speech reported in this book, are passed through the simplifying filter of English.

I have tried to be as simple and direct as I could. It may not have been part of my job, but once I returned home it became inevitable that I would write *Coming Back*. Doing so prolonged my Afghan mission by another two months. It was my final contribution to the aid effort, a contribution in words alone, but one which I hope gives the reader at least a glimmer of what I witnessed and spurs him or her to take action, each in his or her own way.

– 11th October 2002

P.S. The first reader of *Coming Back* was also the person I hurt most in writing it. I'm sorry, darling.

The second reader pointed out that this is a book about children, the real protagonists are the children of Afghanistan. It's true, and I hadn't even realised it.

Abbreviations

ACF	Action Contre la Faim
ASCHIANA	Afghan Street Working Children and New Approach
CIC	Children in Crisis
DACAAR	Danish Committee for Aid to Afghan Refugees
EU	European Union
GTZ	Deutsche Gesellschaft für Technische Zusammenarbeit
HRW	Human Rights Watch
ICMC	International Catholic Migration Commission
ICRC	International Committee of the Red Cross
IOM	International Organisation for Migration
ISAF	International Security Assistance Force
MSF	Médecins Sans Frontières
NGO	Non-Governmental Organisation
OMAR	Organisation for Mine Clearance and Afghan Rehabilitation
TDH	Terre Des Hommes
UN	United Nations
UNHCR	United Nations High Commissioner for Refugees
UNICEF	United Nations International Children's Emergency Fund
WFP	World Food Programme

Coming Back

APRIL

The briefing I was given in Pakistan was very perfunctory. But I'd asked for it: I wanted to get to Kabul as soon as possible.With the words 'God forbid!' a stressed Finnish lady ran through a list of all the disasters that could possibly happen to me during my mission, and ended by suggesting I learn as quickly as possible three sentences in the local language (there are basically two in Afghanistan, Dari – that is, Persian – and Pashto).

'Get them translated and learn them by heart. Don't think they're foolish or pointless.'

The three emergency sentences, in the order in which I'm supposed to use them, are:

I AM A GOOD MAN
I WORK FOR THE UN
PLEASE DO NOT KILL ME

Streets of Kabul
There are usually four or five policemen at every crossroads, but the traffic meanders all over the place and everyone cuts straight across without circling the roundabout.

Children of two or three cross the street on their own between lorries hurtling along at high speed. Some make as if to throw themselves under the wheels, and the lorry drivers swerve just enough to avoid crushing them.

The vibrating, syncopated sound of the motor horns make a particularly irritating noise. The city swarms with Toyota pick-ups, which formed the motorised division of the Taliban army. Groups of men with rifles over their shoulders travel in the open part, holding on to the sides: they all look at you at the same time, a dozen eyes trained on you.

Every now and again, about once every half hour, you hear an explosion that seems quite distant and yet quite near: it's the mine clearance people cleaning up the area around the airport.

The general curfew in Kabul starts at 10:00 p.m., but for UN personnel it starts an hour earlier. To reach the house where I've been assigned a room, I have to walk two or three hundred metres. The houses are marked with letters. Mine is the last one, G. I ask someone to go with me because I'm not sure I can find it at night. A woman offers – strange that a woman should want to go out and walk in the dark, especially as she'll have to walk back by herself. There's a strong wind, but it isn't cold. The sky is full of stars, but I'm too tired to notice, she's the one who points it out. 'That's Orion,' she says. It takes us a few minutes to get to guest house G. There, I find an Italian carabiniere who's cooking pasta with bolognese sauce. What's he doing here? He's the friend of a girl who works in logistics. She's wearing a black T-shirt, tight over her breasts, and the words on it bounce so much I can't read them. Gennaro has been at the Italian embassy in Kabul since last December, and can't stand it any more. But then he says, 'It's a great experience, I've learned a lot of things,' as he tips the spaghetti into a colander made from a perforated basin. 'Anyway, I chose to come here, so I can't complain.'

Noisy American journalists at Kabul airport, trying to recover their baggage. With their boots, their trousers and jackets covered with pockets and zips, their loud chatter, their laughter, their forearms covered with blond hair, and the way they're either swaddled in quilted jackets or stripped down to T-shirts, irrespective of the actual temperature, they're like parodies of American war correspondents. The baggage carousel is half-destroyed and isn't moving. Four or five Dersu Uzalas in overalls emerge from the opening the bags normally come out of. Squatting on the carousel, they hand the bags to the travellers more rapidly than if the carousel was working.

There are 870 lorries full of returnees waiting at Torkham, on the border between Pakistan and Afghanistan. The border has been closed after the attempted assassination of the minister Mohammad Fahim. The poppy growers are blocking the road in protest against the eradication programme announced by the government.

A night full of dark thoughts. Wake up at four, the sound of crowing cocks and the muezzin in my ears, despite the wax earplugs.

Wearing earplugs is against security regulations. You're supposed to keep the radio on at all times, even at night. But even when the radio's off, it gives me nightmares. (During my first month in Kabul, I wake up five or six times every night.) The flashing light of the battery being recharged makes me think I have urgent messages, quick, get up, you have to answer, I jump up with a jolt, grab the radio, switch it on and turn the knob, running through the channels: 3, 2, 4, 5, 9. Of course there's no message. At this hour the whole country is asleep. The dust raised by the wind has settled. Snow falls on the mountains in the darkness. I turn off the radio, put it back on recharge, and go back to bed. I throw a sweater over it so as not to see the flashing.

The first stories I hear are about animals. The one-eyed lion in Kabul Zoo, one eye taken out by a piece of shrapnel. The eagle thick with oil from the Persian gulf: an Austrian boy scrubbed the feathers one by one with solvent, until the eagle was completely clean, but it felt cold, because in rubbing away the oil he'd also taken away the natural film that protects the plumage, it was huddled and shivering, left to its own resources, they thought it was going to die, instead of which it got proudly to its feet in the middle of the night and the next morning it was gone: it had flown away.

I gave one of the drivers two ten-dollar bills to change, and he brings me back a pack of 640,000 afghans in bills of 10,000. I do some calculations in euros and old lire.

Wednesday. Things are already getting better, much better. Very strong light, blinding. They've given me a desk. I have a look around the office of a colleague who's on R&R, Rest and Recuperation. All UN personnel have to take a vacation every eight weeks and leave the country for five days. To rest and recuperate. Many go to Islamabad or Thailand, shut themselves in a hotel, and do nothing but eat and sleep. On the office wall, photographs of children with nicely combed fair hair, in the garden of a beautiful house, and a blonde woman with a neat hairdo, the photo of the woman is actually a slightly crumpled black-and-white photocopy, which distances the image even more, as if it were thousands of kilometres, tens of thousands of kilometres away, as if the man whose office this is were an astronaut who's left for Jupiter on a mission that will last decades... maybe he's been frozen, and is sleeping packed in ice.

I'm given a taste of the typical situations the job entails, starting with the centre at Pul-i-Charkhi, about ten kilometres outside Kabul, where returning refugees arrive. It's an encashment centre as well as a centre for distributing aid. The refugees receive money, mainly to cover the travel expenses they incurred getting here from Pakistan. Those who are stopping in Kabul also receive aid in the form of grain and utensils, while those who are heading for other parts of Afghanistan will get them further on in their journey. The centre consists of two enclosed areas plus two huge parking lots: the lorries and buses stop there first to be inspected by various teams of checkers, who have the task of establishing if the documents are in order and actually correspond to the families who've arrived at Pul-i-Charkhi. There are always a few without documents, and they start crying and begging us to help them, too. Many are ill after the journey, many are dehydrated, and the children's faces, which are often very beautiful, are disfigured by leishmaniasis scabs.

Those whose papers are in order are admitted to the

encashment centre enclosure. The sick stop off at the *Médecins Sans Frontières* clinic, the others hurry to the big tent to receive a briefing about mines by experts from an Afghan organisation called OMAR.

There's a table covered with coloured shapes which look like cakes at a children's party.

At this point the groups divide, to be reunited at the exit: the heads of families enter a hall where they're given their money, the children, accompanied by their mothers or their elder brothers or sisters, receive vaccinations in smaller tents. The people are guided along the route by young Afghan men shouting instructions through megaphones.

The distribution centre run by GTZ is two hundred metres away. The heads of families hand in their forms at the entrance, and the staff transport the sacks of grain and the utensils on wheelbarrows to the lorries, which have moved in the meantime from the first to the second parking lot. Once the stuff is loaded, the refugees are ready to resume their journey. If there's not too much of a crowd, the whole procedure takes an hour. For this first tour of the centre, I'm accompanied by an Afghan engineer, who explains to me how the centre works and the kind of problems that occur.

Example
The Afghan engineer doesn't like the fact that some refugees start selling the sacks of grain as soon as they're distributed. It isn't right to put the aid straight onto the market. Of course, the refugees are free to do whatever they like with the grain and the blankets and the utensils, but they could at least wait until they get out of the camp. Some need ready cash and the grain is of no use to them, the sacks are heavy and take up space. Often, this turns out to be a serious mistake: in a few weeks they'll need the grain to make bread and they'll have to buy it back at two or three times the price they're selling it for today, which means they'll have to buy the same grain again or the flour ground from that grain or

the bread made with the flour of the grain they're selling today…

It isn't a pleasant thing to see this instant market. From the warehouse to the wheelbarrow and then directly into the hands of the merchants. The grain is supposed to be enough for a family's needs for a period of one or two months. The people who buy it from the cash-strapped refugees do a roaring trade.

There are many complaints. The Afghan engineer is incredibly calm and kind, he listens to everyone's tales of woe, caresses the backs of their necks while they scream and wave their hands, takes hold of the tips of their beards and tries as calmly as he can to convince them, repeating his words slowly and gently. The incredible thing is that in 99% of cases he succeeds, I don't know what he says to them but in the end the petitioners resign themselves, cheer up, and even smile, they come and shake my hand gratefully despite the fact that the engineer has refused point-blank… When they get angry, the engineer places his finger tip on their heart, and all at once they calm down, even those with grim faces and fiery eyes.

While they speak, the men hold each other's hands. They hold hands when greeting each other and in conversation, and they also walk hand in hand.

A man arrives. On his form it says there are five people in his family, but only four are here. Who's missing? Let's see… a girl. His daughter. Why? Where is she? 'She stayed in the lorry, she's ill.' 'Very ill?' 'What's the matter with her?' 'So ill she can't get off the lorry?' They go and look for her. They find her and bring her here. The money can only be distributed if the family registered in Pakistan for repatriation is all present and correct. In fact, she isn't ill at all. Quite simply, she didn't have shoes, and was ashamed to be seen walking barefoot.

A man whose three-month-old child died last night in the lorry coming from Peshawar.

A girl in a black veil comes up to me. How do I know she's a girl? From her voice. She's dragging along with her a woman whose face is uncovered – her mother, a widow – who's probably younger than my wife but seems like an old woman, in fact she is an old woman. The girl tells me in clear English sentences, punctuated by sobs, that she's a medical student from Mazar-i-Sharif who had to suspend her studies when the Taliban came to power and flee to Pakistan, now she'd like to resume them and graduate because she has only a few exams left to take, but she has no one to help her except her mother, who's more of a burden than a support, and she has no money to get to Mazar, what we've given her (forty dollars for the two of them) won't even be enough to pay for the transport as far as here, she has nowhere to stay in Kabul, and doesn't know where to go. The old woman nods but seems absent. She looks towards the snow-covered mountains in the distance.

The girl insists she's studied and is almost a doctor. Because I can't see her face, I have the feeling I'm talking to nobody. But a nobody who's desperate. While she's begging, a dark patch appears on her veil at eye-level, it's wet with her tears. The patch gets bigger. By the end the veil is completely soaked.

More tears, from the children coming out of the tents where they've been vaccinated. They hold their little arms and scream, drag their bare feet, lose their sandals. What distresses them more than the pain is the sense of betrayal: they've been taken inside, seized, held still, and jabbed before they knew what was happening. It's hard to describe just how dirty some of them are.

Medical problems: diarrhoea, respiratory difficulties.

Two earthquakes during the night, one at midnight, the other shortly after, but I was asleep, they told me about them this morning. I did, as it happens, dream about an earthquake, or rather a seaquake. I was on the shore in a place somewhere like Nice, where the town is directly adjacent to the beach.

After the tremor, a huge wave formed on the horizon, came towards us and swept us away, it was like one of those disaster movies in which the Earth is struck by an asteroid, but this wave was more revolting than anything else, it reduced everything to a whirling mush, like a toilet being flushed, and scattered us in the most distressing way: that was the real anguish of it, the way everything was mixed together and engulfed in that filthy tide.

Clash of Civilisations

Last night's earthquake destroyed the urinals at Pul-i-Charkhi.

A slack afternoon. A big rush until one o'clock, then no more new arrivals. Some of the Afghan staff play volleyball, and they're really good. They bump the ball, lift it and make a textbook spike. Others kneel on the carpets and pray.

In the big tent where we give money to families, they've brought out the chessboards.

I use the time to go over my Dari lesson, which is scribbled on a sheet of paper:

Khoshamadi = Welcome
Chi tor asdi = How are you?
Khop (or khub) = Well
Drostast = OK
Bass! = Stop!
Khana = House
Khaima = Tent

There aren't any cars available, so my combative English female colleague suggests we go out in the street and get a taxi.

It's evening. Actually, it's already night.

We take up position on the edge of the pavement, ready to signal our presence.

Heavy traffic.

The lights of the cars emerge from a curtain of dust.

Blurred yellow circles.

Dozens of cars stream past and vanish into the haze.

The dust of Kabul is thick and heavy like fog, we're immersed in it, impossible to make out the shape of a taxi, the cars are dark shadows.

I don't know where my colleague has got to, I call her name anxiously, then I see her silhouette outlined against the lights of passing cars.

Streets and other places in Kabul are named after something that's located in them. The mountain with the TV mast is called TV Mountain. 'But what did they call it before they put up the TV mast? Or before they invented TV?' Nobody knows. 'No idea! It's always been called TV Mountain.' In a street that cuts through areas which are nothing but ruins, there's a huge Soviet-era silo torn apart by rockets and cannon fire. The name of the street is Silo Road.

Training ship

Morning at the ex-Soviet Compound. As the name indicates, it's a Soviet-style estate, enclosed like a factory. Twenty-four apartment blocks of which only the brickwork is left. 2,500 displaced families lived there, most of them from the Shomali Plains, a plateau north of Kabul. They're the wretched of the earth. A programme was started a month ago to help them return to their places of origin. There are still thousands of people in the Compound. A big convoy of 220 families is leaving today, heading for the villages of Shomali. Before going, they've torn everything out: doors complete with the frames, windows, railings, pipes, lead and electric cables. They've even pulled out single bricks. A few squares of a dark substance indicate the place where the toilets were until a few days ago, before they were dismantled piece by piece. Fresh layers over solidified layers. At least the stench stops us from falling in, but it's difficult to keep a sense of direction in the middle of this crowd.

Jette moves about constantly, she never stays still in one spot for more than a minute, changes direction unpredictably, says what she has to say then breaks through the crowd and zooms off to another block. The families have gathered their meagre household belongings, plus the fixtures and fittings they've managed to pull loose from the apartments, and now they're waiting to load them onto the lorries. Women in burqas crowd around Jette, waving crumpled pieces of paper. Their names don't appear on the lists drawn up the day before. They don't live here, they're from Kabul, and slipped into the Soviet Compound this morning while it was still dark in order to receive aid. J. takes these home-made papers and throws them theatrically into the air to make it clear that there's no point in cheating, they won't get anything. Instead of getting angry, everyone laughs, and for a moment the pressure eases. J. takes advantage of the moment to move off again. I'm afraid, and tag along behind her. Whenever I lose her after one of her sudden sideways leaps and find myself surrounded by the crowd, I feel a certain anxiety and a chill goes through me. This crowd really scare me. When one of the beggars becomes more threatening, raising his hands and shouting, Jette reacts by shouting back at him angrily: 'If you think we're going to carry you as well, you're an idiot! Because if we carry you there'll only be one litre of water per family today instead of two! And your children will be thirsty! You have to wait for the next convoy!' Indeed, water is rationed. Jahid translates, and the people calm down for a moment. Jette sets off for the next block, and again I tag along. 'They may not understand what I'm saying, but at least they understand my tone!' She walks on, head down like a rugby player, sidestepping pools of mud, jumping over holes and carpets of excrement.

Veiled women and children look down from the railless balconies. Almost all bear signs of disease: red pustules on their faces, if they don't have them it means they've already had them, and what's left are bruise-like scars, the inner part concave and lighter in colour. Jette tackles head-on a couple of young men who are chasing after her. 'Who are you? What do you want? Show me your hands. Show me the cross.' She turns to me and whispers: 'I hate being rough with them.' Then she radios to the girl from the IOM. The girl joins us, radio in hand, talking to the lorry drivers in an agitated tone. English, I guess, with a beautiful schoolgirl's face and a scarf rolled round her beret, which bears her organisation's initials. She's a bit worried, and begs Jette not to go just yet, to stay at least until all the people are on. 'It's worse than usual today.' Her nervousness is evident in her smile. There's a light pink chapping around her lips. Jette doesn't wear anything on her head. She was the one who walked me to my digs along the dark street on my first night in Kabul, and then went back on her own, with her faithful radio.

Jette loves the radio. Everyone knows her call sign, which starts to circulate on Channel 3 from early in the morning. Hotel Alpha 6.4. It's the most famous call sign in Kabul.

Drive up TV Mountain, between ragged young men who greet us in a threatening manner. The Mountain cuts the city in two. 'It was our Berlin Wall,' says Mohammad, the Afghan who's returned from Canada, I don't know if he's serious or joking. This is the only place from which you can see the whole of Kabul. The area to the west and south is an expanse of rubble. In the distance are the remains of the famous Museum, shattered by bombs and looted.

Going through the western districts, which have been reduced almost entirely to ruins, I'm reminded of Ostia Antica.

Visibility
Our staff wear jackets full of pockets, with a big UNHCR logo on the back, and a small square of leather in front bearing the Calvin Klein logo, I suppose it's a donation. As a joke, I tell Sarujeddin he's very fashionable because he's wearing CK,

but he doesn't know who that is. I explain, and instead of one of the other articles produced by the brand, like the famous jeans, I mention the perfume 'Obsession'. Puzzled, Saruj asks me what exactly the word means. Hmm... let's see... obsession... it's when you think about the same thing all the time. What kind of thing? Well, there are different kinds of obsession, but as it's a perfume I think they're probably talking about an amorous obsession. When you can't get it out of your head... when you think only about...

I see Saruj stiffen. He's not smiling any more. His puzzlement has turned to dismay. He's a serious, devout man, and I've forgotten for a moment where I am and who I'm talking to. I stop before getting into a description of Kate Moss rubbing her lips with ice cubes, the husky voice repeating: 'Obsession... obsession...'

Later, Anne and I joke about it, imagining the engineer will turn up tomorrow with a hole in his jacket instead of the CK logo.

$7 \times 20 = 100$

Before I got used to bending, I banged my head badly several times on the door frames. I've also injured myself on the shower head. My skin is covered in scabs. Most Afghans are tall – why is everything so low? Today I bang my head again as I enter the urinal at the distribution centre. I start bleeding, and have to go and be disinfected. There must be some significance in the frequency with which I bang my head.

It was after I banged my head that I started making mistakes in the sums, or rather, started getting them right. I'll explain. The sums (which are very simple) are messed up by the fact that as there's an upper limit of a hundred dollars per family even if the family has more than five members, we have to write on the form: 7 (members) $\times$ 20 (dollars) = 100 (dollars), or $9 \times 20 = 100$, but sometimes our minds wander and we automatically write $140 or $180.

The cashiers have often brought me back the forms to correct and sign again.

When you see the ages on the forms, it really hits you. You have an old man in front of you and on the form it says 46. A little old woman: 51. They take out the forms rolled up like parchment. Sweat has faded the ink and the stamps.

The 100-dollar bills distributed by the cashiers, on the other hand, are often crisp and brand new.

There are passport photos attached to the returnees' documents, showing either single family members or the whole group: those in black and white seem to be printed on thermal paper, after a few days the faces begin to change and fade. By the time they arrive here they're already ghosts.

In Kabul today: 803 repatriated families, 4,775 individuals (2,405 male, 2,370 females, 84,160 dollars distributed).

There are two more tremors, the second while I'm putting on my pyjamas.

The children going to school or coming back from school are a lovely sight – especially the girls, who were forced to stay at home during the time of the Taliban. With their UNICEF bags and satchels, they walk by themselves or in single file along the muddy paths, or are carried on the crossbars of their elder brothers' bicycles.

Saturday 13th April. Morning at Pul-i-Charkhi. The cashiers haven't started work yet but the special cases are already appearing: like the family of a mentally ill man who's torn up the precious forms. They want to give us the fragments in a bag, like the pieces of a jigsaw puzzle.

All right, I tell them, try to solve it. With scotch tape, they manage to stick together just the green sheet, the one they need for getting money.

The old men queuing to receive money look embarrassed. They hand over their forms with both hands, holding themselves at a distance from the table and bowing. They touch their chests and whisper 'salaam', and I can only answer 'mez doum' – 'next table' – where the cashier is waiting with the packet of money.

Today we're asking the women to lift their burqas to check if they correspond to the photos on the forms. A sample survey, just to see what they look like. They readily agree, revealing real faces, the faces of human beings, sometimes the surprised, round, pale face of a thirteen-year-old girl. At that age they are already heads of families. There are many widows with five or six little children. Many are disabled. All without exception in abject conditions.

But the place I prefer, the liveliest, is the vaccinations tents (polio and measles) where the children enter unawares, get their jabs on the production line, and come out screaming: it's a real vale of tears. Many of the herd of burqa-clad women, alerted to what's happening, try to slip away to avoid their children being injected, and we have to wave our arms and shout through the megaphones to bring them back into line.

To the Ministry of Education in the afternoon to negotiate for girls and boys to be taught in mixed classes until fifth grade, that is, until the age of ten. What if they fail before then? Well, let's say they can be together either until fifth grade or until they reach the age of ten, whichever is first. How about that? No, definitely not. Can't be done.

Dull evening. I don't feel like seeing or speaking to anyone. At a pinch, I wouldn't mind chatting a bit with the young Afghan men on the staff at Pul-i-Charkhi, but in the evening the Afghans and the internationals go their separate ways. (Except during field missions, when we have dinner and sleep together, I won't spend a single evening with the Afghans.) I retreat to my room. On the floor below, there's a dinner going on. Every twenty seconds or so, thirty at the most, I hear a burst of cavernous masculine laughter. I put the plugs in my ears.

I've sent an email to Leone, who's seven and a half. I hope he replies. I've heard from B. that he's missing me and cries a lot, he's just as worried as an adult might be, for specific reasons: because there's still a war on here and the situation in Afghanistan is unstable. He watches all the TV news bulletins. There's a rational component to his child's sensibility that makes the emotional response even stronger.

14th April. A really beautiful Sunday. I watch the convoys leave the ex-Soviet Compound for the Shomali Plains, the Windy Plateau.

During the war, Jahid worked for the Red Cross: twice a week fighting was suspended and the ambulances were able to pass along a boulevard (the one we're on now) which constituted the line between the forces of Massud and those of Mazori. The truce would last half an hour. Exactly half an hour? Well... more or less. The ambulances would hurry past with the wounded on board, and it was quite a spectacle, says Jahid, watching Massud's troops on the north side of the boulevard and Mazori's troops on the other take advantage of the truce to reposition themselves. It was like a chessboard where all the pieces change squares in a split second: the men would rush from their positions and find other cover, carrying their heavy machine guns and rocket launchers with them, and at the end of the half hour would immediately start firing at each other again. (This part of the city has in fact been completely destroyed by those troops: it's like being in the middle of an archaeological site.) In spite of the ceasefires, Jahid's ambulance was fired on by the militias several times and was once even hit by a rocket. (He laughs about it now, and slaps his thighs.)

Because of the burqa, identifying the women can be a complicated business, and there's always the possibility of mix-ups. Jahid, who loves things to be regular, claims to have discovered a woman in the Soviet Compound who turns out to have a different name from the one she was registered under yesterday for free transport to her home village. Is it the same woman? Is it a different woman? With the burqa on, who knows? Jahid wants to get a good look at her, so he tells her to lift her burqa, but the crowd around us start to get heated, they close in on us, raising their arms and screaming – I'm not sure how much of a threat they really are, nor am I sure if the woman is really trying to cheat or if it's just a mistake – Jahid turns and throws me a look as if to ask (or suggest) 'Shall we drop it?' I nod and he drops it. He swerves to the side and cuts through the crowd, which opens to let us pass.

It's strange how even this early in my time in Kabul, I should have to make decisions about things that the Afghan staff understand better than I do. It's to do with hierarchy, as well as that element of colonial mentality that runs through all human relationships, even within aid organisations.

But actually the way it works is like this: I ask the Afghan assistant what, according to him, would be the best thing to do, he tells me, and I repeat it to him word for word as if it was my idea. Or else he informs me of a problem, but in a more or less coded way that contains within it the suggestion of a solution.

All poor people are skilled in the art of complaining. Complaining gets results sooner or later. In the ex-Soviet Compound, I come across an old woman I saw the other day at Pul-i-Charkhi, crying and begging to be helped. She'd managed to get a free ride on a lorry from Pakistan, but now she was alone and had no money to continue the journey. She had to get to Qara Bagh, some forty kilometres north of Kabul, and in the end my colleague, feeling sorry for her, gave her money from her own pocket to pay for the coach. We thought we'd solved the problem, and we had her taken to the city, from where she'd be able to take the bus. But now it's two days later and she's still in Kabul complaining, and begging for money. She comes up to me and pulls me by the sleeve, then when she recognises me, and realises that I've recognised her, her expression changes and she vanishes again into the crowd.

Another old man who's been asking to be taken, weeping bitterly and dogging the heels of our group – myself, engineer Jahid, the English girl from the IOM (much more detached and ironic today than she was the other day), plus a young Afghan girl with a resigned face, who I had to grab by the waist at one point and push away, violating all the rules of etiquette, because, walking quickly with her head turned to me, she was going to end up in one of the deep round holes, like uncovered manholes, that riddle the ground in the Soviet compound – anyway, this old man has been galloping after us from one block to another, never letting up for a moment, every time the crowd of petitioners thins out and we stop to catch our breath, he returns to the charge with his pleading. In the end, after consoling him ten times, stroking his beard and then pushing him away, Jahid (with my approval, which I give more out of boredom than anything) makes sure he's taken on.

Destination: Chaharikar, Jabal Saraj, Gulbachar.

The road that goes up to the plateau is flanked by the carcasses of burned and decomposed tanks and military vehicles. Men squat beneath them, sheltering from the rain. Others lean out from the side of the road as if to grab vehicles as they rush past. It isn't clear what they're after. Do they want to touch the cars? Are they trying to tell us something? To greet us? To ask for information? It's hard to know. Hands reach out to the passing cars, hands of children and adults. In fact, they're beggars and they're waving their arms to get flying handouts.

A few drivers slow down a little and throw them banknotes, and they run and pick them up wherever they've landed.

There are stones on the side of the road, painted half white half red: the red side indicates a minefield.

In the vineyards, famous for dozens of different kinds of grapes, the vines have been reduced to contorted stumps.

We're in the jeep, a few minutes ahead of the rest of the convoy. We stop in an open space between demolished houses to distribute the plastic sheets, two for each family. Better to do it in open country than in Kabul, there are fewer opportunities for cheating, and no crowd around to insist on having one. (These are the kinds of details you learn after the first few logistical fiascos – and I'm still learning.) We distribute them directly to the buses as they arrive and park in the muddy space, we count the families on board, making them show their tickets for the umpteenth time, we unwrap the sheets, two… four… six… eight… and then they're loaded inside the bus.

It's raining, but not heavily. I use the Swiss knife. It's fun. Slicing with the thick blade through the scotch tape on the sides of the wrapping, cutting the yellow tape which holds the sheets together in packs of ten.

Do it this way! Come on, we're in a hurry! Tell the bus to reverse. The Afghans are really surprised that I want to do the work myself – unloading the bales in the muddy square, opening them and counting the numbers of the sheets to be assigned to each lorry, getting wet and muddy – they can't understand the perverse pleasure I feel in being here. They're even more surprised when I tell the swarm of little boys who've appeared from out of nowhere that if they want to keep the plastic wrapping (almost as valuable as the contents) they first have to collect for me all the pieces of yellow tape that have been left lying around, which makes the onlookers dissolve into laughter. Maybe they're right to think that in a plain infested with mines and bombs, a few scraps of plastic are nothing to worry about, but maybe I'm right not to leave this mess of yellow tape lying around, 'Otherwise,' I tell them, 'your goats will nibble on it, and in a year you'll be eating plastic kebabs.' (Ecological propaganda: the image works every time.)

Taking the displaced families to their houses, we drive through villages that are little more than mud tracks. Very small girls coming back from school skip beside the tracks, with their satchels on their backs or over their arms. Some families have found their houses more or less as they'd left them, apart from the usual signs of neglect, the broken windows, the weeds that have taken possession of the yards and the roofs. Others, though, are nothing but heaps of mud.

Gulbachar, at the entrance to the valley of the Panshir: a row of shops. A human torso leans out of a room, a young man without arms or legs, probably no more than eighteen, with a sparse goatee on his smiling face. He drags himself out to get a bit of rain.

The carcasses of tanks litter the sides of the road. Some have been pushed off the road by bulldozers, others have been flung there by explosions that have put them out of commission. I wish I had with me the little illustrated manual of tanks I gave Leone, so that I could identify them. Most of them are Soviet-made T-57s. There's one on the right-hand side of the road, whose turret has flown to the other side.

We pass a textile factory built by the Germans, surrounded by model houses for workers, like a Utopian village. Abandoned and destroyed. All the factories in Afghanistan have been destroyed.

We eat kebabs on a little terrace overlooking the fast-flowing river, then when the fog condenses into rain we go back to the inn and lie down on the carpets to finish the kebabs.

As we've been on the trot for about ten hours, Jahid asks me if he can buy a fish to take to his seven children for dinner, but he can't find a fresh one.

In Chaharikar we visit six or seven shops, which look very beautiful, trying to find a particular kind of raisin that ripens in the shade, not in the sun, which gives it a special yellow-green colour. But although Jahid examines at least twenty varieties of grape, none of them satisfy him. He wants a very specific, even paler type. These markets are revolting (I think of the mutton we ate at lunch, and how long it must have been hanging there, collecting dust and flies) but fascinating, too, and full of beautiful things: the vegetables, the harsh colours of the spices, the grains spilling from the sacks like precious coins. After paying for my lunch (*he* pays, though I get ten times his salary!) Jahid also wants to buy me a huge, sticky bag of roasted peanuts.

At six in the morning I go down to the street, greet the guards in the sentry boxes, who are boiling water for tea and listening to the radio, I walk with my rucksack on my back, and suddenly I hear the shuffling of shoes behind me, a very beautiful beggar girl is following me, God knows where she sprang from. All the street children ask for money. The boys have crates for polishing shoes, with a brush and a can of almost dry polish inside. If you don't want to have your shoes shined, they ask you for money. If you don't give them money, they at least want a pencil or a pen. They make it clear that they don't have pens for school, so if you don't give them a pen, they won't go to school.

Blue jays walking in the gardens of the Institute for Street Children. The garden is in bloom. The windows of the classrooms are open: you can hear the children repeating a sentence in unison: OUR TEACHER IS HERE TO HELP US. Compared with European countries, the thing that strikes you the most here is the number of children: there are children everywhere, children on lorries, children under lorries, children working, greeting each other, squabbling, throwing themselves in front of cars, children looking after other children, throwing balls of paper or balls of mud.

Someone sums up the lives of the international staff like this: 'Our children hate us, our wives leave us.'

The Albanian girl speaks very good Italian. I ask her how she learned it. 'Oh, same as everybody.' In other words, watching

Italian TV. It was something I discovered last year when I visited Tirana: the only person there who didn't know Italian was someone who'd spent ten years in prison. When I get back to guest house G, the TV is often tuned to an Italian channel showing some crappy programme. Incredible to come all the way to Kabul to see the same old faces. Fortunately, the dish often can't receive the signal.

Z.'s Conscience[1]

Twelve years after I stopped smoking, the craving has returned. It crept up on me gradually, and now it's very strong. I start begging around for a couple of drags, before the cigarette ends up on the ground or crushed in the ashtray. The ashtrays are usually overflowing with cigarette ends, because everyone here in Kabul smokes like mad, the women even more than the men. It's the first visible effect of working in an emergency: everyone chain-smokes. Z. tells me about when she was assigned to Rwanda: the terrible things she saw happening, the relentless work, but she got through it and didn't break down. At the end of every day she'd say: 'Thank God I'm a heavy smoker.'

The most beautiful – but also the most sordid – moment of the day is when we go to the UN bar for a drink at about seven-thirty. There's only whisky – Red Label or Black Label – and orange juice to choose from, and you have to hurry to get a sufficient quantity of alcohol down you before eight-thirty, when it's time to go back. This interlude brings out the best and the worst in people. On Thursday nights the bar is also open to the staff of the NGOs. In my first weeks in Kabul, I try to discover the ideal number of drinks, one or two aren't enough, you polish those off in five minutes, it's almost as if the glass has emptied itself (despite the expedient of adding enough ice and water to the Red Label to fill the glass to the brim). Four or five whiskies, on the other hand, are too much on an empty stomach: it's embarrassing to go to the canteen half-smashed and sit elbow to elbow with people who are perfectly sober and who know where you've been and how many you've drunk, however straight you try and sit, however nonchalantly you handle your knife, however affected and tight-lipped your English, they'll still notice. No, you can't do it. Three. Three glasses is the right number, the perfect number to get rid of the day's rage without ending up completely wrecked.

But you can't really get rid of rage. It just accumulates.

At the UN bar, loud chatter about nothing very much.

Everyone talks and talks. ('We can talk ourselves to death', Roxy Music.)

Then a moment comes when you fall silent and stare into space.

Outside the perimcter wall is Afghanistan.

Curfew at nine. To bed with the hens.

Do the right thing
People busy collecting money. People busy spending money. However elevated our humanitarian spirit, the measure is always money. It's a necessity that shatters illusions and high-flown clichés. The best and noblest aid worker is – indeed, has to be – an accountant who can balance the books. Money badly spent = money thrown away = people dying. The obsession with accurately identifying the people who need help, with observing absolute priorities. Because if you help the wrong people, you're automatically taking money away from the right people. You're robbing the poor to give to the rich. I can already feel this obsession inside me like a throb, and it will stay with me for the rest of my time here, will make me sour and mistrustful and cause me more anxiety than actual poverty, war, death and hunger put together.

Don't throw money away. Use it wisely.

Six in the morning. It's a really beautiful day. Three little birds are perched on a wire. I don't know what they're called in any language. I really wish I were in bed with B. now and our kids would come into the room and jump on top of us. As I walk to the guest house where we have breakfast every morning just after six, the little beggar girl follows me, catches up with me... whenever I hear slippers shuffling behind me, I know it's her.

From the data of the MSF clinic at Pul-i-Charkhi: in a week spent examining the returnees, 183 children with diarrhoea, 253 cases in all.

Nursery rhyme
The sun is god
it's afraid of the clouds
the clouds are afraid of the wind
the wind is afraid of the wall
the wall is afraid of the mouse
the mouse is afraid of the cat
the cat is afraid of my wife
therefore the sun is afraid of my wife.
(Not Afghan, but Vietnamese)

1,350 families have arrived at Pul-i-Charkhi in a single day. I don't have the number of individuals to hand, but there may be seven thousand or more. The grain flows slowly from the 50-kilo sacks, like liquid. A mountain of sacks in a tent eight metres high and thirty metres long. Every half hour, boys bring tea, which we sip from unwashed cups. At about five the sun goes down and everything around us – the ragged, veined mountain tops, yellow and ochre and grey, the sky drained of its brilliance, the distant mountains of the Hindu Kush, the flags of the international aid organisations and the fluttering rags of the poor (always a little resentful, always a little scared when faced with their current benefactors) – suddenly becomes very beautiful, legendary...

Hi, B., I'm just writing you a few lines before work. The king is supposed to be landing in Kabul today, and there's a lot of excitement. Daily life has settled down, I wake up at five, toss and turn in bed, thinking about you (all of you) then go to one of those centres I've told you a little about, where people arrive and leave. I have to deal with the so-called vulnerable groups, that is, families without adult males able to provide income, very poor families, widows, disabled people, etc. I've spent the last few days looking all over Kabul for an NGO (non-governmental organisation) to assist these particular cases, given that the UNHCR has to think about the mass of repatriated people (who in the jargon are called returnees). The flood of people returning to Afghanistan is enormous: 250,000 in five weeks. I'm also supposed to deal with the emergency in the Shomali Plains, which is a (very beautiful) plateau to the north of Kabul, where there's an enormous amount of devastation caused by the war and the people going back to live there have nothing. These field missions are very interesting. All in all, things aren't too bad even though I'm still beset by anxiety, which comes from three sources: the problems of this country – my work – and the fact that I'm missing you… All the same, I'm muddling through: I get on very well with the Afghan staff and I'm doing fine in my field activities. Private life is non-existent, apart from a little bit of socialising at certain times of the day like mealtimes and before going to bed. The food (decent enough, though without wine it has no taste) is served in the central guest house of the group of little two-storey houses where we sleep, in an area that reminds me of Labaro. I live in the furthest one so I have to go two or three hundred metres on foot. The first evenings I felt a bit anxious walking in the dark, but don't worry, the area is very safe because all the international organisations are here and they all have their sentry boxes. The sky's very beautiful, by day and by night, the mountains too. Kabul is a foul place but the people are extraordinarily beautiful. Yesterday I went to visit a centre for street children, there were classes of 20-25 girls who were learning a sentence by heart, something like 'Our teacher teaches us good things', and I

*swear to you they were all very beautiful, the first few days
I thought I was hallucinating, but it's true, you know those
photos you see in the newspapers of wide-eyed children,
they're all like that, even the old people, fantastic, with those
impressive beards. They often have dark eyes with green or
purple on the outside, and red or blonde wisps in their black
beards and hair. A lot of them have blue eyes. Very long lashes.
Very beautiful hands with long fingers. The various ethnic
groups have very marked physical characteristics, the
Hazaras for instance, they arrive at the distribution centre in
families of eight or ten people, all looking the same, with flat
faces, protruding ears, Mongol eyes, in other words, they have
their own distinct character. At the guest house we have two
Hazara cooks who are twins. They're thin and quiet and
really nice, I must have my photo taken with them. Anyway,
I'm starting work now, so I have to stop, I'll continue tonight
or tomorrow morning when I wake up. Lots of kisses. Love, E.*

18th April. The king is returning today, after twenty-nine
years in exile. The streets are blocked, and people have to go
on foot or by bicycle. I accompany a UNHCR woman who's off
to talk to another woman, from the European Community,
about human rights. This other woman is leaving for Kunduz
and Mazar-i-Sharif on Saturday and needs information. It's
the first time I've been around Kabul on foot. I'm just along
as an escort. Ironically (or perhaps not), that was one of the
tasks mentioned in my job description. The weather is very
fine and the streets silent apart from the whoosh of the bicycle
tyres in the dust. Men carry burqa-clad women on the back
wheels. My companion, a bold English feminist, whose blonde
hair emerges from under her black shawl as she walks, like
a kind of heraldic crest, seems as happy as me to be walking a
little. At the EU we're thoroughly searched. In the courtyard,
German soldiers in vests are underpinning a ledge with a
row of wooden beams. We're received by the EU lady, who's
Swedish and dynamic. They're all dynamic here, the women

even more than the men. In a small, shaded room, the UNHCR lady gives her a briefing of exactly two hours about the situation in some of the villages in the Kunduz and Mazar areas. What's meant by 'situation' is the complex conjunction of ethnic identity, class, sex and family ties through which men and women, Uzbekis and Tajiks, Pashtuns and Arabs, rich and poor, natural brothers and foster brothers, bosses and tenant farmers, former killers and current killers, are inextricably bound together by a history that's largely oral. Who really owns the houses and the land that the refugees are returning to? Giving them back to their former owners, which seems at first sight the obvious thing to do, may simply be perpetuating old injustices, themselves brought about by wars, deportations, one group's oppression of another...

(A few days ago, as Jahid and I accompanied a displaced family into the yard of their house, which was quite well maintained, I thought: who can say off the top of their head that this house really belongs to them and not to other refugees who haven't yet returned, who won't return or may even be dead?)

While the UNHCR lady speaks, mentioning a number of Afghan names and nicknames, I try to follow the briefing but after five or six minutes, my mind starts to wander. Behind the EU lady's profile, beyond the barred window, the German soldiers are rubbing their arms with Nivea cream.

When we return to our compound, I go in search of a TV set, and just as I set foot in the small press office, where about fifty people are crammed, some sitting on the floor, most of them Afghan staff members, at that very moment the TV shows King Zahir appearing at the door of our military plane, an Italian plane. His bald head emerges from the shadows. Applause breaks out in the room. But not everyone applauds. Not everyone is equally happy and some probably aren't happy at all. The king steps forward unsteadily. He's wearing a leather jacket. Those Afghans in the room who are moved by the sight make comments but nobody asks them to translate.

I've decided to have at least a few Dari lessons, though God knows how long it'll take me to say even a few sentences. This morning, Daniel, who's been studying for a few weeks, managed to converse with the shoeshine boy outside the guest house, after giving him 10,000 afghans for his work. I pulled up my trouser legs and had my shoes shined too. They were incrusted with dust.

The king disappears beneath the throng of military caps and the turbans of the dignitaries who come forward to kiss his hands.

Strange to be here in Kabul and watch events on TV just like the rest of the world.

Criteria for identifying vulnerable groups and individuals
- Widows and women who are heads of families containing no males above the age of twelve.
- Families whose head is mentally or physically disabled and which contain no other males above the age of twelve.
- Families with one or more mentally or physically disabled members.
- Families with one or more members over sixty and no other males above the age of twelve.
- Families with five or more members below the age of ten.
- Orphans and unaccompanied minors up to the age of eighteen.

At the second stage of identifying EVIs, groups or individuals who nevertheless have ties with other family units able to support them will be excluded, as will families in which one or more members have completed further education, or possess professional skills that may ensure their survival.

The orphanage
We visit the Alaouddin orphanage, which houses 670 children. As it's their free afternoon, when they're allowed back to their relatives' houses, there are only about a hundred children in the orphanage today, those who really don't have anyone in

the world. Many of the orphans do in fact still have one parent, or an uncle, but they're too poor to keep the child at home and that's why they entrust them to the institution.

We inspect the dormitories, the classrooms and the playing fields. Hygienic standards are adequate. We note, though, the total absence of toys. The assistants tell us that many of these children suffer from psychological problems as a result of witnessing acts of violence, in some cases the deaths of their parents.

When Anne enters the dormitories, the girls start singing to her in unison. They try to take her by the hand and lead her to see their beds. They want physical contact, they want their hair to be stroked, they want to touch this smiling blonde lady, to tug at her skirt. In the bare rooms, which are fairly clean, there's no sign of a toy. Not even a doll.

On the wall there's a letter from an American boy, dated 15th November 2001, and written in block capitals with some of the s's and r's back to front:

DEAR FRIEND MY NAME IS BRANDON I AM IN A GRADE – I'M WRITTING THIS LETTER TO YOU BECUSE YOU DON'T HAVE A MOM OR A DAD – I KNOW THAT YOU ARE FELLING SAD BECUSE MAYBE YOUR MOM AND DAD ARE DIED – I WANT YOU TO FELL HAPPY – OUR CLASS IS DONADING $50 TO CHILDRIN WHO NEED MONEY TO BUY FOOD AND WATER – I HOPE YOU ARE BETTER I WISH I CAN SEE YOU – YOUR FRIEND – BRANDON

In the hall leading to the dormitories I have to hold my breath, so strong is the stench of urine, it's like the smell you notice when you enter a zoo.

Visit to district 3 (completely razed to the ground) where a university NGO are hoping to open a kind of students' house in the only building still standing, which was rented at three hundred dollars a month before the prices in Kabul soared (in a couple of months it'll cost a thousand), but restoring it to a fit state is really going to take a lot of money. In the middle of the inner yard there's a huge pile of stones, fifteen metres by five, and at least three metres high. If you placed it in a museum – in London or Frankfurt, say – it would be taken for a work of conceptual art, maybe a metaphor for war. Almost the whole of the western part of Kabul is in this state. For years, all those heroes pounded it with artillery, rockets and bombs rained down on it. The reinforced concrete buildings have crumpled. (Mohammad points out the cinema, where he used to go and see Indian films when he was a little boy).

My next-door neighbour, an Armenian woman, has received an animated card by email from her daughter who lives in the United Arab Emirates and is studying at the conservatory. When I tell her that the reason I don't come down to the sitting room in the evening to chat to the other people in the guest house is not because I don't like them, but because I feel sad and tired and prefer to be alone, she shows me the card. It shows a rose covered in dew and floating on water, which sways to the sound of a poignant tune for piano and orchestra. Beneath it are the words:

I MISS YOU

19th April
I cried last night. On the little sofa where people usually have coffee, Jette held my hand and told me not to worry, not to feel ashamed. The others kept their distance, I suppose they didn't want to embarrass me. From the canteen, I could still hear chatter and laughter and the buzz of the TV.

When I'd come in a little earlier, the BBC news was on, with a still image of an urban panorama and a smoking skyscraper. The image was distant and unclear. Beneath it, the caption: AIRPLANE CRASHES INTO THE MAIN TOWER OF MILAN, ITALY. I stood there frozen. I thought… I thought… I can't say what I thought. Kamel saw me grow pale and lent me his telephone. 'Call. Call straight away.' I called my wife. It was the first time I'd heard her voice again. She didn't know anything about the skyscraper. She'd been at the children's five-a-side football match. In Italy, it was the afternoon. Her soft voice shook me even more.

They're attacking my country and I'm in Afghanistan. That's when I let it all out. Tears streaming into my mouth, I murmured: 'It's the only bloody skyscraper we've got…'

An hour later, I was calm and went back to the canteen. As the food was all finished and cleared away, I asked the cook to make me something. He suggested an omelette. I'd got my hunger back. The omelette was yellow, light and fluffy. I ate it in silence as I continued to watch the images of the punctured Pirelli building.

For the rest of the evening, after it was clear that it was an accident, and that the plane was small and not a Boeing, after I'd relaxed to the point of insensibility (helped by the vodka I'd been given to help me overcome the crisis), tears of exhaustion and emotion continued to stream of their own volition from the corners of my eyes.

Peace

Flash of inspiration on a boring morning (they exist here, too): suddenly, as I was saying 'Salaam aleikom' to a driver, I remembered the Hebrew words 'shalom aleichem' from the songs they made us sing in church when we were children, with the same phrase repeated in every language as a sign of brotherhood… 'la paix soit avec vous', 'la paz sea con vosotros', etc. etc., maybe we said them in German and Russian too.

Hackneyed phrases, maybe, but with such a profound, mysterious meaning.

Peace be with you

(and with your spirit)
Peace be with all of you
Peace…
Peace…
Salaam.

All morning I've been studying maps, reports, treatises, statistics, the history of the Afghan political parties and their historical leaders – amazing partisans, marauding gangs organised by so many Ali Babas – or genuine popular heroes, in the old sense of the term: men like Ahmed Shah Massud, the Lion of the Panshir, killed by kamikazes disguised as journalists two days before the attack on the Twin Towers in New York, Gulbudin Hekmatyar, who reduced Kabul to a heap of rubble, the Uzbek generals Dostum and Malik, the Shiite chiefs Mazori and Khalili, and so on.

Since the war in Yugoslavia, I've been haunted by these Homeric figures, these ruthless commanders leading their ethnic groups. It's as if they'd left thorns in my hands. I find them repugnant and at the same time, looking at them objectively, I have to admit there's something heroic about them, as demonstrated in fact by the inhuman acts they commit: looting, reprisals, the liquidation of prisoners. I'm talking here in strictly philological terms. If they were human, they wouldn't be heroes. The hero (Ajax, for example) isn't a champion fighting for an Olympic ideal, but a man who slaughters his enemy even when that enemy is unarmed, a man who slaughters the largest number – like beasts in an abattoir. As in a story by Fenoglio[2], they want to bathe up to their elbows in the blood of their enemy (Ratko Mladic stroking the children of Srebrenica before having their fathers killed, Achilles himself killing Penthesilea and then raping her – in that order – though that's something they never teach you at school). There's very little that's chivalrous in any of this. Talking of school: reading Homer to my classes in Rebibbia prison, I came to the conclusion that if Ulysses hadn't massacred *all* the Procians he wouldn't have been a true hero. The book has to end with that massacre. Just like the Ring of the Nibelungs or the Mahabharata. Otherwise the story wouldn't finish, would remain incomplete, incomprehensible. Later (as collateral damage) men of letters come along, like Peter Handke, moved by the sound of Serbian ballads sung by the wife of Commander Arkan.

The prisoners, who haven't been as corrupted as honest people and are capable of understanding reality as it is, grasped all this immediately. They didn't need me to explain it to them, they just had to read the texts. Respectable people would be scandalised – rightly so, perhaps. That's why they often understand nothing about literature. (I've discovered that nobody reads epics, nobody gives a damn about them – after high school.) Sometimes, the greater your culture, the more impoverished your point of view, because your culture distances you from the real forces that shape the world, draws a veil over them, as does a comfortable life. True culture should bring you closer to these forces, reveal them to you in the clear light of day.

Late in the afternoon, a dust storm.

(20th April)
I banged my head in the middle of the night getting up to go to the bathroom but I was too sleepy and only realised the following morning that my hair was caked with blood.

From the document *Paying for the Taliban's Crimes* by Human Rights Watch, April 2002, vol. 14.

A Pashtun peasant beaten by two Tajik militiamen in the province of Baghlan, to the north of Kabul.

I was working on the land. It was midday. Two men arrived – one was armed, the other picked up a stick from the ground. They beat me on the head and shoulders. My face was covered with blood. They hit me on the back and on the legs with their rifle butts. When they struck me on the head I collapsed. They hit me so hard with the stick that it snapped. Then they hit me with stones. They wanted money or weapons. The beating went on for more than an hour.

December 2001. A forty-six-year-old sheep farmer from the Faryab region, north-west of Kabul, two months after being beaten and tortured by Tajik militiamen from the Junbish party answered the questions of the HRW inspectors from his bed, where he is still recovering from his reported wounds. He knows his attackers well, they come from a nearby village.

I was on the way to feed my sheep. Two men – S. and N. – arrived on a motorcycle. First they tried to strangle me with my own turban. I fainted and they tied my hands. Then they started to beat me with a kardum, a length of cable with a metal ball on the end. I don't remember how many times they hit me, on the back, the legs, the hands. They broke one of my arms with the kardum. The beating went on for an hour. Then they carried me home on their motorcycle, and I gave them money and my motorcycle. I said to them: 'I'll give you money, don't kill me.'

Armed Hazaras enter the village of Spin Kot, near Balkh, on 12th December 2001. They burst into the house of M.J., forty-five years old, and take him away. M.J. is led to the nearby Hazara village and put in the donkeys' enclosure.

One of them twisted my head and the other two beat me on the back. While they beat me with a shovel, they asked me for money and weapons. They threatened me, saying: 'You're a Pashtun, which means you're a Taliban. We're going to kill you, but not right away. We'll do it a little at a time. You have to feel really bad before you die.' They beat me for two hours, two and a half hours.

21st April. Rome's foundation: I explain about the foundation and where Rome is. Ten kilometres outside Kabul, traffic is slowed by a terrible accident between a taxi, which is completely wrecked, and a lorry full of refugees. It must have happened not so long ago. The lorry has turned over on its side, and the belongings that were tied to the roof have scattered over the road. Big bundles, all shiny with rain. Doors, windows and wooden planks among them. Screaming children are being pulled out like fish through the rear door. A Red Crescent ambulance has arrived.

I count the burnt-out shells of tanks, but by the time we reach Kalakan I've lost count and stop. There are too many of them. Blankets hanging on the guns to dry. The magnificent plateau, bounded on the sides by the snowcapped mountains, is dappled with gentians and red with little poppies, not opium ones. I feel the impulse to go into the fields to pick them. Never having been crazy about flowers, I realise that the only reason I'm drawn to them is the fact that the fields are mined and the flowers forbidden. A pity, though: it would have been nice to carry away bunches of flowers to brighten the canteen in Kabul. Now the American helicopters appear, flying low as usual, no more than thirty metres from the ground, God knows why – to make their presence felt and show the population that they control the territory, I suppose.

Six transport Apaches and two fighters.

A message to the local militias patrolling in their pick-ups: watch out, the helicopters are saying, we've got our eyes on you. But we're more impressed than they are. The militiamen, with their Kalashnikovs, don't turn a hair: the sides and roofs of their vehicles bristle with rocket-propelled grenades, which are answer enough.

One of those things can destroy a house.

(On passing armed men on lonely roads in Afghanistan: Who are they exactly? Good guys, bad guys? What do they want? Unarmed as we are, we greet them with a certain apprehension, raising our hands stiffly and waiting for a peaceful gesture in response. Impossible to tell anything from their uniforms.)

First stop, the distribution centre, which is inside a hangar with a sheet-metal roof riddled with holes. Inside, the mountains of grain sacks I saw last week are only half the height they were before, which is a good thing, because at the end of the hangar, where the sacks are heaped, the roof is intact, so they won't get rained on. On a line of wheelbarrows the provisions for each repatriated family are ready: bars of soap, a bucket, a shovel, blankets, plastic mattresses, a couple of jerrycans. These are the last of the jerrycans, and we've run out of buckets, too, there's been a larger influx than expected in the last few days, and the young Afghan men who run the centre weren't clever enough to order a new consignment in advance. So the next families who arrive will have to go away without jerrycans, which are essential, to judge by the lines of children going back and forth along country tracks and city streets, holding the jerrycans in both hands or supporting them between head and shoulder. To the children, they're more familiar than toys: one day in Jabal Salanj we were talking to a woman with a child around her neck, about one year old, carrying an empty jerrycan – practising already. The young Afghan officials roll their eyes in embarrassment. Jette reminds them for the umpteenth time that they must be prepared to receive up to three hundred families a day, and as it takes three days to get a new supply, they must have in stock at least 3 (days) × 300 (families) = 900 packs of provisions, let's round it up to 1,000 packs (that is, 3 × 1,000 50-kilo sacks of grain, 2 × 1,000 blankets, 2 × 1,000 jerrycans, etc.) and as soon as they realise they're getting below 1,000, order the stuff from the warehouses. The young men nod contritely. One of them is short and has red eyes. The other looks like he's top of his class, with long hair and a pimply face, and a threadbare blue jacket over his shalweer kameez. It's clear they're both willing but a bit messy, and they dread us checking up on them.

J. goes over the procedure with them, forces them to repeat to see if they've absorbed it, like a prayer to be learned by heart.

Under the somewhat dazed eyes of the supplier, the Australian engineer checks a couple of thousand timber beams from the Bamiyan area. Some are cracked and we have to settle on a criterion for discarding the unusable ones, which would split as soon as they were put in place. They're used for rebuilding the roofs of houses. The ideal circumference is about 35 centimetres. As we don't have a tape measure, I measure them with my hands. The beams ought to be checked when they're unloaded, but last time they were all wet and it was necessary to wait until they were dry to make sure they were all right. Of course we don't take out the bad ones in front of the beneficiaries, otherwise they'd start to say that those we give them aren't any good, that they want them straighter and smoother.

Some of the beams have spiral cracks. They're still usable, says the engineer, unlike those with straight cracks.

The supplier haggles and proclaims his innocence, putting his hand on his heart. If he didn't look so dodgy and flushed, he'd be rather a handsome man, his beard and hair reddish blond, his complexion ruddy but basically clear, his green eyes tinged with red. In the end, he's persuaded to take back several of the beams, which he'll try to palm off on someone else.

Poplar wood: straight, light, easy to strip, fast-growing.

I know a bit about the seasoning of timber, from the days when my father used to make wooden doors and windows.

Opposite the hangar there's the usual tank. It's intact and well preserved, as if rust-proofing has been applied to the carcass. The door is open. The interior is blackened, and the parts have fused together beneath a kind of lacquer. It doesn't seem like a weapon any longer, more like a toy or a monument. I come out onto the turret and have myself

40

photographed by my Nepalese colleague with my fist raised towards the mountains.

We enter the village of Khwaji Khel (approximate spelling) at about one o'clock, taking a detour along a dirt track away from the main road, where a platoon of soldiers are marching somewhat unenthusiastically in a kind of cramped goosestep: at least half are out of time, and can't keep in a straight line. We bob up and down in the jeep until we reach the enclosures of mud bricks that mark the entrance to the village of Khwaji Khel. Three mine clearance experts are working here in transparent masks and blue smocks. They say the machines are arriving next week and then they'll really be able to clear the area in a hurry. The mud on the heath has congealed and hardened in uniform waves a metre high. We pitch and toss. As soon as we get out of the jeep in the village, we're surrounded by dozens of children, laughing and joking and wanting pens. There are the usual military salutes and cries of HOW ARE YOU? They seem like Jack-in-the-boxes, they get on my nerves. They tag after us and don't give us a moment's peace. The brightest of them addresses me in English and explains that he's been to school and that he likes it, then to show me he's in third grade he counts the numbers with his fingers tied in a dirty, frayed gauze. The others cling to me and try to grab the pens from my breast pocket.

When I see that the children aren't going to leave us alone and that we can't move without tripping over them, I try to chase them away by pulling faces and jeering at them. But they simply move back and return soon after, running ahead of us and yelling.

Finally the village elders arrive. They have few teeth and long beards, except for one who's very tall and looks like the French actor Fernandel. They, too, find it impossible to leave us alone. While we talk, and while the other elders raise their voices and strike dramatic poses (the problem discussed: the chronic shortage of water), Fernandel looks down at us and smiles calmly, showing his prominent teeth. Every now and again, when the children get in between our legs or push us from behind, making Jette gesticulate impatiently as she tries to clear a bit of space around her, one of the elders rescues her by threatening the children with the raised handle of his shovel, in such a way as to suggest that he has, in fact, applied it several times to their backs. But all this melodrama with the shovel doesn't keep them at much of a distance, only a few metres, after which they return to the attack like hungry little animals. Hungry for what? Attention, I'd say, more than anything else.

Here, too, many children have leishmaniasis pustules on their faces, which have been coated with a violet-coloured medication: we have various ideas about what it is, possibly a paste made from gentians. Behind the earth walls, mulberry trees.

Who these village leaders are, what they represent, and what real authority they have is hard to grasp, both in general and when we meet them in the flesh. An Afghan friend has explained to me how the communities function, with their rais, the malik, the mir aab, who is the man in charge of providing water, the community's greatest treasure, the shura, made up of respected men, and then the masters, the secular and Koranic teachers, the mullah, all influential figures in the villages. You have to recognise them and listen to them even when what you'd really like to do is pull their beards.

In this village, we want to find out whether they have water or not. Apparently, they have it three days of the week, when a village higher up opens the tap. Negotiations are under way with the heads of that village to persuade them to be more generous. It seems they're blocking the source with a boulder and diverting the water. Long discussions follow between the elders and our Afghan colleague, who doesn't want to translate it for us or only partly, as if he preferred to conduct the investigation by himself. The elders want us to put in a pump downstream, but it'll take time: the plans, the contract, the work itself, it could be months. What is possible in the short term is to drill some new wells, but a pump is out of the question, and J. wants our Afghan colleague to make it quite clear to the elders that they can forget about a new pump for the moment, NO PUMP, she says, miming it theatrically and shaking her head, but the Afghan seems reluctant to pass on the idea, he talks and talks and talks to the elders without translating anything back to us and we're not sure that he hasn't softened the harsh lines of what we've said, maybe because he doesn't want to take responsibility for the refusal himself or because he's openly taking their side. Well, we're on their side, too, to an extent, but we must keep strictly to the protocol that says we shouldn't create 'false expectations', 'expectations that cannot be fulfilled', etc., etc.

Anyway, it's obvious that these poverty-stricken people are trying to get us to cough up as much as possible.

It's also obvious that resources are not unlimited.

(On my first day in the field, I laid a plastic sheet on the ground so that the children shouldn't have to wait in the dust for their vaccinations, but a female colleague made me fold it up again: we don't have that many of them, she said.)

We're haggling now, in the most classic style.

While the animated discussions continue, I watch the line of children carrying water and wonder where they're coming from. They leave with their jerrycans empty and return with them full. They disappear behind a hillock. Let's drop this, I say to J., and go and see for ourselves. I slip away from the debate and start walking back along the line of water carriers. My eyes, accustomed as they are to clearly defined urban landscapes, find it hard to orient themselves in this disordered panorama, where everything is brown, where the paths lead nowhere and there's no network of streets and houses and squares, merely a succession of depressions, hillocks and earth walls. I don't know if it's the colour or the shape, but by the end of the day I'm left with the feeling that I've crossed a single compact landscape of mud. Fresh mud and dry mud, moulded in unpredictable ways. Only the trees interrupt this monologue in brown.

The trees burnt by the Taliban on their punitive expeditions. They simply sprinkled them with kerosene and set fire to them, for no reason, to increase the effect of waste land left in their wake. They chose age-old trees which had many association for the villagers.

The terrain is perforated with wells, part of an old irrigation system called kariz, which was partially destroyed and filled up during the war. They're now trying to restore it, cleaning the channels which run ten metres below the ground. Crouching men slip inside to free them of mud.

In the evening, someone lends me a phone and I call home. My children come on the line one after the other, one minute each. You can tell over the phone that they're embarrassed and don't know what to say. Just hearing the other person's voice, his unmistakable tones that you love so well, ought to be enough, but you need words, too. Anything will do, like trying out a keyboard by typing the first sentences that come into your head.

Leone: 'The goalie missed the ball, and then he couldn't believe it, he saw Ronaldo run to the goal and just knock it in...'

Total lack of physical contact, tenderness, release. Personally, I miss hugs: embracing and being embraced. We search in vain for compensations: that's why people prop up the UN bar after seven and talk and talk and talk and tell jokes and smoke and smoke and talk and talk and laugh and drink one glass after another and laugh their heads off without a pause. At the end of a hard day's work, we deliver the knockout blow with whisky and words. We think it's a way to relax. Real pleasure ought to be much simpler, not so boisterous.

My next door neighbour, a giant from Newcastle, goes running every morning at six: up the dusty hill behind the last houses, down again, a final lap around the guest houses and then back to his room, drenched in sweat. I see him on my way to the bathroom, through the half-open door, sitting on his bed and lighting a cigarette, and I greet him under my breath. He shakes his long, wet hair and says that he feels much better.

22nd April. I've been all over Kabul trying to get myself vaccinated – the booster for hepatitis B. The last place I tried was a military garrison with a mysterious acronym on the other side of the city. Nothing. The road was blocked and we had to make a detour through a vast ruined area, where the Taliban, Al Qaeda militiamen, Pakistanis and Arabs were all concentrated before their defeat. It was a place the Americans really went to town on. There was hardly a stone left standing. We had to climb little hills along the dirt road. The reason for the detour was that military manoeuvres were taking place. Apparently, there's due to be a ceremony next week, but I have no idea what it's about or why it's being held in such a grim place. We saw the soldiers marching along the street, looking down-at-heel in their grey-green uniforms, many of them with trainers on their feet. No offence meant, but I've never seen soldiers marching in such a listless, casual manner. All the soldiers had beards except for a couple who seemed not to have them because they hadn't grown yet, because they were in fact children. It took us a long time to get back, the streets were swarming with people, a non-stop bazaar.

Worst Case Scenario
I'm supposed to be going to Chaharikar but at the last moment there's a security briefing. I'm sorry not to be going to the plateau, but finding out more about saving my skin

might turn out to be useful. The lecture is given by a policeman, who starts off with a dramatic flourish, writing a number on the board:

205

and asking the audience what the number means. Nobody answers. 'Well, my friends,' the policeman says, 'that's the number of United Nations workers killed in the last ten years.' Many died in road accidents, but some were killed in clashes and ambushes. 'Unfortunately, this isn't the final figure, we have to bring it up to date.' He rubs out the 5 and substitutes a 6 because someone else (I don't catch who or where) died recently. This switching of numbers is meant to drive it home to us that if we aren't careful one of us could be number 207.

24th April
(notes for an unwritten letter to Adelaide)
Trip to Chaharikar and Qara Bagh (Shomali Plains). Stories told by Wazi, the driver. The first kidnapping near Sorubi (1997 or 1998). He hadn't been a driver for long. Two lorries and two MSF cars, eight people + the interpreter. The interpreter disappeared and was never seen again. The others escaped in the dark, taking advantage of a quarrel between the kidnappers. They spent the night in hiding while the kidnappers searched for them with torches. Then they returned to Jalalabad. At Sorubi there was a warlord called Zardat who had a bodyguard nicknamed Sag, i.e. Dog. Whenever Zardat said to Dog: 'Bite', Dog shot someone dead. Zardat and Dog ended up in London. Another attempted kidnapping in Hazarajat: the Taliban stopped the car, one of them touched a Frenchwoman's thighs, she started to scream and then the Taliban also started to scream. He was shaking, and even more terrified than she was. MSF's policy was to treat all people, even the wounded Taliban, and the Taliban let them pass.

The number of children Wazi has: his original family, his poor mother's death when she was still young. We arrive in Chaharikar (offered tea and sweets). Then we turn around to go to Qara Bagh. Sitting on carpets in the tent. The village leader (taller than Uncle Riccardo). His son, who waits on us, looks like Giuseppe's schoolmate David. Discussion with the chief about the number of tents, papers written in Arabic by his son, tea with cake, sitting in the lotus position. 96 villages, 200 tents. He wants 2,000. The discussion goes on for an hour, during which I eat three pieces of cake. We go to a village. A kind of walled farm. They want to invite us in for the umpteenth tea. The little girls run away from the Englishman, who roars and pretends to bite them. A little dog. A well. Shops bulldozed to the ground. Bicycle parts sticking out of the ground, a chain guard, a handlebar. The factory of cement moulds. All around, bombs dropped by the B52s. (Those old planes? Yes, they celebrated their 50th birthday in Afghanistan). The bomb disposal experts exploded a huge bomb yesterday. Another village, a hundred metres away. Old men with beards, only old men and children here, the old men want to shake your hand, the children want to play. They go to school in tents. I tell the chief I'd like to meet the poorest of all. Large ruined compounds. Two families in each tent. Two children are sleeping in a tent, swaying in a hammock. Anne wants to speak to the women, but it isn't possible. I get them to tell me who they are, where they're from. The old man shows me the documents. Little houses with pieces of plastic on the windows. They've begun to clean up. Gardens of war. Fruit trees. Scabs on the children's faces. Seven or eight women in another tent. Very beautiful girls who in a few years will disappear behind veils. The sky is magnificent, the sun very strong, every now and again it rains.

The head of the village gives me five when I ask him if he'll agree to face his people with just two tents per village. We don't have any more for the moment.

Little girls at the side of the road offer bundles of violets to the lorries that speed past them. I'm sorry I can't buy them, but if I did the girls would go back into the minefields to pick more. Divided feelings: you always have to think before doing anything. (Like when A. gave money to the children: was it the wrong thing to do or not?) Half a loaf of bread to the driver, who's hungry. Talk about religion. A good Muslim, a bad Muslim. Meaning of the word itself: 'religion'. I think of Alessandra F., who doesn't eat sausage. True Islam. Oppression of women. Wazi's mother wore miniskirts when the Russians were around. Did the Communists have any good points?

I think the day is over. But it isn't. Two people leaving tomorrow are buying drinks at the UN bar and I have to go. There are toasts and souvenir photos with Pashtun hats, which look like pizzas or cakes when they're rammed onto European, Japanese or African heads. Then a listless dinner. Home at last, I find a little party in progress, with three Russians drinking like fish, they're very pleasant people but all I'd like to do is go to bed, instead of which I have to guzzle vodka and be pleasant like them and join in discussions of who the laziest people in the world are, who the most dishonest, and which countries have the most beautiful women. The thought of Russian girls in spring, when they start to dress in light clothes, leads them to the verge of sexual lyricism. One of them is a Tartar with a huge belly contained inside a leather waistcoat, the second an Armenian with a crew-cut, the third a genuine Russian with watery blue eyes, red hair and moustache, and a subtle, blasé sense of humour. Tired as I am, my curiosity forces me to keep listening to this cornucopia of jokes and stories, culminating in the achingly funny image, evoked by the Tartar amid much laughter, of Pinocchio (my most famous compatriot) feeling very alone and jerking himself off with sandpaper.

Over and out
Pul-i-Charkhi. In the distance, the immortal summits of the Hindu Kush.

I touch the biceps of our driver Farid (green eyes behind green glasses) to verify that he goes to the gym regularly. He practises every kind of sport: football, volleyball, boxing, bodybuilding. He says that when your nose is broken in a boxing match, you become a Hazara.

(The H. have naturally flat noses.)

The engineer who works for us, who graduated in Russia and has eight children, earns two hundred and forty dollars a month, plus a risk indemnity of another seventy or eighty dollars a month. In all, that makes 3,600 dollars a year. Not bad, considering that an Afghan state employee earns between thirty and sixty dollars a month.

Apparently, there are lakes near Kabul where you can bathe and swim. I ask the girl who works in my office how you get there, but she doesn't know, maybe it's a delicate subject to talk about with a young woman. A swim in the lake, that's all. I haven't yet grasped how far you can go without offending anyone's sensitivities.

At Pul-i-Charkhi I go and take a look at the lorries while the returnees are loading the stuff, the sacks of grain, the blankets etc., and are getting ready to climb on board and leave. At the moment there are about thirty of them, some with their engines running, ready to go. Children climb like squirrels onto the sides of the vehicle, gripping the decorations, which are heavier and more fanciful than those in a baroque church. It's incredible, the amount of stuff that somehow manages to get crammed in along with the people. I finally understand the purpose of the racks over the lorry driver's compartment, which jut out like the figureheads of ships and are also fantastically decorated, with stars, hearts, diamonds, swords, waves, hawks and doves, fish, camels and lions, footballs, aces, planes, crosses, sentences in Arabic, monsters and sages, gods and dancers. These roof racks suspended four metres from the ground are like extra baggage compartments packed with all sorts of objects, completely incompatible in terms of shape: bicycle wheels, fans, rugs, sacks of grain with the initials WFP, doors and windows, and the heads of children, their streaming hair white with dust. It's almost impossible to look up, the enamelled blue of the sky reflects the light, the whole field of vision is bright and sharp, without shade. This Afghan light seems to penetrate or avoid every obstacle, like the light of God. It isn't enough just to wear sunglasses. Everything shines, and the brightness is unbearable. The fronts of the Pakistani lorries are painted in bright colours, green and blue, and the rest sparkles with varnish and inlaid lacquers, like a dazzling veneer over these clapped-out old machines. In the middle of all this decorative junk I try to find some indication of the make and model of the vehicles, but I can't find any: personalised as they are, they're also anonymous. Real collectors' items. Every now and again, you see one of them that's broken down at the side of the road with a steaming engine or more often with a broken suspension, tilting to the side and ready to topple over. The potholes and the dust are lethal, you'd need to change filters every 2,000 kilometres...

The rims of the wheels and the arches that support the covering tarpaulins are also decorated with flowers and pictures.

I try to imagine the journey at night, everyone crouching on those tarpaulins...

The flies have arrived.

26th April, a feast day, when I go down to the street I hear ducks honking. It's half-past eight, later than usual. But it isn't ducks: two sellers of coloured balloons are playing trumpets and the children are running towards them. The balloons are small and flaccid. Two of the children have bought long narrow balloons and are crossing them like swords in a duel. Meanwhile other children dig the muck out of the gutters and heap it on the sides of the street. The neighbourhood is beautiful today, I realise how many trees there are along the sides of the street and emerging from the inner courtyards.

1,560 families have arrived from Peshawar. Pakistani lorries like rococo churches. Amazing stories in the evening from a Norwegian policeman who was crowned prince of North Cameroon and was smeared with palm oil by naked girls. Eight hours' sleep, thank heaven.

Proper nouns
Oyvind means 'wind on the island'. Gri means 'dawn', but being a verb and not a noun ought to be translated as 'dawning'. Jahid means 'the man who tries'. (He tries and tries, but does he succeed? Jahid laughs fit to burst.) Nuria is the equivalent of Lucia, Nur means 'light' or 'brightness'. The name Yasuko contains a Chinese anagram with various meanings, among them 'peace'. Massud is the lucky man. Edoardo 'he who guards the treasure'.

Michele was an archangel. Mohammed the prophet. Ibrahim the patriarch. Sebastian a Roman soldier pierced with arrows.

Abdul and I talk about the death of Najibullah (February? 1996), tortured and killed by the Pakistanis (we usually think of the Taliban, but it seems they really were Pakistanis, they spoke Urdu). He was there, he saw the whole thing. When they pulled the former dictator out of the UN compound, struggling with all his might, Abdul took fright and ran away. Returning an hour later, he saw Najibullah hanging next to his brother. Najibullah's police tortured people in indescribable ways. Najibullah died in one of those ways. Abdul promises to take me to these places next week. At the moment the area is completely surrounded and cordoned off for Sunday's festival.

I ask him what to call that day: Liberation Day? (Like yesterday in Italy, 25th April, I'd have loved to celebrate it, I know Giuseppe wrote on the class register: DAY OF LIBERATION FROM THE NAZIS AND FASCISTS.) Or Revolution Day, as I heard someone say? Independence Day? Very coldly, Abdul gives his own definition: 28th April, 1992, the day the mujaheddin seized power. It wasn't in any way a liberation. On that day we Afghans lost a state, we lost a nation, we lost everything, and thousands of people were killed, thousands of houses looted, that's what happened. The dictatorship was overthrown, but the civil war went on.

(I've heard that Abdul's parents were killed during the fighting between the various warlords. But I don't have the courage to ask him about it directly.)

Here's the chronological summary I've made for myself:

1973: While King Zahir Shah is in Europe, a coup led by Daud Khan, who declares a republic.
1978: Communist coup against Daud, who is killed with his family. Taraki is named president: he signs a friendship treaty with the Soviet Union. The anti-Communist mujaheddin resistance is born, soon to be financed by the USA.
1979: Taraki is killed and the presidency is assumed by Hafizullah Amin. Amin executed and replaced by Babrak Karmal. At the end of the year, Soviet troops invade Afghanistan.
1980: Najibullah returns from the USSR to lead the secret police. Mass arrests and torture of opponents.
1986: Najibullah president.
1987: Najibullah proposes a ceasefire but the mujaheddin refuse to negotiate.
1988–89: Peace treaties signed in Geneva. The Red Army withdraws from the country after suffering losses of at least 50,000 men. The mujaheddin continue to fight against Najibullah's regime.
1992: The mujaheddin take Kabul. Najibullah seeks refuge in

UN compound. Rabani elected president of the Islamic State of Afghanistan.

1994: Military anarchy. The various warlords, among them Dostum and Hekmatyar, fight against the Rabani government. The movement of Islamic students, the Taliban, spreads (especially among the Pashtun), supported by Pakistan.

1995: Taliban victories. Increased intervention by Iran and Pakistan.

1996: Hekmatyar comes to an agreement with Rabani and returns to Kabul as a minister. The Taliban take Kabul and execute former president Najibullah. The anti-Taliban forces form an alliance.

1997: The Taliban take and then lose Mazar-i-Sharif. Many Taliban prisoners liquidated by General Malik.

1998: The Taliban reconquer Mazar-i-Sharif, massacring thousands of civilians, especially ethnic Hazaras.

1999–2000: The United Nations impose sanctions against the Taliban regime for its support of Osama Bin Laden and his terrorist activities.

2001: The Taliban destroy the Buddhas at Bamiyan. The Tajik leader Ahmad Shah Massud in Europe to obtain help against their regime. Massud assassinated 9th September...

But when Sunday comes, our staff are forbidden to go out. Kabul is swarming with armed people and any of us could be mistaken for a Russian and get shot at, just as a way of celebrating. The ISAF peacekeepers are nowhere to be found. Actually, by the time Najibullah fell, the Russians had been gone for three years. I protest mildly that nobody would take me for a Russian but I know it's pointless arguing about security measures.

I talk on the phone to my mother for the first time since I came to Afghanistan. She seems calm and happy, as if I were phoning her from home. We talk for five minutes about this and that. She wants to know if I've seen 'terrible things'. Well, I don't know about that, I've seen things that have struck me greatly, I've seen enormous poverty, but terrible things, no. Maybe they happened during the war, but things are better now, what we're seeing now are the long-term consequences of those terrible things. It may be that I've quickly become inured, or it may be that they have. Even in the most wretched villages, even covered in filth and pustules, people's main concern is survival. What little grain they have is ground into flour, what little bread they have is baked and eaten. They sleep twelve to a patched-up tent. But the flow of pain seems to have been reversed. We were joking yesterday at Pul-i-Charkhi with the young men on the local staff that if the historical cycles of bad luck and good luck balance out in the end, for the next thirty years Afghanistan should be the happiest and most prosperous country in the world.

The only terrible thing I've seen was that father who was sobbing for his three-month-old child, who was found to be dead on arrival. Terrible in its very purity. I never saw the child, only the father weeping. When the dead arrive at the distribution centre, we don't know where to put them. They can't stay in the lorries but we don't even have a car to take them... to take them where? To the Kabul morgue. Five or six days ago, a lorry arrived carrying a man who'd died before leaving, they'd brought him all the way to bury him in the land of his fathers.

Maybe the child would have died anyway, even without making the journey, maybe not.

I told my mother I was fine.

When I reached out my hands to the child's father and stroked his tear-stained face, I felt as though a cold wind were dragging me into an unreal world. The landscape around us lost its solidity, the man himself seemed to vanish, driven back inside his grief, and all that was left of him was the trace of wetness on the palms of my hands.

26th April, public holiday, balloon sellers in the streets. It's like the first day of normality in Kabul. Some children shovel dirt from the drains, while others play with balloons.

In the afternoon, as we're closing the encashment centre, a line of ten helicopters emerges from the mountain gorge through which the mysterious road winds towards Jalalabad and the Pakistan border, the road taken by thousands of refugees fleeing Afghanistan or returning there.

A woman from the Red Cross shows me a report (confidential, please!) in which they've requested forty body bags for the corpses exhumed from a mass grave in the province of Bamiyan. But then she adds that when they send body bags the local people don't use them because, being good Muslims, they don't want to wrap their dead in plastic. They prefer to carry them wrapped in the traditional white shroud, even when there's hardly anything left of the body. I'd prefer cotton, too, if I were dead. It can't be nice to end up in a rubbish bag with a zip. After the earthquake in Mazar, in which at least eight hundred people died, two hundred body bags were sent but many were left unused.

Every day at Pul-i-Charkhi we distribute between 100,000 and 200,000 dollars: if I were a bandit I'd know where to head for.

After the morning rush at the encashment centre, a moment of relaxation in the yard of a warehouse for storing utensils: I'm lying in the minibus with the reclining seat. The sliding door is open. I stretch my legs. I can hear the little birds, I can see the sun, the snowcapped mountains in the background. It could be anywhere in the world.

This evening, there's going to be a little party at an NGO of mine clearance experts. Mines manufactured in Italy are exploded by other Italians and the arc ends five thousand kilometres from where it started. No message from Italy today.

A Japanese colleague asks me if I can accompany her on a shopping expedition, because a woman mustn't walk in the street unescorted. OK, let's go, it's five o'clock, we've worked enough considering it's a public holiday. Negotiating in a supermarket to buy a small Sony TV set and a Hitachi video recorder (she's here for two years so she has to be well equipped), she does rapid sums on a calculator: they're too expensive, they don't work too well, there are no cables, forget it. The Afghans embarrassed at discussing Japanese products with a woman – a Japanese woman at that. In the back room we haggle over the exorbitant cost of alcohol: twenty-five dollars for a bottle of Australian Cabernet, eight dollars for a beer, we take away a bottle and two cans. I make a move to take the basket from her and she says she's not used to such kindness in Japan. Then she wants to buy a blouse. OK, I'll go with you. We buy the blouse, the smallest size we can find ('I'd like to be tall but I'm so small…'), and I buy three little silver rings with lapis lazuli and amethysts for eighteen dollars. I wanted to try them on the Japanese girl's hand but her fingers are too thin. B.'s and A.'s fingers are long and strong. The atmosphere at the Italian NGO is very friendly, like a teenagers' party: the little garden, the little table with the drinks, the music played loudly to encourage the wallflowers to dance, songs interrupted suddenly by those who are fed up with them and want to change the kind of music. Someone puts on the *Moulin Rouge* soundtrack: nobody can resist the call of *Lady Marmalade*. Miniature bottles of Borsci cordial (I hadn't drunk cordial since my military service, when they gave it to us in plastic sachets before we went on guard). Artichokes' hearts in oil – they, too, look greasy and homesick. At seven, the Japanese girl goes to tell the driver that she'll go on the eight o'clock car, and when she returns she asks me if it's an Italian habit. Is what an Italian habit? The fact that the Afghan at the door asked her if he could give her a kiss. She told him no. I tell her no, too: an Italian would have given her a kiss without asking first. I'm joking, but she's confused. I'm beginning to think that the Japanese are really different. Soon after we arrived, we were sitting on a little sofa chatting to other guests about the various reasons we were here in Afghanistan and to amuse them I told them what Benedetta had said to me on the way to the airport, which I'd found both touching and ironic: 'If you find you really can't stand it there, don't hold out, come back after three days if you have to, it doesn't matter, to us you'll still be *a hero.*' Yasuko was amazed: 'In Japan you couldn't express your own emotions in such an intimate manner.' What, not even between husband and wife?

Afghanistan is turning out to be an excellent place to get to know people from around the world.

One of the young men from the NGO must have stepped on a mine, I think. He has one eye missing and his face is disfigured. I'm moved at the sight of his face.

These bubbles of Western life in the heart of Kabul can either give you a sense of relief or irritate you. But it's nice to see men and women dancing together like this, forgetting all the fuss they make about it out here. French women doctors and nurses who look after the refugees by day and dance rock'n'roll (something the French have long been crazy about) in the evening.

NOTICE TO HEADS OF FAMILIES REGISTERING FOR REPATRIATION AT TAKHTA BEIG (PESHAWAR, PAKISTAN)

– *Be prepared to a longer trip than you can imagine: even if your last destination is close to the border your travel could be slowed or stopped by strikes, block of the roads and others unpredictable accidents*
– *In order to that, provide your family with enough drinkable water: one of the main dangers especially for the babies is dehisidratation*
– *Try to eat some food during your travel: if you don't have*

it or if you have finished it ask the driver to stop to buy it
- Keep on having your medical treatments, don't stop to take your pills for any reason
- Any 4–5 hours of travel ask the driver to make a stop in a safe area (10–15 minutes could be enough) to allow the members of your family to have a breath in open space, stretch their limbs and have a little walk around. It's no use rushing to arrive an hour earlier but exhausted and sick
- Be sure that the members of your family, especially the elder and the babies, are not suffering too much for the travel: check often their condition of health

Black Hawk (Down?)

We spend the morning at the encashment centre dealing with one problem after another: some of the grain sacks are broken, the people doing the vaccinations ask us humbly for uniforms and for another team to be hired because they can't vaccinate all the children at peak times, MSF want to find a doctor in the area to treat emergencies among returnees arriving at night, but how are we going to find him? and who could possibly get the sick to his surgery at three in the morning? who'll pay him and how much? where exactly should the UNICEF tent be put? there are too many cases of diarrhoea, both watery and bloody, there's been a shortage of jerrycans for a week now and giving out buckets instead of jerrycans isn't the same thing, if you have to carry water in a bucket on foot for a kilometre, there's not much of it left by the time you arrive. We weren't expecting many people today, as yesterday was a public holiday and the registration centre in Peshawar in Pakistan was closed, and yet quite a few people have arrived who left Karachi two days ago, which has caused a glitch, as our cashiers had ten-dollar, twenty-dollar and fifty-dollar bills but they've got through the one-dollar bills very quickly, as the returnees who arrive from Karachi are entitled to a supplement of eight dollars a head, producing a total which isn't a round number, so the cashiers have had to go back to Kabul to stock up with small denominations. The idea (in itself a very good one) of putting up a big tent for women and children who arrive during the night to sleep in instead of being crammed in the lorries has a lot of disadvantages: problems of security, cleanliness, possible harassment, lighting, legal responsibility, and anyway we don't have a rubb hall – that is, a maxi-tent with a tubular structure – available at the moment and we'll have to put it off. When there's a rush some children and whole families avoid vaccination, so I suggest that the slogan we need is NO VACCINATION NO GRAIN. The UNICEF information campaign on the necessity of sending the children to school (especially the girls!!!) can't be optional, it's meant specifically for those who want to escape it (as I've observed at school open days, the parents who don't show up are the very ones whose children are doing badly...).

While we're dealing with all these things, a plane crashes into a mountain about ten kilometres away. Some people see it with their own eyes, I leave the tent in time to see smoke rising from the side of the mountain and the pilot's parachute slowly descending.

Responding to a basic instinct to help, I tell the driver to call the base, who in turn will tell whoever's on duty (the ISAF?).

But this seems to cause a problem: it's a military matter, nothing to do with us. It isn't for us to worry about a plane crashing into a mountain.

This morning there was also a gorgeous Japanese girl with freckles.

Back in Kabul, we drink coffee in the sun. But the helicopters fly back and forth over our heads, at a low altitude, and we can see the light guns and the machine guns rotating, as if they're taking aim. The procession is led by a very beautiful helicopter, which Gri says might be a Black Hawk, even though the Black Hawk ought to be bigger and more solid, while this one is a nervous grasshopper. This intimidating parade is being put on for the benefit of a mosque near here packed with warlords and their soldiers, who are getting ready for tomorrow's celebration.

I ask Gri if she's seen *A Bug's Life* where the grasshoppers scare the ants to death by taking off vertically. 'Let's buzz!' and their wings start turning. Of course she's seen it.

Except that here the ants are equipped with AK-47s.

Later, in the car, we compare Osama Bin Laden with Kaiser Sose.

A quarter to seven in the evening. The solemn call of the muezzin mingles with music from the party given by A., who's leaving on Monday. She's happy to be going home, but sad at the same time. For the moment, the Oasis tunes are winning out over the muezzin. Pink-bellied clouds fade away in the sky. Right now, anyone in Afghanistan with a house and food to cook is going back home.

28th April. Last night's party (continued). I get back home half-dead, throw myself on the bed. I'd like to go to sleep, but A.'s farewell party is just starting, so I stagger downstairs, I don't feel much like seeing people and talking in different languages, on top of which a cold wind has risen and though the sofas have been carried with great effort (who by?) into the garden, nobody will sit on them. People are starting to arrive, the usual faces from the various UN and NGO circles, but I'm really only interested in the girls, thanks very much. In fact I do say thanks – I think I should be thankful (to whom?) for the presence of girls. It's only when they're around that I can open my mouth, joke, tell stories, express my thoughts. I'd like to be able to do that with the Afghan women, but unfortunately it's not possible, it's forbidden. So during the day, at work, in the field, all my affection, my playfulness, my thirst for knowledge are lavished on the male Afghans (drivers, money changers, engineers, refugees, shoeshine boys, village leaders, children) and in the evening I can't help devoting what's left to the girls on the international staff. French women doctors and nurses arrive, always quick-witted and friendly, the gorgeous Japanese girl from the morning, a couple of Italian girls I've already seen over and over again, plus a girl from Sarajevo who danced at the party given by the mine clearance people. What I say and do for the next couple of hours before they all leave because of the curfew is a bit of a blur. Gennaro, a carabiniere who works at the embassy, has made – guess what? Pizza. Good. And there are drinks: Russian beer, vodka from Kazakhstan and a single bottle of wine that's just enough for one round. I find out from a couple of Americans a few inches taller and fifteen years younger than me that the plane that came down in the mountains was a thirty-year-old Mig 21 which was practising manoeuvres for the parade. They went to the scene of the crash – it isn't clear if they're soldiers or journalists – and basically there wasn't a piece left of the plane bigger than this, it had disintegrated. It wasn't until they were leaving that they realised they were treading on a minefield. Wasn't there a film where Alberto Sordi[3] spent a whole night not daring to move because he was afraid of being blown up, and then realised he was in a field of watermelons? Talking of Sordi, I'm introduced to an Italian who's said to be an excellent cook but unfortunately for his friends he's leaving. Everyone leaves Afghanistan, all they ever do is leave, with farewell parties, gifts, photos, tears. Anyway, the Italian immediately starts flirting with the Bosnian girl, singing her praises to me as if he needed me as a support for his serenading of her, at the culmination of which he describes her as The Absolute Woman, a title that may have been inspired by the vodka. He kneels in front of her, and it becomes clear from a number of things, including the tired but amused gaze of the woman herself, that the siege has been going on for some time and tonight's his last chance. Some Italians are sitting on the only sofa left in the sitting room, gawking at a channel showing videos of Raf and Articolo 31[4]. I tell a girl from Udine that the lyrics of Raf's songs are always very sad and talk about the solitude of the universe or time passing without leaving a trace (*What will remain of the Eighties*, but just think about it, a lot of time has passed since that song and the answer is nothing, nothing of those years has remained) and the existential angst of the lyrics makes a strange contrast with the dance tunes they're attached to.

...as curfew time approaches, I exchange a few tentative glances with a nurse who looks like my sister-in-law Anna, but I don't pursue matters, though the atmosphere seems favourable and my room is just one floor up, it isn't that I don't like her, but she's sad because she's leaving next week, not to mention that this is a bit of an expatriate cliché – I even laughed about it with Benedetta before I left, she asked me: 'Are you going to find someone else?' and I said yes of course, I'll soon find a nurse.

But when the guests leave, the hard core of those who live in the UN guest houses remain, determined to stay on until after midnight. I don't know how I'm going to manage it, since I'm dropping with exhaustion, or maybe it's this very exhaustion that makes me go through everything that follows with a little smile on my face, like a kind of Buddha anaesthetised not by wisdom but by tiredness. Everything seems distant and unreal. Someone puts on a karaoke CD bought in East Timor: covers of Whitney Houston-style ballads and that kind of junk, with a sprinkling of golden oldies. Behind the lyrics, images of beaches, exotic landscapes, soft-focus fountains. *Yesterday, Only you, Without you*. With a smile, the carabiniere whispers in my ear that all that's missing is the game where you turn a bottle and kiss the person it ends up facing, and I suddenly remember that the first time I played that game, Harry Nilson's heart-rending song *Without you* was playing in the background, too, and I'm transported back to the terrace of a house in the Coppedè district of Rome, where to my great astonishment a girl I'd never seen before thrust her tongue in my mouth, I never knew a kiss could be like that. The carabiniere guffaws. 'Wow, that must have been three hundred years ago,' he says in an accent from Campania he's kept under control until now. *No, I can't forget tomorrow / When I think of all my sorrow…* The merry crew stare at the screen and sing at the top of their voices. Even the wife of the head of security, who's just arrived from Pakistan, has joined in. A little earlier, when she saw her husband lifting the sofas to bring them back from the garden into the sitting room, she begged him: 'Darling, please don't hurt your back, not *tonight*.' After the karaoke we switch to discs of Greek and Albanian music, and our colleague who's leaving dances to them, brilliantly, with a sardonic look on her face like an ancient statue, crossing one foot in front of the other, and making vaguely oriental hand movements. There are also a few hints of belly dancing, and people start throwing 10,000-afghan notes (thirty cents), as if we're in a strip club. The carpet is soon awash with notes, which she kicks away gracefully with the tips of her bare feet as she dances, she's clearly euphoric but at the same time very sad because they're playing music from her country and because she has to leave. To leave Kabul. Life draining from a bottle, drop by drop. Finally, the carabiniere says he's ready to cook the midnight spaghetti, I can't believe it, it isn't possible, I never imagined that five thousand kilometres from home, with missiles being fired at the airport (two today: they missed), such innocent rituals could be replicated with such care. I go and keep him company while the water boils and he unburdens himself to me, he's been here since January and will stay until Christmas, in other words a whole year. To think they offered him a choice between Kabul and Buenos Aires, 'and being the fool that I am, how could I not choose Kabul?' He shakes his brilliantined head. 'Well, it was a good choice after all. I've had a lot out of it. Where else in the world could I have had this kind of experience?' he says, as he stirs the spaghetti, and I feel very fraternal towards him. Just as if he were an Afghan, a prisoner, a friend in need. Then he says something surprising: they're ready to evacuate the embassy tomorrow if the mujaheddin's celebration should turn nasty, and I wonder if he's exaggerating or if things have really got that bad. This bloody Liberation Day is turning into a nightmare. But I find it hard to get worried. The pasta's ready and strained through a big pan, where the holes have been made with a hammer and nails, then we add the sauce out of a coffee pot and carry it into the other room, but Gennaro has overspiced it: it's so hot that the first forkful takes everyone's breath away. I don't care: I'm hungry and I eat, though my lips are burning. The angry pasta.

Full stop. I swear I won't write another line about the social life of foreigners in Afghanistan.

On Sunday I lie down in the sun on the silk sheet in the garden. There are many birds eating the crumbs from the party. Other birds singing all around. Children's voices from the nearby houses. The wind keeps the air cool and clean, the sun isn't too hot. Then the helicopters and jets start flying overhead.

Before dawn. Reading by the light of a torch, I stop because I've suddenly recalled an encounter in Pul-i-Charkhi a few days ago. While I was inspecting the lorries, a boy rode up to me on a bicycle. He was about fourteen, though you can never be sure with the Afghans. He was clean, his clothes were tidy, he looked well fed, there were no blotches or boils on his face. He addressed me in reasonable English, but first of all he wanted to shake my hand. Why not? We shook hands and placed them ritually on our hearts. He was a student from the neighbouring village, he had nothing to do with the returnees, that much was obvious. He told me about his studies, which were going quite well. Why on earth aren't you at school now? He told me lessons finished at eleven today. I complimented him on the way he'd personalised his bicycle: he'd meticulously bound the frame with adhesive tape, as tennis players used to do with the handles of their rackets. The tape was phosphorescent green, I've seen other bikes decorated with yellow, gold or sand-red. He's hung reflectors and iridescent plastic stars on the wheel rims. Two mirrors, like a motorbike, and a horn instead of a bell, with a big bunch of plastic poppies next to it. Very nice, I said. At which point he asked me if I could give him money. What do you want – money? He nodded. He must have been used to begging because he didn't seem at all embarrassed. I'm sorry, I can't give you any. No money? No money. Why? You help people, he said, slightly disappointed. When I went back to work among the lorries, he followed me, circling slowly on his bike.

Record
A very busy morning at Pul-i-Charkhi. Two hundred and fifty lorries yesterday, but the centre was closed because of the military parade and only the teams of checkers went out into the parking lot to do their usual work: going from lorry to lorry checking the documents issued in Pakistan, telling the heads of families to come back tomorrow (i.e., today), alone, without old people and children, to get their money and other things. Now, it's seven o'clock and we haven't even opened yet, but we can already see a very long line of people squatting outside the enclosure, and beyond them, at least another hundred and fifty lorries crammed with people who arrived between yesterday evening and last night, which in all should make 2,000 families, at least 10,000 people. In her pep-talk to the staff, who stand in a circle, the Afghan women kept well apart from the men – an important ritual that's meant to get the work off on the right foot – our Field Officer, a woman, warns us this is going to be a hard day for everyone. She sounds like a coach before a championship match. And it does indeed turn out to be a big day. After the men have briefly gathered in the big tent to pray, a line of tables is set up, four tables – two more than usual – placed at right angles to the direction from which the heads of families will enter. It's like the divisions who have

to withstand the first assault being laid out on the scale model of a battle. (I'm not too happy about the fact that, despite having done my military service, I haven't had a scrap of real military training, which would prove useful today, especially the rudiments of tactics and logistics.) There are just three internationals here today, me and two others, and we work hard to fill in the gaps, irrespective of our roles. We have to check the stamps and signatures on the forms, calculate the amount to hand over to each family, from twenty dollars up to a maximum of a hundred (with a supplement of eight dollars a head up to a maximum of forty dollars for refugees returning from Karachi) and sign the encashment forms, pressing down hard so that the signature shows clearly on all four duplicate sheets. Dealing with the outstanding cases: people who've lost one or other of their documents, people whose forms have stuck together and which tear when they're unstuck, people who aren't registered, people who are missing a stamp or a visa, people who've come from Iran – no idea how they've ended up here (about sixty of them today, there'll be a hundred tomorrow) – single women protesting because they have to share grain with other families that aren't so big and naturally the numbers don't add up, because there are three sacks for four or five people and we may end up with something like the famous story of Solomon and the child with two mothers – keeping an eye on how things are going in the vaccination tent: there's such a crush of women and children that from outside the tent appears to be moving like when there's a fight in a Popeye cartoon, it's the heads of the screaming women and children who don't want to be jabbed – making sure the people doing the vaccinating put the needles and syringes back in a hygienic place instead of throwing them under the table until they form a mountain, as happened the other day – grabbing the young men with the megaphones and reminding them they must keep an eye on those children and whole families who try to slip past without being vaccinated – they must catch them and bring them back into the corridor – going to the French women doctors to find out if any tricksters from the neighbouring village have mingled with the crowd of refugees today in order to get a free examination, and also to tell them that the idea of marking people entitled to an examination with a coloured sign on the wrist, as they do at the entrance to a disco, isn't a good idea. Tagging along with ICMC, who are inspecting the centre, and UNICEF, who are supposed to be pitching their tent here. Calling the WFP and telling them we're almost out of grain, calling Care and telling them there's no more water in the tanks, putting our foot down to GTZ about the jerrycans and about turning on the pump at the well because people are thirsty. Putting up sheets of plastic to give shade. Complimenting some families on how large they are and at the same time warning them not to be pissed off if they receive the same money as the others. Being prepared to do all this in rotation, like members of a Utopian commune – in fact, Saruj and I laugh about it: he's an engineer who graduated in Moscow, and I studied contemporary art, we would never have thought that we'd end up as bookkeepers-knife-grinders-campers-endocrinologists. But of course this is what makes the work interesting. And I'm proud of it, I enjoy bustling about, being useful, giving orders. And the Afghan staff are even more childish than us, and are delighted when you give them the thumbs-up sign to tell them they're doing a good job, now that everything's working.

The cashiers have been asked to carry a lot of money on them. A lot.

4,809 50-Kg sacks of grain
2,853 blankets
1,603 buckets
well over 6,000 bars of soap

and these figures don't cover the whole process because more than three hundred families have taken the money but not the supplies: they'll get those later, in Chaharikar, closer to home. (I always use this expression to indicate the place of residence, given that the house itself – walls, roof, windows – often no longer exists, just as I tell the inmates of Rebibbia, 'Do this exercise for homework,' the first time it was a slip of the tongue, now it's a kind of ironic signal used to underline the significance of what we're doing, the challenge to logic, the idea of a pure action that has to be performed even though external conditions prohibit it: here in Afghanistan, repatriation could be defined as a Return Home Without a Home, like the man in a novel by Flannery O'Connor who wanted to found a Church of Christ without Christ.)

but the most impressive figure is the money: 180,662 dollars in cash – which makes Pul-i-Charkhi the place where the most money changes hands in the whole of Afghanistan.

Some people smile and thank us, others – predictably – complain. They pass before my eyes, all neatly noted down on the forms, hundreds and thousands of names, family names, numbers to indicate the children's ages, the boxes showing the ethnic group.

To the Red Cross in the afternoon, to ask about the procedures for reuniting families, unaccompanied minors, etc. It turns out they don't have a single outstanding case involving children. This is confirmed by the discovery I make in the Kabul orphanage: the family network, however shattered, is still capable of holding its members in an almost invisible but strong embrace. The branches of kinship, drastically pruned by twenty-five years of war, grow again in profusion, twisted but alive. A mother is replaced with an aunt, a brother with a cousin or brother-in-law. A scar tissue of new relationships forms over the wound, and those who've suffered losses are compensated and revived by at least a degree of affection, care and protection (and a proportionate number of blows and other domestic punishments). Of course, as we learn from fairy tales, some adopted children end up like Cinderella or Harry Potter, enslaved by their new parents.

This solidarity was created by the misfortunes of war, but now it's the only thing capable of resisting them and finding a cure for them. Interestingly, the largest number of people being searched for in Afghan territory are Pakistani. The Red Cross get a lot of requests from Pakistan to trace missing relatives. Some of them are probably in prison, but I'd guess that many of them are buried under a blanket of rock and American bombs, they don't exist any more, pulverised, melted.

30th April. Same scene at the distribution centre. By midday I have a blister on my middle finger from pressing down hard on the pen while signing forms.

Total Number of Families: 1,472
Total Number of Individuals: 7,803

(From now until mid-June there will be between 7,000 and 10,000 arrivals per day, in Kabul alone.)

MAY

Musical evening. Two musicians, one a tabla player, the other a virtuoso on a kind of lute shaped like an elongated raindrop, with eighteen strings that have to be retuned between one piece and the next, even though he uses only the six lowest while the other twelve are used for contrapuntal chords.

We lie on rugs with geometric patterns, listening to music which is wonderfully repetitive, like the telling of rosary beads.

The ladies of the international staff wear fixed smiles on their faces and sit with their legs demurely crossed and their backs straightened by years of yoga. On the walls, there are pictures for sale: landscapes, minarets, portraits of children and corn vendors, donkeys, mountains, still lives, the inevitable Massud, a very bold *Die Brücke*-style painting of blue and purple horses, their long necks spiralling into a vortex. The carabiniere from Salerno tells me that the other day they came out of the embassy to discover that the gate and the walls had been covered with posters of Massud, and woe betide them if they'd tried to take them down.

'If you try to remove them we'll kill you,' said the billposters, who were armed with Kalashnikovs.

'But this is an embassy!' they protested. 'The Italian embassy!'

'So what?'

(3rd–5th May) Bamiyan, Egypt
It's the best car journey I've ever made in my life. A brief stretch on asphalt, followed by seven hours of dirt road. I couldn't believe my eyes. I couldn't even believe words. The landscape changed constantly. Valleys filled with Indian mist, rocky canyons, gullies blocked by landslides, mountain passes streaked with ice, ravines, streams to be forded, dust and snow, and quivering birches everywhere. Peach and almond trees in blossom emerging from walled farms.

Long deserted stretches, but even in the middle of nowhere, we pass an old wayfarer, or a soldier carrying a Kalashnikov decorated with phosphorescent adhesive tape.

Hazara women with fire-red shawls bending in the fields to pull up weeds.

Their faces are uncovered.

It's not such a problem here, the necessities of work come first.

Often a man comes up the path leading a donkey ridden by a woman, holding a Mongolian-eyed baby wrapped in her shawl. The shawl has fantastic shades of blue and red. The baby's eyes are heavily made up to the temples.

With the head of the mission (an Italian), the inevitable iconographic references are: *The Flight into Egypt* (see description above) and – at the sight of a nomad lying near his flock on the desolate heath – *The Night Song of the Wandering Shepherd*[5]. But the character that most often comes to mind is Wyle E. Coyote. Of course! Many peaks in the canyon culminate in just the kind of flat rock or towering boulder that's destined to fall on his head as a result of his experiments with ACME products: catapults, jet-propelled rockets, crossbows, glue, ostrich feed, etc.

We use a map drawn by hand by the driver's father: it's more precise and more reliable than the printed ones, apart from which Waisuddin spices it up with information about the places we pass, for instance, the fact that the village of Chekali has the most beautiful girls in the province. All the Hazara bachelors come to Chekali to find wives. At the moment, all we can see are little girls, and with their Mongol faces and their colourful clothes they are indeed stunning.

We pass a convoy on its way back, the most clapped-out buses imaginable, with signs in German and English: *Modern-reisenbus, Have a Nice Travel, Wellcome!*

Half an hour from Bamiyan, we cross a valley which is the most extraordinary collection of rocks of every conceivable colour: ochre, grey, ink-black, slate-blue, brown, pink, though the main colour is red, a red gorge. Halfway up the mountain, there's a dead town, red too, with dead castles and towers, everything dead and eternal, and in the distance, where the valley opens out, the usual barrier of snowy peaks sparkling in the sun. Everything here was destroyed by Genghis Khan eight hundred years ago. The inhabitants had killed his favourite nephew during the siege, and he took his revenge by exterminating anyone left alive in the valley. The thousand-year-old civilisation of Bamiyan came to an abrupt end. All that remained were the silent Buddhas fifty metres high. Until the Taliban used them for target practice in March 2001.

When, far in the distance, the two great empty niches come into view, I catch my breath. From now on, I'll refer to them as the non-Buddhas, because the negation of something still, in a way, affirms its presence. Those niches are not just empty, they've been 'emptied'.

I can't help commenting almost admiringly on that fanatical gesture by the Islamic students, that perfect, destructive faith that has no qualms about being insensitive.

Not a bit of it, my chief retorts, it was just a way of black-mailing the international community: the Buddhas were used as hostages in the negotiations to obtain political recognition for the Taliban government.

The last stretch of the journey is of dizzying beauty. It's time to stop making comparisons. We're at the foot of the wall of red rock where the giant statues of the Buddha stood, until a year ago. First they carefully mined them, then they had fun firing rockets at them from below, and finally blew them up. The UNHCR compound is on a plateau: if you stand on the roof and turn 360 degrees in a clockwise direction you can see: the walls of the non-Buddhas; the old city, which is a conical mound, ash-yellow in colour, honeycombed with caves, a dead and mined city; the brightly coloured pinnacles of the gorges we crossed to get here; an expanse of bare hills, the mountains silhouetted behind them, crowned with dark clouds; and far off to the west a line of jagged peaks on which the sun is setting. In the wind, the blue UN flag flaps against the sparkling white of the snow. From November to March, this place is covered in snow. We're at an altitude of 2,400 metres.

The stone wall that used to house the giant Buddhas is perforated with hundreds, perhaps thousands, of caves. It's like an anthill. Displaced families live in them. The authorities want to evacuate them, in theory to protect the archaeological site (let's hope the insane idea of rebuilding the Buddhas doesn't come to fruition). They've given them an ultimatum. If they don't leave, they'll be evicted by force. We want to know where these people come from, why they're here, and how we can help them. The caves were once inhabited by the monks who excavated them, before Buddhism was eradicated by the spread of Islam, which happened much later here than in the rest of Afghanistan. Since then, these holes have been occupied for centuries by all sorts of poor and derelict people. In the Bamiyan area, successive waves of war and ethnic cleansing have forced practically every group in turn to flee, return, leave again, try to return again, but often they've found their houses no longer exist or else they're occupied by other cuckoos-in-the-nest who are not very keen to move. We climb, out of breath, along the limestone ledges, until we reach those caves which bear the marks of recent human presence: walls blackened by fire, fresh animal shit. But there doesn't seem to be anybody here today, the mouths of the caves (which are tiny, like something out of a fairy tale or a horror story) are all blocked, and it must be because of the gathering we notice a kilometre away, near the junction between the rock façades of the male and the female Buddhas. Something is happening, something that's smoked the people out of their caves. We see two people trudging up from there, and we follow them as they climb, it's an old man, with a pair of brand-new jogging shoes under his arm, and his granddaughter, who has frighteningly blue eyes. They're happy to let us into their cave: it's a low, dark hole with sloping walls, like the inside of a pumpkin in a fairy tale, or an animal's lair. The old man, who's an elementary school teacher and hasn't had a fixed abode for more than ten years, says that nine people live in this cave, but I can't begin to imagine how nine bodies could lie down in these few square metres, not even slotted together like the pieces of a jigsaw puzzle. The old teacher puts his new shoes away neatly in a corner black with soot.

We interview other families living in the caves, and I have my photograph taken – to send home – with two snotty-nosed but very beautiful little Hazara brothers. They have fair hair which is just starting to grow again after being shaved off, and their eyes are two narrow slits between the cheekbones and the eyebrows. I ask the bigger of the two how old he is, he looks six or seven, but he replies that he doesn't know and doesn't even know how old his little brother is.

Distribution
The walls of rock behind the non-Buddhas are like a big wide-open stone book, two inclined rectangles connected at an angle of 140 or 150 degrees. The sun, as it moves through the day, strikes them at different angles, turning them into two unsynchronised sundials. The surfaces are dotted with black cave mouths and marked by towers at the top. When the shadows are sharper and more dramatic on one side, on the other they shrink and fade to orange and red.

About halfway between the niches of the two non-Buddhas, which may be a kilometre apart, or perhaps less, six or seven hundred metres, we see a crowd gathered around a heap of cardboard boxes. It looks as if some kind of humanitarian aid is being distributed, that's why there's nobody in the caves, they've all run down there. Our curiosity aroused, we approach the crowd.

Items of clothing have spilled from those boxes that have already been opened or in some cases turned upside down. They're similar in quality to those you find in Italian street markets: trainers with fancy soles, jackets with lots of zips, military-style trousers. There's no orderly queue, everyone's crowded round the boxes, and as usual the women are being kept at a distance, which makes it seem unlikely they'll get anything in all this chaos. The stuff is being distributed by four or five people of uncertain nationality. One of them is sitting inside a box, talking on a satellite phone. Every now and again he fishes a pair of shoes from the box next to him and throws them in the air. They land in the middle of the crowd, causing a great commotion. The young men fight over them. This seems to amuse the guy, who keeps throwing things in an arc, just as if he were throwing bread to ducks in a pond.

We ask who's in charge of this gang. It's a little guy with mirrored glasses and the after-effects of acne, Asian but not necessarily Afghan – hold on, he might even be Latino, the kind who plays the stooge to Al Pacino in movies about Cuban gangsters. He has a thick American accent, that's for sure. He says he was expecting to find someone else to distribute the stuff, he was only supposed to handle the transport to Bamiyan, and now the lorries have gone back to Kabul. He'd be glad if we could take charge of the stuff (it would certainly be in safer hands…), but as we have no transport, we can't do anything. One of the Afghans in our group whispers in my ear that he knows these guys, they pocket most of the money and almost nothing gets to the 'supposed beneficiaries'. The money's lost on the road. In the meantime, other shoes fly up in the air. Young men armed with Kalashnikovs keep the other young men – not so different from them – at a distance with leather whips. The women sit motionless, not daring to ask questions.

Amid all the confusion I go and speak to one of the men unloading the goods, a Filipino with gloves and a woollen cap. He's opening the boxes with a paper knife. The name of an

American Protestant association is stamped on the boxes. I imagine devout ladies making the collection after Sunday mass or over tea. He's from California. The shoes are from California, too – they're really good shoes, he says, and he bursts out laughing. Then he goes back to disembowelling boxes. The fact that this chaotic scene is taking place at the foot of the holy mountain makes it all the more vivid. The shouts fade away on the air. It's too late now to stop this ceremony. The crowd would be furious. We turn our backs on them.

The smaller of the two Buddhas is a woman. I don't understand the significance of that, but everyone calls it the female Buddha. It's thirty-five metres high. On both sides of the niche where it stood before they blew it up, there are tunnels at various levels through which you used to be able to climb up alongside the giant. I duck my head and squeeze inside. There's a spiral staircase cut into the rock, with very high steps. Climbing each step requires a real effort, which we'll pay for later with cramps in our thighs. The first flight of steps leads to a rock terrace overlooking a chapel that used to be decorated with statues and frescoes. The paintings have been rubbed out with manic precision. Now all that's left are the inscriptions on the wall: names of people who passed this way and wanted to be remembered. A second flight takes us another twenty metres up, and I'm starting to feel dizzy now because on one side there are full length oval windows from which you could once look out at the statues, and I suffer from vertigo – what's more, the stone is all cracked: it doesn't even deserve to be called stone, given that it looks like some kind of crumbly, clayey dough with crushed pebbles inside. I find it hard not to think of the kilos of dynamite that blew away the Buddhas and shook the whole mountain. (Parenthesis for bomb disposal experts and all admirers of work well done: the removal of the statues succeeded one hundred per cent, it's as if they were torn out and scratched away with a huge knife, leaving a scar on the rock.) This second flight, which I climb leaning with my hands on the rock and trying not to look out, also leads to a cave with a view of the valley, and encloses another circular chapel, its vault dominated by smoke-blackened relief decorations shaped like triangles and lozenges. Five or six of us have climbed this far. Some start to massage their thighs: in my opinion, it isn't just the dispro-portionate size of the steps that's played a nasty trick, it's a question of nerves: we're tense and excited, and waste our energy making uncoordinated movements. I think I'm going to stop here, at this intermediate level. Vertigo prevents me from going any higher. I know the way it works, it's pointless trying to overcome the fear: I simply can't do it, I lose balance, I feel as if I'm falling, and it's even worse when I see someone else on the edge of a precipice. The last time was in Chartres, watching my children strolling around the walkways on the outer flanks of the cathedral, and we weren't even halfway up. I persuade myself it'll be different this time and try to follow the others up the third flight of steps, which leads to just above the head of the Buddha. Two turns of the spiral, and suddenly I'm blinded by the light, and find myself in front of another opening that looks out on the void, this time the hole reaches right down to below the step where we're putting our feet, so it's impossible not to look down. I do so. I'm paralysed. If I keep looking down I'll fall straight through the hole, if I look towards the interior I'm afraid I'll take a wrong step and slip anyway. Leaning both hands on the stone, I carry on climbing, until I realise that the whole staircase is separated from the rocky wall by a vertical fissure, as wide as a palm, as if it's about to come away altogether. (The Fall of the House of Usher.) This is completely idiotic. The whole thing is sense-less. To die in Afghanistan as a tourist. I'd like to run back down, but that would mean I'd have to pass the two-metre-high hole again, and I'm sure I'd be sucked through it, like the little metal balls in one of those games riddled with holes – no point turning the knob, the ball is already in it. So I turn and go down backward on my hands and knees, testing each crumbling step.

When we get back to the distribution site, the scene is still more chaotic. A lorry has arrived and they've loaded half the boxes on it, as well as three or four people who are trying to keep them steady. The lorry heads for the slope, but as soon as it turns, some of the boxes fall and roll down the hillside. A couple of the armed young men, who've been trying somewhat ingenuously to keep the load together by putting their arms round it, have to jump down before they fall. At the sight of the lost boxes, some people come out of the crowd and try to grab them, but the armed boys whip them on the face and arms – not that this discourages them, they must be used to this kind of treatment, they go nearer to the lorry, waiting for something to fall off.

Still losing items, the retreating lorry edges its way through the crowd, who step aside at the last minute before they end up under the wheels, until at last the lorry manages to get onto the track leading down into the valley.

The mine disposal people are at work in the area, only a few strips have been cleared of mines, and yet the people run all over to follow the lorry.

Our chief goes to their chief and tells him he'll report this sordid business. 'Go ahead,' the man with the mirrored glasses sneers.

5th May, afternoon. As we reach the governor's office, the reliefs on the red stone façade look all the more dramatic in the glow of the sun. As on many of these official visits, hammer blows and other sounds of work in progress can be heard from the next room. The building is being restored while still in use. An even louder noise is made by the flags on the roof, beating furiously in the wind. The governor: a shrewd-faced man with a pointed goatee who speaks in measured tones. On his dusty desk, a vase of artificial flowers (tulips and irises), three handwritten sheets of paper and an amber rosary. The interpreter translates in a low voice, and his faint words are covered by the flapping of the flags and the jangle of the window panes. The head of our delegation asks for protection and security for the Tajiks who want to return to Bamiyan, and the little Hazara nods, with a gleam in his eyes. You can't talk about minorities in Afghanistan. 'Every ethnic group is a minority in one place and a majority in another.' The governor bemoans the fact that there are so many armed men on his territory who aren't easy to identify and control. Our chief negotiates a solution for the families living in the caves near the Buddhas. The governor has a beautiful silver ring with a red stone. 'Don't push them out before finding a shelter for them.' On the wall, a classic photo of Chairman Karzai: a black jacket slung over his shoulders, a buttoned-up shirt, an astrakhan cap on his bald head.

Bad grace
When we greet someone, instead of gently putting our hands on our hearts like the Afghans, we internationals beat our chests as if accusing ourselves of a sin.

At the end of the day, a brief excursion to the third missing Buddha. We follow a stream until we're beneath a rocky hill riddled with a fantastic number of holes and surmounted by old towers. When the rays of the setting sun suddenly hit the hill, it glows yellow against the white of the snowcapped mountains and the violet sky.

M. makes tagliatelle while listening to Eighties Radio, which broadcasts old hits by Police, Spandau Ballet, Huey Lewis (*I Want a New Drug*). I help him by filtering the flour through a colander which is full of small stones, fibrous flakes and little balls of some pink substance: we'd prefer not to think what it might be, given that in Afghanistan there's only one pink thing – which is used but is never mentioned by name. While M. works hard at spreading the pasta with his sturdy arms, I skim through the video music channels on the satellite. On my right forefinger I'm wearing a ring with a blood-red stone held by two little silver hands.

On the way to the third non-Buddha, Rafiq asked me about the king of Rome who fought against the Muslims. Hang on a sec... are you sure it was a king of Rome? We have some difficulty getting through to each other, then he makes an effort to remember the name of this famous warrior... his name was... Iraches, Iralches... and at last it turns out that he means Herakles, Hercules. *Hercules against the Muslims*: that could easily have been the title of a Fifties B-movie. He's no more confused about the history of my part of the world than I am about the history of his. I tell him that Hercules comes before Rome, before history, he's the link between the world of the gods and the world of men. But for Rafiq there are no gods, and history begins with the Prophet. Rafiq is a somewhat intransigent Muslim. In the office, he keeps an eye on the female Afghan employees, how they dress, how they behave towards the internationals, who carry germs of corruption, or are themselves those germs. He complained to his superiors about one girl who was wearing tight-fitting trousers – 'sticky pants', he called them.

Hazara women, short, sturdy and big-breasted, carrying bunches of firewood on their heads.

The Ambassador arrives in Bamiyan. He's a handsome man with combed-back white hair and something of the yachtsman about him. When his plane emerged from the clouds and dropped hard onto the gravel runway, parallel to the white profile of the mountains, we watched with a certain amount of apprehension, because it's this same little nine-seater plane that will take us back to Kabul this afternoon. He's escorted by two carabinieri, handsome, athletic men with satchels and the relaxed air of people who have everything under control. We accompany him to see the governor, the same man we saw yesterday. While he's inside, we catch sight of a colourful crowd gathering beneath the niche of the Larger Buddha. It's the preparatory assembly for the Loya Jirga, the great tribal parliament which is meeting in Kabul in a few days' time. We drive down there, I stay behind and find myself in a river of women and little girls descending into the valley to take up their places opposite the men lined up on a rise at right angles to the Buddha. Behind them, the dozens of lorries with which they arrived at Bamiyan. These mass movements are accompanied by loudspeakers blaring out orders and music. The government representative for the Loya Jirga tells us that the Tajiks (not all, but some) are boycotting the assembly because one of their chiefs has forbidden them to go. The divisions here are not just ethnic, they also follow religious lines (Shiite and Sunni), with further sub-categories based around villages, mountain vs valley people, etc. The spectacle beneath the niche of the non-Buddha is a grandiose one: donkeys without masters running everywhere, adolescents with Kalashnikovs lying in the grass, women with uncovered faces, children laughing and jumping over the ditches, we internationals, who have no idea what's happening, a TV crew with a long fuzzy microphone fishing for comments from the people, and up above the crowd, more pyramid-shaped groups of women who've scrambled up the sides of the mountain, dozens of motionless and colourfully dressed women who've emerged from the caves next to the huge black hole, the shadow of the Missing Buddha.

I have no wish to pose as a negative theologian, but the presence of the Enlightened One can be sensed even more strongly in the darkness of the niche. That emptiness draws to itself the turbulent forces of the valley and absorbs them.

We're supposed to be going to Shaidan. An hour's drive through red desert and canyons. We cross two passes: from here, the track looks like a strip of white dust. We bounce up and down, hanging on to the handles. At last, here is Shaidan, a plain with a tangle of villages in the middle: roofless houses interspersed with white tents of the kind you can stand upright in, with a hole at the top for the flue. We stop near the most conspicuous group of houses. There are mostly children and a few old men here today, everyone else has gone to Bamiyan for the assembly. A few women in red veils peer at us from between the blocks of houses, children come out onto the little terraces and the few intact roofs, laugh, disappear, then pop up again. Others are down in the valley, washing and scouring pans in a little river. We talk to a man who looks like a chief. Our local officers know him and embrace him. It's common here for men to embrace and kiss three times, but in fact it isn't a real embrace or kiss, they lean towards each other so that their temples almost touch but don't, it's enough for their beards to graze each other. It all happens very slowly and they keep that position for a long time while they exchange news and compliments in each other's ear. They place their hands very lightly on the other person's sides, rather than on their shoulders as we do. It's an important ceremony. Early in the morning at Pul-i-Charkhi, when about fifty people greet each other as enthusiastically and passionately as if they hadn't seen each other for months, and start on a knock-out round of embraces, it takes a quarter of an hour to get through the civilities. This reminds me of the opening scene of Monty Python's *Meaning of Life*, where the fish in an aquarium say 'hello' every time they pass each other.

The chief from Shaidan takes us to see a few abandoned houses. The marks of reprisals are quite evident. The houses were deliberately set alight, the walls are intact but the roofs have collapsed and all that remains are a few charred beams. One of these houses clearly belonged to a rich man. The rooms are large and one of them could even be described as a drawing room: big windows, solid walls at least half a metre thick, and the interior walls are plastered in two different shades of blue, darker on the skirting board and light at the top, like a

Greek house. It's the first time I've seen such sophisticated brickwork in any of these villages.

We return to Kabul in the little plane. There's a full complement of us, but a well-built gentleman from the WFP is already sitting in the plane and won't budge. Outside, it starts to rain and the wind's blowing. In the end he's asked to get off, and from the way he grabs his briefcase and his leather bag and goes off on the runway, with the heavy step of a navy veteran, it's clear he isn't happy. We've made ourselves a friend. Then something happens, there must have been a radio message, because one of the pilots changes his mind and goes to find the veteran, brings him back to the plane, and puts him in the spare seat, where he falls asleep as soon as he's fastened his belt. Beyond the rain-streaked windows, we see the UNHCR staff, who don't want to leave until we take off, we signal to them not to stand there getting wet for our sakes. The governor's also there: while we were shaking hands, he pulled me to him for the triple kiss.

The flight is as bumpy as the car ride was.

The nosedive down to Kabul, with the figures on the altimeter rolling so much you can't read them, is not the kind of experience you want to repeat often.

I asked the carabiniere how much he earns: 143 euros a day. Then he told me about his four years in Palma di Montichiaro and the mafia war between Gela and Agrigento.

Hi, M., thanks for your message, sorry I'm in a bit of a rush. The country is very beautiful but conditions are inhuman. The curfew's a great nuisance, there's this endless obsession with security, though I'm sure when you're really in danger you don't even realise it. Like the people who pick flowers in minefields. We went on a three-day field mission to Bamiyan (where the Buddhas were) and it was a bit of a breather after four weeks in Kabul. Most of the international staff are

neurotic, with a few exceptions. But it's impossible to describe
life here, I'm sorry, I can't do it in a few lines and maybe not
even in many lines. As I'm only here for three months, I'm
really breaking my balls, using all my strength and imagina-
tion, but I'm always afraid of doing or saying bullshit, which
at this level could actually harm a lot of people. My favourite
place is the reception centre just outside Kabul where every
day the returnees arrive from Pakistan: between five and
ten thousand people a day – spectacular – extremely difficult
working there – but interesting and dramatic. I'll send you
a few notes I've managed to make, especially early in the
morning, I wake up at five and have a free hour before I go out.

Last night I was up until late watching the match high-
lights on the satellite TV in the guest house next to mine. I'm
genuinely sorry for the Inter supporters, even though they
don't really deserve a thing, losing four goals to Lazio in the
last game. The only entertainment (?!) is one evening a week
when the UN bar opens to the NGOs and from half-past seven
to half-past eight we have a kind of imitation of a Western
cocktail party, chatting a bit to the girls from the various aid
agencies. And that's it.

The following day, 6th May, I'm in the office writing my
report.

In the afternoon, there's a really spectacular storm: wind,
dust and rain. I think of the cyclists riding around Kabul.

I wake up in the middle of the night because the bed is
shaking. It must be an earthquake. The cover on the stove's
air vent has come away from the wall facing me, and a black
sludge has spilled out onto the floor. I try to clean the silk
sheet I'd laid on the floor, and only succeed in making my
hands black. I can't get them clean even after washing them
three times with soap and water. It's an oily, sticky substance,
like shoe polish. In the morning, I ask around, but nobody else
noticed any earthquake. Maybe I dreamed it. Nuria says it
was my private earthquake.

The international news from the BBC. I've been watching it for a month at meal times. It's always the same. The world seems to repeat itself. The same things always happen. There's an angry crowd, or an enthusiastic crowd, pouring down a street. People get beaten and carted off. A political leader has been shot somewhere in the world. Houses swept away in a flood. An explosion, bodies covered by sheets hurried into ambulances. Other people protesting, lifting banners, but if I don't have my glasses on I'm not sure if they are in fact protesting. They may even be celebrating. A great victory. On the banners they carry there's always a stylised portrait of a man, sometimes with a turban, often with glasses. He's definitely a leader. Maybe he's alive, maybe he's dead and they're mourning him. The people love him and think of him as their father, their saviour, or else they hate him and call him a butcher and a bastard, and spit on him. Anglo-Saxon or acceptably coloured newsreaders. The women journalists, strictly career women, move their mouths as if they were chewing. More clashes with the police. Water hoses. I look down at my plate and concentrate on my cucumber salad. The images on the TV become blurred. More ambulances or presidential cars. They beat on the bonnet with their fists. If the crowd consists of men in white shirts it means we're in Asia, if there are also women it means we're in Europe. They burn flags, or wave them. Somewhere in the world, Agassi wins a tennis match with a sensational backspin ball.

8th May 2002, no light, all day at the desk writing reports in English, searching for each and every word.

But just before leaving – seven thirty, dark outside – I go into the office of my woman boss, who listens to music as she works:

Time has told me... not to ask for more...

Wake up at four forty-five. At a quarter-past five I'm walking down the street. I'm probably breaking the curfew, but it's too late to turn back now. We go to Kabul stadium. On the terraces above the football pitch, today's problem is camped, complete with household belongings. The French doctors say there are four hundred families, we didn't believe it at first, but we walk and walk and the camp goes on and on, there really are a hell of a lot of people. Their meagre belongings are rolled inside bags and blankets. They've slept in the open air, on the pavement, beside or on top of their stuff. We try to talk to some of them, but we choose the wrong people: they don't understand our questions, answer without thinking. It isn't enough to be an old man with a beard to have authority. Finally, a clever kid goes to fetch the chief – God knows where he comes from: unlike the others he's clean, fresh, dazzling in his white clothes. He gives us the information we need. We don't have time to check how reliable it is, but offhand I can't think of any other way to find out more. There are about three hundred families (the French weren't far wrong), all Uzbekis, on their way from Karachi, south Pakistan, to the north-eastern province of Sar-i-Pul. They have travelled more than 2,200 kilometres and still have 500 or 600 to go, on terrible roads. They received money when they reached Kabul but they say they've spent it all paying for the journey here, which is plausible. The lorry drivers didn't want to take them any further. They've been camped in the stadium for two days. They won't move from here until someone helps them. Who? Maybe the Minister for Repatriation, or maybe us. If someone gives you the money for the journey – we ask them – you'll leave, won't you? You aren't going to stay in Kabul, are you? No, no, we want to return to Sar-i-Pul. The chief has the registration forms of five or six families. I take a look at them, check the figures and the signatures. Everything's in order. They all received 140 dollars in Pul-i-Charkhi. They haven't been given grain and utensils, because they're supposed to get them further on in their journey, at the distribution centre in Pul-i-Khumri, Baghlam province, but if they don't leave here they won't receive anything. We don't want all returnees stopping in Kabul waiting for something to turn up. The city is growing by two or three thousand people a day. I give the forms back to the chief, who rolls them up and slips them into a plastic folder, the multi-purpose container used in Afghanistan to protect important documents from sweat and dust. Without plastic, the sheets of paper get stuck together and are ruined. Then he slips them inside a hidden pocket. Are you all Uzbekis? Yes, all Uzbekis.

My female colleague tells me a policeman followed her yesterday, blocked her path, and fondled her breast. She punched him in the face.

Jette says we can give the Uzbekis an extra allocation: ten dollars per person, let's say, up to a maximum of fifty dollars per family. But who's going to give them this money? Where? How? 'Simple,' Jette says, 'I already did it once for a similar case. We don't even have to get out of our car. We open the car window, the heads of families come one at a time, we write thirty, forty or fifty dollars on their forms and give them the money, and on to the next one.' I'm taken aback. I'm sure it can be done: the fact that J. has already done it is the best guarantee of that, because our Danish carpenter is the toughest and most serious of us all, but I don't like the idea of being on a street corner in Kabul with 15,000 dollars in a briefcase and hundreds of people watching you give them away.

My suggestion is that we make sure they have transport and leave it at that. That way, we're sure they'll really get to their destination and we won't have to handle cash. Mind you, it's become very difficult in the last few days to organise a convoy, since the principal agency transporting refugees and displaced persons has practically declared bankruptcy. If the donors don't put more money in…

All the agencies are in the same situation. The WFP have almost exhausted their stocks of grain: since yesterday, just one sack of grain per family, after that we'll see. We have enough funds to see us through to 15th June.

About half-past six we are outside the entrance of the ex-Soviet Compound. We've had to come because today the last convoy of displaced persons is leaving. It's a small convoy, forty-seven families, just a few buses are enough, plus three or four lorries for the baggage. It was only the last three blocks that still had to be emptied. Now that the Soviet Compound is almost uninhabited, it's become even more ghostly. Twenty-four blocks, burnt and riddled with holes, not a single door or window remaining, railings torn out piece by piece, the open air cinema with a few metal seats that have obstinately resisted attempts to uproot them. The final removable items have ended up in sacks, and will soon have to be lifted, with great difficulty, onto the backs of the lorries.

That's what the Soviet Compound resembles now – the village in the second half of *Full Metal Jacket*, where the battle is fought. The place is impressive because it gives you a glimpse of what was an attempt to provide planned housing – the outpost of Communist bureaucratic functionalism trying to stamp its mark on the swarming anthill of Afghanistan, squashing a good few ants in the process, but at the same time providing a semblance of order (something which, paradoxically, like all remnants of the Soviet past, it's possible to feel nostalgic about). But it's impossible to describe the Compound, when you're inside it a hundred eyes turning in all directions wouldn't be enough to grasp all that's there, all that's been there and all that's missing: it's too big, too desolate, too foul, to let you go into details. Of all the places I've ever been to in the world, it's the one that's given me the strongest sense of my own limitations. A failure of perception rather than of expression. If I can't describe something I've seen, I feel as if it hasn't really passed through my senses, or rather, it has passed through and immediately come out the other side. Like the horse on that record of fairy stories we listened to as children, the horse that was cut in half: '...the water that the horse... drank with his mouth... fell out again... through the cut-off part!!!'

Just going in through the big gate sends a shiver down your spine, but of course that's not enough to convey the atmosphere of the Compound. The first and second and third time I went there, I thought the difficulty I had in making sense of my impressions was due to the sheer number of new things, the frightening crush of strangers, lack of sleep, fear. I really was afraid, physically afraid: the day after receiving my security briefing on things that are *not* to be done in Afghanistan, it seemed to me we were doing *all* of them, in one go.

Avoid gatherings: and yet there were a thousand people around us, screaming or whimpering unintelligible things.

Keep as far as possible within sight of UN staff: how could you do that in this crowd?

Signal your own position frequently: but I was hopeless using my radio, stammered my call sign – Kilo Hotel 1.4 – and forgot to press the button.

The worrying thing was that to reach the furthest blocks we had to go quite far inside the Compound, putting hundreds of steps – and above all hundreds of potentially hostile people – between us and the only exit. No escape route. No possibility of *retreating quickly in case of danger* (another *elementary* security regulation – broken).

IF IN DOUBT – BUG OUT!

(In other words, if you have the slightest suspicion that the situation is getting worse, get out of there before you're trapped like a maggot.)

And yet even today, when there's hardly anyone about, no screams echoing between the shattered walls, just the bleating of some calf to be loaded on the lorry, entering the Compound provokes a very strong emotion. I pretend that I'm fine, but I feel like an astronaut leaping onto the moon and holding his breath in order not to hyperoxygenate.

The displaced families are already waiting, their belongings beside them sinking in the dirt: bales of rags, sacks full of scrap metal, door frames and window frames sprouting nails as big as fingers.

There's a Macedonian doctor who, before examining the serious cases, kindly lets me take the last drags from his cigarette.

Unregistered women emerge from God knows where, waving pieces of paper which are supposed to be documents. For two months, we've been registering the people who are actually living in the Compound. The fact that these women haven't been registered means they don't live here, they've sneaked into the Compound with their things in order to get a free passage to Shomali. Supposedly, the entrance is guarded, but there are quite a few places where the perimeter wall has been chipped away and you can slip in without being spotted. We've seen people pushing their barrows early in the morning, ready to enter with a couple of mattresses and a bale of rags and pretend to be refugees so that they can cadge a ride to Shomali and maybe get a couple of plastic sheets. (We used to give those away, too, but we've stopped in order to discourage bogus refugees and scroungers.) These burqa-clad women do their squawking very professionally. They're extremely poor, too, let's be clear about that. One of them has a towering load on her head, wrapped in a blanket, and a baby boy in her arms. The baby is wearing a woollen cap which is too big for him, with little red and blue ribbons, and his nose is eaten by leishmaniasis. The red scabs make it look longer, like a kind of beak, or rather, like the carrot on a snowman. With the same hand she's using to support her disfigured child, the woman waves a dirty and illegible piece of linen paper, supposedly a document. I learned a lesson in prison some years ago:

whatever piece of paper they hold out to you, never take it in your hand to look at it, because that means you've accepted it as genuine, you've committed yourself – and giving it back becomes an impossible task.

While the beggars jump on anyone who seems to be in a position of authority (all you need is a jacket or a beret with some initials on it), the lorries have reversed and parked in the middle of the square with their engines on, ready to load the heaps of baggage. This barrier of vehicles confines hundreds of people in a small space and makes the whole scene even more chaotic, what with people loading bags, people writing or checking forms, little children crying or quarrelling or playing, completely indifferent to the fact that they're just about to leave, the filthy burqas constantly on the attack, the genuine ones screeching like eagles and the fake ones screeching even louder. Inside the lorries, the people from the transport agency have set about loading the things, joined by a couple of enterprising barefoot teenagers: I shudder as I watch these two boys, standing there in their bare feet, grabbing frames bristling with nails and throwing them to each other. Attached to a pole, two cows have started to moo. Maybe they're conscious of the fact that they might be crushed when the lorry hits the first bend or the first pothole and the rest of the haphazardly piled load collapses on top of them. The man directing the operations is a nervous Spaniard with a limp, who seems impatient to be finished with all this shit. The UNHCR are only here to register the displaced persons, loading and transport are supposed to be the responsibility of the Spaniard's organisation, but we do what we can to limit the damage and make sure things are done properly. The problem of bogus refugees is exacerbated by the presence of a TV crew, which is going to make a meal out of this situation – nothing wrong with that, if they confined themselves to filming the muddle, but no, they want to join in the work, their chief has got it into his head to collect the women's names, he thinks he's making a humanitarian contribution, without realising that every time a name is written on a piece of paper here in Afghanistan, that piece of paper immediately assumes a magical significance, it becomes a lottery ticket guaranteeing unlimited food and transport, like a six-zone annual travelcard!

Idiot! (I say it in Italian, and he smiles and hands me his list, which I tear into pieces and throw up in the air).

Everyone's amazed.

The scene is caught by two girls with TV cameras on their shoulders and figures like models, dressed like locals, that is, in dusty gabardines and plastic sandals, as if they're trying to convince people they're Afghan women. They're taller than me and wisps of blonde hair escape from beneath their headscarves.

That's another ridiculous thing: the attempt – half naive, half malicious – to merge into the surroundings by dressing like Afghans.

There was one guy who grew his beard and put on a Pashtun hat to make friends with the people. And in fact, for one day they took him for a real Pashtun and gave him a good thrashing. You can make friends that way – but you can also make enemies.

Perhaps it's best to stay neutral and visibly different.

While my battle-hardened Danish colleague gives the journalist a dressing down in front of the TV cameras, using the impeccably democratic argument that if we give aid to bogus refugees we take it away from real ones – not that it'll make any difference, given that the TV people will edit the report as they see fit and make her look like a hysterical monster – I deal with the two cows. They're small and dusty and really don't look comfortable inside the lorry. I tell the boys to at least swaddle their sides with a few padded blankets so that they don't hurt themselves against the spikes. They have to get through sixty kilometres of potholes before they'll be able to graze on the plateau. When our Afghan interpreter translates, they burst out laughing. What are they laughing at?

I ask. If the cows get hurt, who cares, they say, we'll kill them. And they pass a finger across their necks. Even the interpreter smiles. Even I laugh, thinking these people are crazy. The dust and exhaust shroud the whole scene in a cloud. The minibuses fill very slowly with women and children. They get on, get off, get on again, get off again, and every time they see me, they take out their travel documents, which by now are reduced to shreds. I climb aboard. These are the most clapped-out vehicles I've ever seen. Broken windows or no windows at all, not many seats and those there are are torn...

The ex-Soviet Compound ought to be sealed off by the guards, because from today it's officially empty and returns to Russian ownership.

2,500 families deported by the Taliban lived there. They have gone home. But their homes have been destroyed.

What will the Russians do with the Compound? It ought to be razed to the ground.

(J. is a carpenter. She's served two terms as a Green member of the Danish Parliament. She's been living in a commune in Copenhagen for thirty years. She works as a field officer for the UNHCR for limited periods only, and has been to some of the toughest places in the world. She's been in Afghanistan since December 2001, and unfortunately she's leaving in twenty days' time. Since I arrived, she's helped me more than anyone else. I've learned a lot from her.)

While I'm writing these notes my room mate is having his Dari lesson. I love the sound of the language. He reads slowly, from a school book printed on pages that look like toilet paper. He spells out the Arabic alphabet, then translates the sentences into English, and I mentally retranslate them into Italian.

THE MUJAHEDDIN... HAVE MADE...
THIS COUNTRY FAMOUS... ALL OVER THE WORLD

THE MUJAHEDDIN HAVE DEFEATED THE INFIDELS
WHO DO NOT PRAY – in other words, the Communists

*Hi, S., things are still tough here. I try to keep busy, but it's
hard to channel your strength. This morning I started at half-
past five, going to see Uzbekis camped in the stadium, who've
run out of money and still have three days' travelling to do,
and then I was around to see the departure of the last convoy
of displaced persons from the ex-Soviet Compound, the shitty
place I think I've already described to you, a complicated job,
what with crowds of beggars, sacks full of stuff, holes, shit,
cows to load on the lorries, and on top of all that a Czech TV
crew (including two gorgeous blondes I might have appreci-
ated in another context) and the usual journalist trying to
make us feel guilty, a real pain in the arse, waving lists of
bogus refugees needing transport and accusing us in effect of
leaving poor people in the lurch – in the end, I had to take the
fake lists, tear them up and throw them away theatrically for
the benefit of the cameras, so tomorrow evening some people in
Brno will see a report about cruel UNHCR officers mistreating
Afghan people.*

*That's the amusing, though stressful, part of the mission.
Apart from that, there's a tremendous amount of paperwork.
We have to read and write reports in English about everything
we see and do. I often manage to wriggle out of it, but not
always. My mood has stabilised, though I still suffer from
lack of sleep. The situation in Afghanistan, on the other hand,
is very unstable and in many areas we're in a state of alert,
especially in Mazar-i-Sharif. I don't know if it's being written
about in the newspapers, but every day quite a few people get
killed, and the fighting isn't between the Americans and
Al Qaeda, but between Afghans and Afghans, Hazaras and
Uzbekis, etc., just like in the good old days. The bomb in
Karachi (13 or 14 dead, I think, all French) has added to
the anxiety.*

Tell me about yourself when you can. All the best.

The big hands of Haider ('snake killer'). He opens his hand and notes down names and numbers on it in biro, as if writing a diary.

The Japanese girl with the freckles has come down with hepatitis and has been evacuated to Islamabad.

12th May, Pul-i-Charkhi
The cashiers work with packets of dollars in their laps.

One of the refugees complains to me that he was badly treated by a cashier for no other reason than that he didn't want to accept notes of low denominations – apparently when you change them at the market, they give you less in return. I ask to speak to the cashier. I tell him he must always be polite to the refugees, no matter what, even when they complain or shout. The cashier tells me that the refugee accused him in front of everyone of belonging to Al Qaeda. (The most common way of badmouthing someone in Kabul these days: you point them out to others as a Taliban).

Cripples, the maimed and mutilated, people on crutches and legs that wobble in every direction.
It must be a hundred degrees in the vaccination tents. Some children fall to the ground when they see the syringes and their mothers – exhausted blue-eyed or green-eyed madonnas – pull them up by the arm.

Leishmaniasis: infectious disease caused by parasites (protozoa) of the genus Leishmania. It manifests himself in various clinical forms: cutaneous leishmaniasis or oriental sore, the most frequent and least serious form, which can nevertheless cause up to two hundred ulcers on the skin of a single person; mucocutaneous leishmaniasis; visceral leishmaniasis or kala-azar, an Indian term that means 'black fever'. This last is very serious because it causes the degeneration of the internal organs (liver and spleen) and has a very high mortality rate if not treated. Death occurs between three and twenty months after the infection is contracted.

There is no vaccine. Children and malnourished subjects in general are the most affected groups.

The leishmaniae are transmitted to humans through the sting of insects belonging to the genus Phlebotomus. It can be difficult to identify them or to sense their sting because they are nocturnal and fly silently. The incubation period of the cutaneous form is variable, and the infection may manifest itself weeks or months after a sting from an infected fly. The lesions consist of red pustules with raised edges, about two centimetres in diameter, which may be either purulent or covered with a dry crust. The pustules usually appear on the exposed parts of the body, the face and the extremities. In general they cause pain and itching, leaving a sunken, depigmented scar on the skin. Healing can take up to a year. Complications may arise, causing secondary infections, bleeding, a ruptured spleen, and the disfigurement of the nose, the lips and the palate.

The spread of leishmaniasis has reached epidemic proportions in Afghanistan. Currently there are more than 250,000 people suffering from the disease, of whom at least 100,000 are in Kabul.

(For a time, it was quite common for a large number of incisions to be made in the hands and feet and infected with scar tissue from sick subjects. This was done to prevent facial scars which might have been caused by a subsequent natural infection.)

Satellite dish
Two lorries full of returnees have satellite dishes on board.
Where are you going?
To Mir Bacha Kot.
Mir Bacha Kot on the Shomali Plains?
That's right.
But there's no electric current there. No TV.
We have generators.

On the way there: flocks of black lambs (hundreds) and goats (thousands) heading for the city. Nomads – Kuchis – on their way to market to sell their animals.

On the way back: shepherds bathing in wells while their flocks graze on what little grass is available.

The type and quantity of aid we give returnees and displaced persons is subject to variation. Indeed, these standards are continually discussed and updated in an attempt to reach a greater degree of fairness (and a greater feasibility: there, I've finally used that ugly word, 'feasibility').

Example: since the end of April we've been giving an extra eight dollars a head (up to a maximum of forty dollars per family) to people arriving from Karachi. This is because when they leave from Karachi they have an extra 1,800 kilometres to travel, and consequently to pay for. However, the supplement is only given to refugees from Karachi, and not to those coming from Kashmir, for example, which may not be as far, but is still 1,000 kilometres further than Peshawar. And yet a refugee from Kashmir and one coming from the camps near the border get the same amount of money. The same principle should apply to those who've come a long way and those with a long way to go. There are people who, once they've arrived in Kabul, have finished their journey, while others have barely started it. We've learnt how to show surprise when we read in the documents that the families are heading for northern and north-eastern provinces like Faryab, Sar-i-Pul or the mythical Jawzjan (a name that sounds Chinese) on the border with Turkmenistan. Until now, apart from the Uzbekis who were camped in Kabul stadium (of whom, incidentally, all trace has been lost, because so far – and it's now 13:00 hours on 13th May – they haven't been through Pul-i-Khumri or Mazar-i-Sharif: where the devil are they hiding? Did they get lost on the way?), apart from those Uzbekis from Sar-i-Pul, returnees who still have long distances to travel within Afghanistan haven't received any extra help.

In addition, humanitarian aid has to be applied with a certain consistency, otherwise the staff in the field would go mad judging the merits of each individual family. There have to be parameters, cut-off points, flat rates, fixed units of measurement. Above all, there should be no room for argument at the point of application. In the field, I've seen how an uncertain reply can immediately cause discontent. The refugees' sense of gratitude can easily tip over into resentment. They're convinced that instead of receiving aid, they've suffered an injustice. And there are people who go around spreading false information, like plague-spreaders. They tell the refugees all sorts of nonsense, and the refugees set off, dreaming of all the things they'll find when they arrive. The cases of this are as varied as the harsh conditions in which the people who believe the plague-spreaders find themselves. Some people return to Afghanistan thinking that the UNHCR will give them food and money for six months (what are you saying? who told you that? Answer: people going around the camps. And who are these people? Nobody knows. People with an interest in the refugees leaving Pakistan in a hurry). Speaking of which, I've heard two opposing theories: one says that the Pakistanis can't wait to throw the Afghans out, the other that they're doing everything they can to keep them. Are the refugees more of a hassle or more of a business? There've been two striking cases in Herat: two seriously ill men returning from Iran sure they would find a centre for dialysis, or rather, three specialised centres. Dialysis? In Afghanistan?

Second example: every family coming from Pakistan receives 20 dollars a head to reimburse them for the journey, up to a maximum of 100 dollars per family. So every family of five or more members receives the same amount, 100 dollars: there may be six, seven or twelve family members, they still receive 100 dollars. For about the past month (and I'm proud to say it was as a result of a proposal of mine), families of ten or more people have received an extra sack of grain and an extra kit of utensils. It may not be much, and of course they'd prefer to take the money, seeing that the kit is worth about 20 dollars. I agree. The fact is that, following these parameters, a family unlucky enough to consist of nine people receives 100 dollars, no more than that, just like one consisting of five people, all for the lack of a single person to make the numbers up to ten and receive the double ration of 'food and non-food items'. All they'd need is an extra little child…

The news of the ceiling of 100 dollars per family has spread down to Pakistan, because for the last few weeks most of the families who've arrived have conformed to virtuous European standards, just five or six members, which means that they've deliberately separated before the registration to receive a larger amount. 'Split families'. Eight people become two families of four and four, so that instead of 100 dollars they scrape together 160.

More opposed theories: the number of returnees will decrease noticeably during the summer; the number of returnees will increase noticeably during the summer. There are valid reasons for thinking that either is correct.

I'm joking
I've noticed that in conversations in which people make a witty remark at the end, perhaps slightly making fun of someone, they immediately hasten to add: 'I'm joking!' They're so afraid of being misunderstood, or being taken seriously, that they haven't even finished their joke before they say: 'I'm joking.' It's due partly to the bastardised English that we speak, partly to cultural differences (what for me is an innocent legpull may be a mortal offence to an Afghan, say, or a Japanese), and partly to everyone's innate need to safeguard themselves, to dare without taking risks.

Dear Dad, I miss you a lot. You always said: either me, or the cat. So, seeing as you're not here, I choose the cat (I'm joking). Bye, Leone

It's raining, and an Afghan is strolling around with his hat wrapped in a plastic bag.

15th May. Visit with Intersos to the slums of Kabul
There are seven of us, driving in the direction of the airport. Qassaba: a line of Soviet-style blocks, housing managers and workers from the adjacent cement factory.

They must have built the neighbourhood with the products of the factory. The blocks are situated on the side of a hill, unconnected by any horizontal structure – pavements, squares, streets.

Many windows have plastic instead of panes of glass, often the black plastic used for rubbish bags.

Everything is patched together and ultra-squalid, flies are buzzing around the drains, but in the end, Qassaba turns out to be more liveable than many other places, almost a model neighbourhood.

A thousand families live here.

We enter the nursery school.

Apart from the devastated entrance, the classrooms are big, furnished with red plastic seats and vast carpets with red and orange stripes.

There are about forty teachers and assistants for the infants. The most self-confident of them leads us through the classrooms where the children are sitting on their tiny plastic chairs against the wall.

Children of three or four, all silent and with their arms folded. What were they doing before we came in?

There are no toys or books or pencils, no other furnishings and fittings to be seen.

All the classes we see are like this.

Clean and bare, with red rugs on the floor.

Quiet, well-behaved children who say 'salaam' in unison when we enter. As we've arrived without warning, it's hard to believe they've been got ready to greet us, maybe they spend their time sitting in silence.

There's also a crèche, for children from three months to a year.

In one room they're all crying at the same time, in the other they're sleeping.

The screaming ones are being rocked mechanically, two by two, by thickset women.

But where are their mothers?

Working in the city.

As if we were in Sweden...

But here it's out of a desperate need to earn money, not to 'find fulfilment'.

Only the toilets are, as usual, disgusting.

Washbasins full to the brim with water. Flies skating on the surface.

The stench turns the stomach.

The good teachers want to show us everything, and they really mean everything. Maybe they think they'll get new funds from us. They bought the chairs and the carpets and the paint for the walls with funds from the GTZ.

I ask them if there's a playground.

There is – they reply – but there's no grass, and I think, smiling inwardly, of the cement playground of the nursery school where my two youngest, well-off children bruise their legs five days a week, while the older ones bear ever more faded marks on their knees, elbows and even on their faces (A. a little white scar, the souvenir of having fallen face down). Does it have to have grass?

In a gloomy basement, its floor flooded with water, there are huge swings of raw iron assembled out of girders and tubes six or seven centimetres in diameter.

Water, iron, *Stalker*.

These things will eventually be used for the playground.

I can't begin to imagine how those mites I saw sitting sadly on their plastic chairs will ever be able to make these works of conceptual art swing with their own weight.

I think of their crushed little feet.

But come on, let's be honest – I tell the people accompanying us – you call this a slum? Qassaba is a model neighbourhood: full employment, work for the women, a middle class, children in nursery school. Apart from the flies in the drains and the equipment that doesn't work and the poverty that becomes obvious as soon as you scratch the surface – it's paradise...

To get to the next neighbourhood, or village, because in this suburban belt it isn't clear whether we're still inside Kabul or outside (I sincerely hope inside, otherwise Anne and I are violating UN security regulations, because we'd have needed a security clearance to go one metre outside the safe area and if something happens to us, even something stupid, I don't mean a mine or an attack but getting stuck here because our car has broken down, it's our own fucking business, our NGO colleagues can go wherever they like, but we can't), we have to take the long way round behind the airport.

Kabul airport is surrounded by wrecks.

Wrecks of planes and armoured cars are lined up on the plain, like toys to be assembled, tails, noses, fuselages, machine-gun turrets, engines.

There's something almost organised about this disaster area, as if the pieces had been arranged by a giant boy.

Driving along a bumpy dirt road which arouses my suspicions, as we don't know where the track – which I'm sure is demined – ends and the fields begin, we see, about fifty metres away, a bloody heap with three dogs around it.

It's a cow blown up by a mine as it was grazing.

Still tossing about in the Rover, we skirt a military depot.

There are rolls of barbed wire on top of the walls.

In front of the entrance, a group of about twenty beggars are held at bay by two soldiers from the Czech Republic with their rifles resting on their forearms.

They have their gloves on, in this heat.

The village of Hojarawash is the usual mass of mud, criss-crossed by crowded and foul-smelling streets.

We talk to some of the poorest inhabitants.

People press around us in the middle of the street, so from time to time I swerve sideways to disperse the crowd.

It's something Jette taught me: 'Move, always keep moving.'

It isn't that most of them expect anything particular from us, but they don't have anything to do, so they cluster around us in an inquisitive circle.

Some of them have only been back a few days.

They've stayed in Kabul instead of completing their journey because their houses, in Qara Bagh, on the Shomali Plains, have been destroyed.

But if you had help in rebuilding your houses, would you go back to Qara Bagh or not?

They all raise their arms to the sky, nod and shout yes.

But the most interesting guy is a tailor who says he came back as soon as the American bombing was over.

When exactly, November, December?…

He can't answer, and I don't think it's because he's lying, but because he really has no idea.

He came back… a long time ago.

In Afghanistan the notion of time is relative: most people, even young ones, don't know how old they are.

The tailor specialised in embroidery, now he sells sweets to get by.

There's no trace of productive activity or of trade in any of the streets.

The third and last slum: Hoja Bughra, an unauthorised shanty town without water or drains. A really unhealthy place, home to at least five hundred families, though nobody knows the exact number. The air is unbreathable, the drains run along the middle of the muddy streets, the flies form dense clouds. As I walk, I suck in the air through pursed lips. At least fifty repatriated families live here, we meet two of them, who arrived in Kabul twenty days ago. The heads of the families have found work in the brick factory. The most immediate problem of the neighbourhood is water. It's going to be hard to get through the summer without water. We need an emergency plan. My report ends with the words: 'Should we follow this up?'

Homesickness focused on certain anonymous fragments of Italian daily life. Not only on people you love, but also on insignificant places, street corners, junctions where you brake on your moped, for example the exact point of Porta Pinciana where the traffic police stop cars from entering Villa Borghese, forcing them to continue along the Muro Torto. It's a place that has no personal significance for me, it's just a hallucination, a particularly pure, primal hallucination.

Elections
The first reform I'd promote as mayor of Kabul would be to give every street in Kabul a name and put up a sign, so that everyone would have an address, even the prefabs, the shanty towns, the muddy open spaces, the heaps of stones would have their civic name and people would no longer have to give directions like 'opposite the Zarghoona school', 'between the Herati mosque and UNICEF', 'near the fifteenth street, in the square behind where the IAM eye clinic used to be', 'next to the Shahr-e-Naw passport office', 'in the vicinity of the Zainab cinema' (I'm quoting from the official address book of Kabul agencies). I ask Harun if he'd vote for me. He turns his handsome, freckled face to me and says yes, he'd vote for me... if I find him a permanent job. I try to explain, in my incoherent

English – a direct consequence of getting only four hours of sleep a night – that this was the method used by mayors to get elected in Rome and Naples. We were together all morning, first at the encashment centre (where UNICEF have put up a new tent for vaccinations and turned the big tent for the 'Back to School' campaign ninety degrees so that the column of returnees goes in one side and out the other – except that the tent posts were put in the wrong places and there was a risk that barefoot children going too close to them would hurt themselves – until we repositioned some and put padding round the others), then we went with an orphan named Najibullah to his home, to try to ascertain what we could do for him and his brother and sisters. Najibullah arrived yesterday with his aunt, who was absolutely determined to abandon him, his mentally handicapped brother and his two younger sisters. She wanted to hand the children over and go, relieved of a burden. Rachel had to plead, threaten, cajole, and resort to moral blackmail ('But an Afghan who throws his nephews and nieces out on the street isn't a good Afghan, or a good Muslim') to convince the uncle and aunt to keep the children with them for a few more days.

From the report
The family consists of: Habibullah, 18, dumb, mentally retarded, probably suffering from pneumonia; Najibullah, 16; Sabra, 12; Rona, 5.

The father apparently died six years ago. The mother last year.

The orphans are cared for by their uncle and aunt, who have five children of their own. They all arrived in Kabul on 15th May. They've lived in Pakistan for four years, but come originally from Wardak province in Afghanistan.

In Kabul they are temporarily housed at Qala-i-Shadi Kohna, near the Ziarat Abulfazil mosque, together with three other families, one of which is related to them.

They are illiterate, none of them has ever been to school.

Apart from the eldest child's handicap, they all seem undeveloped for their ages, both from the physical and the psychological point of view.

There are no obvious signs of abuse.

The aunt has stated several times that she has no intention of looking after them any longer.

We have put pressure on the aunt to make sure she will share with the children the food she received at the distribution centre.

The only one capable of generating income is Najibullah, who worked as a carpet weaver when they lived in Pakistan.

Next Wednesday, Najibullah will come to our office to give us news of the family and receive information.

Harun is given the job of finding a sufficient supply of medicines for an entire cycle of treatment for pneumonia.

Agencies to contact immediately for both short-term and long-term support: ASCHIANA (Association for Afghan street children), Children in Crisis, UNICEF, the Red Cross (Edoardo is dealing with it).

18th May. Cutting corners. I go all over the city trying to find a solution to the problem of the orphans. Maybe we could get the two middle children, who are easier to place, admitted to a day centre, where they would study, work and be given something to eat, so that when they return home in the evening they would already have eaten (two less mouths to feed – two less reasons to throw them out of the house).

But the problem isn't Najibullah and Sabra, but the other two, the eighteen-year-old mentally handicapped boy and the little girl. We need to provide the aunt and uncle's family with financial assistance so that they don't put them on the street. The already heavy traffic in Kabul is being slowed down even more by roadblocks. Soldiers are stopping cars at road junctions, their Kalashnikovs at the ready. I'm not sure what they're checking, since all they seem to be doing is sticking their heads through the window and chatting to the driver, the way you do when you see a friend in the street and you stop your car and the other people behind sound their horns. Our driver wastes no time: he climbs the centre strip, takes the other lane in the wrong direction, gets to the roundabout and cuts left without going round. Here in Kabul, nobody goes round a roundabout in the right direction.

(Little boys playing football in an open space which is also used for beehives. Dust Honey. A Pashtun Maradona is performing miracles all by himself. I stop for three minutes. Later, it occurs to me it's the same thing I do when I ride home alongside the river at Tor di Quinto, and I look down at the fields where different generations are playing football. I've discovered that the bees are Italian. I intend to ask the Italian mine clearance people if they can take me with them some time.)

The curfew has been put back to ten o'clock. On Friday we watched a DVD of *No Man's Land*, a black comedy set during the war in Bosnia, about a man lying on a mine which will explode if he stands up. Typical humour from former Yugoslavia… The audience laughed their heads off, especially at the fun that was made of the UN: the Frenchman in the blue helmet who keeps poking his head out of his armoured car, like a kind of Punch, and asking 'Parlez-vous français?' but nobody ever understands him. Last night they showed *Amélie*, in a French version subtitled, curiously, in French. I watched the first ten to fifteen minutes again, which I'd remembered as being amusing (the way the characters were introduced through what they like and don't like), and then went to bed.

Discussing the World Cup with Mohammad Yama. He doesn't think much of Italy. Neither do I, to tell the truth, but I tell him how things were in '82. World Cups are long competitions that go through various phases, the initial positions can be reversed. He listens with interest, turning his ring with its sky-blue stone. On the radio, they continue to play repetitive music, often embellished, over a very sad accordion accompaniment, interspersed with political proclamations in which the word 'Afghanistan' is repeated in every sentence. Listening to these speeches also produces a hypnotic effect. The gates of all the international organisations bear signs saying that it's forbidden to carry weapons inside. Quite often the signs are put up in the waiting rooms, too, just in case anyone hasn't understood. It's the classic red circle with a diagonal line over the forbidden object, in this case the unmistakable silhouette of a Kalashnikov. Waiting rooms in Kabul are furnished with collapsed sofas, and men sit on them with apparently nothing else to do but greet each other and embrace warmly and drink tea with loud sucking noises. It isn't clear who they are: guards, friends, people waiting their turn, petitioners. I've never seen one of them entering or leaving.

20th May. Wake up at 4:45. Hallucinations. The guard presses a handkerchief to his mouth.

To Pul-i-Charkhi first, in the somewhat clapped-out Italian NGO car. On the way there, we see a terrible accident. A lorry of refugees has swerved into the left-hand lane and crushed a car. Maybe the driver fell asleep, or thought he was still in Pakistan. The weather is fine and cool but very dusty because of the wind. As we sign the forms, I chat away to Harun. I talk to him about Venice, I don't know why but I'd love to be in Venice today, with this wind and this light it'd be beautiful. He doesn't know what Venice is. Hasn't he ever seen it in a photo, in a film, on TV? No, never.

I show him my little notebook. It's covered in newspaper with an image of New York and the Empire State Building on it. He doesn't recognise the city. While we carry on working at full stretch, checking and signing forms and handing them back to the old Pashtun men, I tell him a riddle. Look, this skyscraper was the tallest in the city... then it was overtaken by two other skyscrapers, twins... but then these two famous very tall skyscrapers collapsed... and now the old skyscraper is once again the tallest of all.

But the game becomes more complicated, because Harun asks me what 'Empire' means. What's the difference between an empire and a kingdom? Gosh, it's like being at school – but I don't mind, I love it, I've explained Greek mythology to Margaret (Kenya), a bit of Romance philology to Bashir and Wahid (Afghanistan), who Celestine V was and why John Paul II is so reluctant to give up the papal throne (Jojo, Philippines), I've recited *Tanto gentile*[6] to David (Australia) and verses by Tasso to...

I go to talk to the French doctors. When I get back, I find that Harun and Bashir have been using my open notebook as a tray for a handful of nuts, raisins and almonds. The usual snack taken with tea. They offer me everything that's left. Earlier, one of the young guards at the main gate, wearing a baseball cap two sizes too large for him, took my hand, opened it, and filled it with nuts and raisins. He didn't say a word, just smiled.

Unlike Yelda, Thuba isn't embarrassed when I sit next to her at work. So Rachel encourages her to take the initiative: tomorrow morning, it'll be her turn to give the opening pep-talk to the staff. Oh, no, says Thuba, I can't speak. But why, don't you feel up to speaking to the men? It's just that there are so many of them, she says evasively, more than fifty... But would you speak to him? Rachel asks her, and points to me. Oh, yes, I'd speak to Edoardo, because there's only one of him.

Look, it's much more difficult speaking to one man at a time than to fifty men who are obliged to listen to you and do what you say.

Afternoon. I go back to the Red Cross orthopaedic centre. The Director, Alberto Cairo, isn't there. 'He's flying,' they tell me. I'm met by Dr Najmuddin, a very kind man, who arrives walking on crutches. They produce ninety wheelchairs a month here, six hundred feet, and Lord knows how many crutches. We go to the carpentry workshop. It smells of wood and glue – a great smell – and there are plenty of feet of every size. All the workers are crippled, too. The wooden foot has a padded heel and the part corresponding to the toes is flexible, thanks to a gasket and a spongy black rubber insert. The foot is then coated in plastic. We move on to the section where they make legs. First they carefully take the measurements, then they make a plaster cast following the contours of the good leg, which is perfected on the spot. The rooms are connected by big swing doors. There's a different smell here, of warm plastic. The shelves are full of feet. Najmuddin shows me how the leg is screwed onto the feet, there's an adaptable mechanism in the middle which is tested and adjusted according to how well the patient walks, and then over that a flesh-coloured plastic covering is laid and the leg is finished. All the legs are numbered so that the patients can be identified. I ask the doctor how long a prosthesis can last. Two years, sometimes more. We walk through the physiotherapy room. Behind the curtains, lying on small beds, I glimpse patients of all ages, with different kinds of deformations or amputations. Gently, the physiotherapists help them to bend their joints – or what remains of them. There's a little girl with an amputated leg, her hair caked with dust, a man with polio whose entire right leg, which is wrapped in bandages and rests on a polyurethane support, is no thicker than a water hose. In a rack there are about thirty legs with shoes already on them. They have to be tested and perfected before the 'cosmetic' covering. In the garden overflowing with roses, the patients try out their prostheses, walking back and forth along two paths bordered with handrails and sheltered by a pergola. The whole place looks like a bowling club, the paths are as long and smooth as bowling greens and the patients walking slowly along them are like pensioners coming to set up the bowls. Many of the legs aren't yet finished and the still uncovered joint can be seen between the calf and the foot, as if at that point the leg has been stripped of flesh, reduced to bone. The space between the two paths is dappled with enormous red roses. There are old people, children and middle-aged men. The amputees are almost all men.

I go to the institute for street children to pick up some documents. They are busy at their lessons: singing, needlework, mathematics, making paper flowers. The girls' voices ring out in a nursery rhyme made up of questions and answers, I imagine they're learning something by heart – a happy way of learning that's been ridiculed and then forgotten in Western education, being supposedly not very educational or not very creative (nonsense!). They all smile at me when they see me and then either burst out laughing and lower their eyes or continue to stare at me provocatively. As a male foreigner, they must find me interesting or even ridiculous. They laugh and can't stop staring at me. It goes without saying that their faces, framed by veils, are very beautiful. The trees in the garden bend beneath the wind. When I get back to the car, I find Hamid asleep in a strange position. I've also dropped off three times in the course of the day, just for a few moments: coming back from the encashment centre (10:30), with my hands in my lap and my head against the wall (13:30), and while writing this (18:15). I don't get enough sleep. It's the fault of the altitude, loneliness, homesickness, lack of love, the alcohol I've drunk or haven't drunk, and worry about work, specifically: the urge to do something, so that when I leave, things won't be exactly the same as they were when I arrived.

In the evening, we drink to mark the departure of a Dutch member of staff. As it's too late for dinner in the canteen (21:15), we go to one of the guest houses, where someone's going to make pasta. A dozen people. The mixture of joy and sadness we feel over Bart's departure leads to an impromptu party. People start dancing. They dance frenetically, while all the hidden provisions appear, stocks of beer cans, the last four bottles of wine. The music is Latin and Arab, which encourages the dancers to indulge in a series of wild and ironic variations, with hints of flamenco, belly dancing, vaguely Balinese hand movements, and imitations of Thursday night fever. The dancers who stand out are a really good Filipino girl (on the way to work next morning – both of us feeling quite woozy – she tells me she's crazy about dancing) and an Italian girl who was imprisoned in the magical but claustrophobic world of Bamiyan for four months of a very hard winter and now lets it all out.

21st May. Visit to the Emergency Clinic. The doctors can't see me, they're operating. They tell me to come back two hours later. By the time I get back – on foot, as the hospital's near – they've finished. I'm met by Marco, a surgeon, and Stefano, an anaesthetist. They've been operating on a man who was shot in the back with a Kalashnikov. Streaks of disinfectant are visible on their hairless forearms. I ask them how it went and Marco crosses his arms over his chest. God rest his soul. 'When we turned him over,' says Stefano, 'the blood gushed out like it does in films.'

We talk about work and it's great to be able to do it in Italian, it's great that Italian isn't only a private language for saying intimate things.

22nd May. The light has suddenly turned pearly, with shades of pink and yellow. The air is full of sand. The garden is obscured. I walk along the street, jumping over the drainage channels, which are clogged with rubbish. In some places they're so deep and so wide, you have to take a running jump to reach the other side. The porters and guards outside the headquarters of the international organisations are endlessly shovelling out the dirt from the drains, because they stink, but of course they don't know where to put it, nobody's going to collect it, so they just heap it up a little further away in the middle of the road, but the heaps are soon knocked down again by the wind and the rain and the passing cars and the refuse ends up back inside the drains. A great deal of shovelling goes on in Afghanistan. The holes in the roads are filled with earth every day. The next day they have to be filled again. All this shovelling comes to have an almost religious significance. On the lines of: nothing is created and nothing is destroyed. I don't think they're even looking for long-term solutions, they don't want a solution to the problem so much as a practical commitment to taking care of it. It's like expecting someone not to be hungry again after one big meal, or not to be sleepy again after one long sleep. If we're looking for a philosophical pretext, that is. This shovelling exercise is also reminiscent of the task you're given in the army: to move some sacks or stones from one part of the barrack yard to another, and then move them back again to where they were originally.

(Unconscious reaction to the atmosphere around me. It's as strong as it's insidious. To all intents and purposes, I've become one with the reality of Afghanistan, and yet I still fight to escape it. I keep my eyes wide open – like the characters in cartoons who prop them open with little sticks – and at the same time I feel as if I'd like to close them, so as not to see, not to know what's happening. Amid all the tragic, intense, moving scenes around me, I'm constantly sucked down into the tepid stew of images splashing about at the back of my mind. Visiting the shanty towns of Kabul, or skirting the minefields around the airport, I've caught myself whistling *Girls on Film*, an old hit by Duran Duran.)

(About the dancing the other night: the Frenchman danced in a studied, geometric way, very much of his generation – the Kenyan, very composed, barely swaying, moving his hands at waist height as if telling everyone to keep calm – the American woman completely wild, etc.)

Curfew

In order to see *Spiderman* (absolute crap) I ended up breaking the curfew.

The evening goes like this: guest house A, eight o'clock, the projection begins after *Spiderman*, in a pirate copy, is unanimously voted for in preference to a Woody Allen film. I sum up the feelings of the audience: at the least hint of a thought, I'll leave the room. I didn't know I was so easy to please… During the screening, poor Paul, an American, has to put up with all our ironic remarks about this consummate product of his nation's culture. 'The only civilisation that's gone straight from barbarism to decadence' ha, ha. Anti-Americanism is as strong in the UN as it is elsewhere. I whisper in my neighbour's ear that after seeing *Spiderman* I'm starting to see Al Qaeda's point of view. But we have to wait until the nerd who can shoot spider's webs from his hands defeats a mad scientist with a sneering iron mask on his face. This takes me through to five to ten and I escape without waiting for the words THE END, because I have to escort a female colleague who recently arrived, but it's only after I've agreed to do it that I realise she's staying in a guest house at the opposite end… It's already ten past ten by the time I call the head of security on the radio (I live with him, so I can't get away with it) to apologise for overrunning and to inform him that I'll be in a safe place in five minutes. The stars are very bright tonight. When I press the bell of the guest house, the notes of *My darling Clementine, London Bridge is falling down* and Brahms' lullaby sound one after the other…

23rd May. Najibullah, the orphan, comes back to see us, accompanied by his aunt, who has the role of the wicked queen in the story of the four little orphans. But perhaps she isn't wicked at all. We ask to speak to him alone for a moment.

He sits down, passive and docile. Rachel has asked the kitchen to keep a meal warm, and a tray is put under his nose, with bread, a plate of meat, rice and vegetables, and a bowl of watermelon pieces. Najibullah doesn't seem too keen on the food, maybe he's already eaten, or maybe it's pride. He won't accept charity. He looks into space and keeps his mouth shut. We have to insist that he eats something, we feel as if we ought to spoon-feed him so that he gets some nourishment. He's six-teen and has hair on his upper lip, but seems no older than twelve. He's short and thin, his handshake limp. We tell him he should at least taste the mutton while it's warm, the meat looks good, it's juicy and tender, but he reaches out his hand shyly to the watermelon, as if expecting to be rapped on the knuckles. He grabs a piece and eats it with greedy little bites. Then he eats another two or three slices. Watermelons are too tempting. I think he is actually hungry. But this whole cere-mony with the watermelon is appalling rather than refresh-ing. He answers our questions evasively, as if he didn't care, in a detached tone devoid of emotion. When he talks about his sick brother, or his aunt who tells him off for the slightest thing, or his work weaving carpets (they took him on straight away, which is a good sign, it means he's bringing money home – one more reason to keep him with them) or when he recalls his life in Pakistan before his mother died, he betrays no emo-tion, he sits there stiffly and keeps his eyes down, his eyes are dull and look as if they'll never sparkle again.

How much do you earn? I don't know. Who takes the money? My aunt. And how many hours do you work a day? I don't know. Do you work in the morning? He nods. And in the afternoon? He nods. And do you work in the evening as well? He's about to nod, then changes his mind and shakes his head.

We've found a centre (ASCHIANA) for him and Sabra to go during the day, where they can work and earn some money, receive education, food and medical treatment, and even socialise and have a bit of fun. The letters of introduction are ready and signed. Do you want to go there, Najib? He nods, but coolly, as if shrugging his shoulders.

We tell his aunt that the family has been accepted on Care's food distribution programme. We've registered her niece Sabra as the beneficiary, firstly because the programme is actually aimed at widows or abandoned women or women in difficulty, and secondly to make it clear to the aunt that the orphans are the reason she's getting the food and they must have their fair share. The woman seems reasonable, and agrees to everything we say, maybe she doesn't want us to know what she really thinks, or maybe she doesn't think anything, but is just tired and wants to go. When she talks to her nephew, she's neither affectionate nor brusque towards him, as if talking to a stranger who's turned up at her door, and he doesn't answer her. Najibullah told us earlier that his greatest wish is to leave his aunt and uncle's house as soon as possible. And we're doing everything we can to make them stay! To keep the four orphans together. Too bad: he's going to have to take responsibility for his retarded brother and the two girls who can't yet work. At least for another couple of years. Then it'll be Sabra's turn.

We talk for a long time, obtaining assurances and making appointments to visit the NGOs together. When Najibullah and his aunt leave the office, my colleague and I look at each other, wondering what we've done, and whether we've really solved anything. We've papered over the cracks, but we don't know how long it'll last. The alternative is the street or the orphanage, and a mental hospital for the older brother.

It's obvious that a millimetre beneath her energetic manner, Rachel is exhausted.

Having waited patiently with my stomach rumbling, I wolf down the kebab Najibullah didn't want.

Today, 23rd May 2002, Olivia Gayraud, the MSF coordinator, told me about the following case. The doctors at the clinic in Pul-i-Charkhi examined a one-year-old boy. He was seriously dehydrated, had a high fever and was suffering from pneumonia as well as other complications. The diagnosis: he would die in a few hours if he didn't receive specialist treatment immediately. MSF tried hard to persuade the parents to get their son admitted to hospital in Kabul, but the father refused because he wanted to continue his journey to his final destination, in Bamiyan province.

Olivia told me there was no chance the child could have survived.

The episode raised two questions that both need to be confronted with equal determination.

The first is about how we can intervene promptly in cases like these. We need a system that allows families in similar medical emergencies to be helped financially, that is, in terms of transport and accommodation. They should be allowed to stay in Kabul as long as it takes for their child to be treated, and subsequently given help to reach their destination. Such initiatives ought to be realised by the UNHCR or by a partner agency chosen for its ability to assist EVIs (Extremely Vulnerable Individuals). I shall go to Intersos tomorrow and hear what they have to suggest.

The second question is about the rights of children in Afghanistan. I believe the primary right is the right to life. Even though children are traditionally considered their parents' property, I wonder if the UNHCR Protection and Community Services can do some work on the legal aspects of the matter, investigating the current legislation as it affects the responsibility of parents towards their children and (if necessary and suitable) giving advice to the relevant ministries (Justice and Public Health) on the rights of children to health and life.

A day in the life of a mine clearance expert
We're driving across the Shomali Plains, north of Kabul. This is a land blessed with beauty and fertility, and at the same

time the most devastated part of Afghanistan. Two out of every three houses have been razed to the ground. For twenty years Shomali was the front line, first between the Russians and the mujaheddin, then between the warlords fighting among themselves, finally between the Taliban and the Tajik leader Massud – and the US Air Force put the finishing touches to it with last autumn's bombing. Every day, hundreds of refugees return from Pakistan to live here, as well as displaced persons from Kabul and the Panshir. What they find is a graveyard of tanks, burnt vines, wells filled with earth, entire neighbourhoods bulldozed in Taliban reprisals.

There used to be a bazaar in the village of Qara Bagh. You can still figure out what was sold in the individual shops from the objects sticking out of the rubble: a bicycle's chain guard, a stove pipe, a tailor's measure.

The whole area is mined. Various organisations are working to clear it, which means that if you spend a morning anywhere near Bagram airport, you're stunned by a shattering explosion every five minutes: the dry thud of a mine blown up beneath the first ridge of blue and yellow mountains, or the tremendous boom of an aerial bomb immediately followed by a great mushroom of silent, swaying dust. The camels belonging to the Kuchis (the Afghan equivalent of gypsies) seem to have got used to it and carry on chewing in peace. In theory we should be used to it, too, but all these powerful vibrations have a direct effect on the stomach. You can train your mind, but not your body.

We enter the village of Dewana, which is infested with American cluster bombs. Clusters are fragmentation bombs used against tanks because of their ability to pierce the shells – but at the same time the splinters will turn anyone within a radius of 150 metres into pulp. They are launched from planes, doughnut-shaped bombs containing two hundred bomblets, which open before touching the ground and scatter them over an area of about 500 square metres. When the first ones explode, they create a cushion of air that slows the fall of the others. Some don't explode and stay there for years, live and dangerous.

If you saw them in the middle of a field you wouldn't think they were worth a penny. Each bomblet is slightly bigger than a Coca-Cola can and hangs from a ridiculous-looking para-chute. They lie half stuck in the ground or gracefully posed on a heap of brushwood. Their yellow colour attracts children, who think they're something to play with.

We put on padded jackets, which weigh six kilos, and set off along the corridor that has already been cleared. The aspect of the jacket I appreciate from the start is the square dangling between the legs to protect the genitals. We have to be on our toes from here on, and keep an eye open for the colours of the little sticks which distinguish the cleared areas from the uncleared areas. I try to put my feet in the same places where Biagio, the Italian mine clearer, puts his, I dog his heels like a shadow. It's patient, methodical work, like a game of spillikins: once a security corridor has been established, the surrounding terrain is subdivided into squares of 25 metres × 25 metres, and the mine clearance people go back and forth over it with detectors.

We reach the famous vineyard. The vines are in bloom, they look wonderful. The owner – the blockhead! – didn't want to let the mine clearance people in at first, claiming the ground was already clear. Well, since they started working here, they've found and destroyed twenty-eight mines, plus four mortar bombs. And beyond that wall, there are another fifty.

Now they're getting ready to explode three of them. We go to have a look at them before they're covered with sandbags. We've suddenly lowered our voices, as if our very words could trigger the explosion.

But before the three cluster bombs can be destroyed, there's another big problem to be dealt with. A thousand-pound aerial bomb has been found in a house in Dewana. It's already been defused but now it has to be moved. We go to the centre of the village, and there, tense as we are, we burst out laughing. I can't believe my eyes…

There are bombs *everywhere*. The walls of the houses are constructed out of bombs placed in rows and cemented with mortar. A group of children are playing and jumping on a bridge composed of old Russian bombs, while a line of women carry water in 120mm. artillery shells which have been sawn off and had handles added to turn them into buckets. Leaning against a wall, ready for recycling, the propellers of some Russian helicopter that gave up the ghost.

The problem, Biagio whispers in my ear, is that with all these bombs around, the locals have stopped worrying about the live ones, they can no longer tell which are which.

We enter the house where the aerial bomb is. It's been there since October: an American MK83, as big as a man, lying in the middle of what must have been the living room. Biagio examines it: its curious position suggests it might have been launched from a low level and bounced without exploding. Before it can be removed, the ground around it has to be very carefully sifted, as it could be a booby-trap left by the Taliban: they might have laid it there with a hidden device underneath it, either a traction mine (a hidden wire) or a pressure mine (as featured in the film *No Man's Land* – when you lift the weight, the mine explodes). The Afghan mine clearance people set to work, delicately scraping away earth from around the bomb with shovels and knives.

Then they come and call us, because they've discovered a store of rockets in the yard of another house. They are stowed away in the darkness of a hen-house. They're half a metre long and shiny. 107mm. BM12s. The yard was used as a training centre by the Taliban, who fired rockets into the front wall, with their detonators removed. Two rockets are embedded in the wall, sticking out the length of a palm. Another one has penetrated the inside wall of a house, and we don't know which side to pull it out from. All this stuff has to be removed before it causes any more damage. But it'll take men, time, money, and a lot of care.

There's a joke circulating among the mine clearance people: of all the errors of youth, they can only commit one.

Meanwhile the refugees continue to return. Right now, three lorries are entering the village and starting to unload belongings, children scatter everywhere, I shudder to think where they're going to put their feet. I ask the old men if they've received the money and the grain, and then I explain that we're forced to distribute only one sack per family because we're running out of food in the warehouses. They'll get the other two sacks... when?

(My God, there's going to be a disaster if more funds don't arrive soon. What are they all waiting for – the governments, the banks, the large donors? Why don't they want to help this country? When are they sending the money they promised? And yet the small donors continue faithfully to support Afghanistan...)

We return to the vineyard. Everything's ready for the 'demolition'. We inspect the three cluster bombs again. Half a kilo of perfectly ordinary dynamite, purchased in Pakistan, has been positioned near them, to be triggered by a detonating fuse the colour of fire. The whole thing is then connected to a slow fuse which looks like a ribbon of licorice and which has to be lit by hand. It takes two minutes to burn – just time to reach shelter before the explosion. Someone yells a warning over the loudspeaker, and we run about two hundred metres and hide behind a wall with our backs right against it. I'm completely soaked beneath my jacket and feel the need to pee. Is it fear? Or the four hours we've already spent in the field? I start to do it against the wall, but then it occurs to me that if the bomb goes off now, I'll never be able to have a pee for the rest of my life. I do it as fast as I can. But nothing happens. It seems to me as if the two minutes are long past, so I turn to ask why on earth the bomb hasn't gone off, and at that very moment the blast rends the air, and dust and fragments rain down from beyond the wall.

One down... The other two, at about twelve metres'

distance one from the other, have to be connected to make them explode together. Biagio shows the Afghans how to make the connection: another roll of detonating fuse is wasted, but at least it's safer because it'll only take one man to defuse two bombs.

This time, we put not one but two security walls between us and the mined vineyard. It's not enough. While I wait anxiously for the fuse to burn down, my Afghan colleague signals to me with his finger. Come, come here, he seems to be saying, behind the tree. I do as he says. And then he motions to me to grab hold of the trunk. I hug it as tightly as I can and rest my face against the bark. It turns out to be an excellent idea: the shock wave from the two explosions (only a few milliseconds between them) is partly absorbed by the trunk, and I feel only a slight vibration in my stomach. I'd never have thought I would hug a tree with so much gratitude.

The collection
37 mm AGS-type Russian grenades which are fired in
sequence from a belt, like a machine gun
HE 37 mm projectiles
F1 hand bombs
40 mm anti-personnel grenades fired from a 'Kalashnikov'
grenade launcher
82 mm mortar bombs
14.5 mm heavy machine-gun cartridges
Almost all of it Russian
Helicopter propellers
107 mm BM12 rockets

Over dinner, we talk about the Taliban era. Several of the UN staff were already working here then, they know that period well, having lived through it. There's a photo at the entrance to the office showing Aziz, Waisuddin and Rahmatullah, almost unrecognisable with long beards halfway down their chests. Josefa tells us about the time the police stopped the car because there was a woman in the front seat. Rahmat had an answer ready. 'What?' he said, pretending to be even more shocked than the Taliban. 'Would you prefer us to put her in the back with all these men?'

And Yoshi, the Japanese, who's smooth-skinned, was constantly harassed by the Taliban guards because he didn't have a beard: they took him for a Hazara.

Uproarious laughter and a glint in the eyes.

Josefa recalls how never once, at any of the official meetings at which she represented the UNHCR, had a Taliban addressed a word to her, not even to say hello or goodbye. And she mimes the sidelong glances that the men threw her: whenever she looked at them they would avert their gaze. So when she spoke, she spoke to nobody. And nobody answered her.

How strange, such stifling oppression of women as to enslave even those practising it.

Multiculturalism

In Sudan, beating the forefinger against the middle finger is a sign of courtship, men make it to girls at dances. In Italy, the same gesture is used by senior soldiers during military service to intimidate recruits.

Rahmat was wounded by a Soviet bullet while he was fighting with the mujaheddin. He was seventeen. The bullet injured the muscles of one cheek, which even now is prone to involuntary contractions.

In the in-patients' ward at the German hospital, we pass close to the beds and see wounded soldiers, lying motionless and silent, staring at the ceiling. We're passing through too quickly to get a good look at the mutilations, the reddened bandages, but there's one man I manage to see, his swollen lips and face daubed with disinfectant and myriads of wounds on the parts of his face not hidden by the bandages.

The Italians

I have dinner with a group of friendly doctors and paramedics. They're all men, and towards the end of the meal the subject of sexual abstinence comes up. Some of them have only been here for a few weeks, some for months. All of us are celibate. I say that the thing I miss most isn't sex, but a certain physical tenderness, intimate sensations, hugs and kisses – in short, I'm talking the way women usually talk. 'Me, too,' says Francesco, the man sitting next to me. 'What I miss most are feelings.'

There's a male nurse, a nice, muscular fellow, who writes email messages to his girl friend. 'Go on, write,' says the anaesthetist. 'She'll read them with her other lover, and they'll both laugh behind your back...' It's true that being in Afghanistan is like being back in the army. For years I had a recurring nightmare: nobody had warned me that you have to do military service *twice* in your life, and now I had to leave for my second stint: pack my bag, take a train, and present myself at the barracks, just as scared as I was twenty years ago. The dream turned out to be a premonition. On the subject of desire, I tell them I was talking to a beautiful black girl yesterday, or rather, she was talking to me, about persecuted minorities, I think, how to protect minorities, Hazaras, Tajiks, Pashtuns, that whole subject, and I was listening to her but after a while I stopped hearing her words and just looked at her beautiful lips as she spoke them and I wanted to kiss them, I was irresistibly attracted to them, all I wanted to do was to give them a kiss, nothing more. I had to force myself not to do it.

Roses

Exhausting day. Emotions constantly bordering on tears. I go to Pul-i-Charkhi in the morning, leaving at six-thirty. I have to make a great effort to do my usual work, checking and signing the returnees' forms. I stumble over words and make mistakes in the accounts. There are the usual exceptional cases: a woman on her own whose baggage has got burned and who has nothing left, not even a change of clothes; a man who wants to offload his widowed sister-in-law and his four little nephews on us here and now: a disabled widower who seems at first to be looking for help with his missing leg (at least in this case we know straight away where to send him, to Alberto Cairo's orthopaedic clinic, where they won't only give him a new leg but will also find him a job), but as he talks it becomes clear that it isn't his leg he's missing, but his wife, in other words, he's looking for a new wife.

Then a woman turns up who gave birth yesterday, or rather her husband turns up, in a hurry to take the money and continue his journey. We beg him to at least let his wife and the baby be seen by a doctor. But we can't convince him. He leaves.

After I get back to the office, an emergency call comes in. The information is none too clear: on the border with Iran a man has fallen into a well and broken his back. Now he's in hospital in Zaranj, in Afghanistan. If he doesn't get specialist treatment immediately he'll die. We have to find a way to move him and a place in Kabul where they would agree to treat him. I deal with the latter, Jennifer with the former. Finally the mission is ready, all we need is a particular kind of stretcher to strap the patient to, so that he can be slotted into the plane, which has a very narrow door. It's a crucial detail. Finding that stretcher turns out to be the most difficult thing of all (after much negotiation, Uncle Oyvind manages to get one from the ISAF hospital, but early tomorrow morning J. will have to procure another even more sophisticated one: we've all resorted to our acquaintances among our fellow countrymen, Italians to Italians, Norwegians to Norwegians, Australians to Australians). We still don't know if the man with the broken back is going to be saved.

In the afternoon, there's a brief ceremony to welcome back a Sudanese who's been away for two months with typhoid fever. I never met him before he left, but it's obvious that he's thinner than he ought to be. In Pakistan, they diagnosed cancer of the colon, but the mass visible on the X-ray turned out to be an accumulation of fluid caused by the typhoid. He went for thirty-five days without eating. During the ceremony, I ask Rahmat to tell me how he got wounded fighting the Russians. He shies away from the question, maybe because it annoys him these days to be taken for a mujaheddin. He talks about it as if it's a very old story that happened to someone else, not the Rahmat of today, which, of course, is true. 'There are things you think and do at that age.' He was seventeen and still in tenth grade at school when he joined the guerrillas. He was with them for three years, and was wounded while attacking an enemy convoy.

Once the picnic for T. is over, the empty cans, driven by the wind, roll down from under the table to the middle of the garden, the table is dismantled, and everyone leaves the garden – all that's left are the very beautiful roses and the Coca-Cola cans on the grass.

27th May. Wake up at four. Sounds of dawn in Kabul: cocks crowing, little birds twittering, a donkey braying beneath the hill, the voice of the muezzin. The other day, the muezzin had trouble with the loudspeaker, it may have been an electrical fault. The amplified voice, loud enough to wake the entire neighbourhood, broke off in mid-sentence, and in the silence the muezzin's natural voice could be heard, much gentler, more private, more distant.

JUNE

A UNHCR vehicle travelling to Ghazni on Sunday, 2nd June, was stopped and robbed by two armed men. One of the robbers fired several shots into the ground. No one was injured during the incident. The attackers made off with the Codan radio. The incident took place at the same location as a previous serious incident on 23rd May, in which a UNHCR vehicle travelling in a convoy from Ghazni to Kabul was fired on by a man dressed in civilian clothing near the town of Salaar in Sayd Abad district, Wardak Province.

Five minutes of perfect lucidity last night. Then they were gone.

It's very hot. Sticky.

At two in the afternoon, we walk through the dusty streets to the Indira Gandhi Hospital. We go on foot because it's near. Anne, Rachel and I. To visit a malnourished child who arrived at the encashment centre yesterday. A case like so many others, perhaps a little worse. He's three years old and only weighs five kilos. His younger brother, who's ten months, is more robust than him. I never saw him, and it's partly for safety reasons that I'm accompanying my two colleagues. We can't find him in the paediatric ward. Nobody speaks English, and to our shame, after all these months we can barely speak five words of Dari. We spell the child's name. Rachel mimes malnutrition, pressing her cheeks between her thumb and forefinger. We are surrounded by eager nurses all talking at once. Then one of them leads us outside into the garden and along a dusty path between heaps of junk, until we reach the main part of the clinic. The nurse trots along quickly and silently between the wards, dashes upstairs and along corridors, turning every now and again to see if we're still keeping up with her. She has a broad face and blue eyes. The hospital seems decent apart from the stench, a mixture of foul odours it would take a refined, obsessive writer pages to identify. In the corridors, the usual dark, turbaned men stand leaning against the walls. At last we find someone who speaks English, he's an orthopaedist but we ask him to help us all the same. A child of three, seriously malnourished. Rachel holds out her hands to show how long the child is, and I think she must be exaggerating the extent of his malnutrition because in the open space between her hands you could barely fit a newborn baby. His name is Bashir. Bashir Daud. The tall, friendly orthopaedist, who's dressed in green, leads us to a ward with the logo of *Action Contre la Faim* on the door. This is where they treat malnutrition. To right and left are rooms full of children and mothers and nurses who are hard to distinguish from the mothers. The smell is the same here, with an extra layer: the sickly-sweet smell of powdered milk. The children are all thin, terribly thin – I apologise for stating the obvious. They have stringy, reddish hair. The unweaned children have hollow cheeks. I've only ever seen children like this in documentaries and TV news reports. We ask the sharp-eyed nurse if they admitted a child of such and such a description yesterday afternoon. Meanwhile Rachel goes around the ward trying to recognise him. The women sitting on the beds are all veiled. I don't go in but stay discreetly outside in the corridor. The children's wards are also women's wards. The only male is a slight young man who greets us, then runs away. When he returns, he's put on a white coat and hung a stethoscope around his neck and looks perfectly professional. Finally, one of the nurses remembers the case: yes, of course, Bashir was here with his parents, but they escaped. Escaped? Yes, escaped. It seems a strong word to use, she could just have said that they went away. Why did they go away, and when? As soon as they found out they'd have to stay for a month while their son was being treated... The nurse goes to fetch his medical record. Meanwhile the doctor, whose name is Zabiullah, answers our questions, as eager as a student anxious to make a good impression.

Do the parents often take their children away before they've been treated?

Yes, especially the immigrants. (*Dr Zabiullah uses this term even about Afghans.*)

Isn't the clinic free?

Oh, yes. But the families can't afford to stay in Kabul long enough for the children to be treated. They have nowhere to go and no money to pay for it.

How many children are there in the malnutrition wards?

At the moment, forty or forty-five.

In how many rooms?

Four.

And the others? (*I point to the rooms that open on the other side of the corridor: the young doctor explains that they are used for other children's diseases.*)

But if we have to, we make two or three children sleep in the same bed.

Which means... that you may be attending as many as 80 children.

Even more. If need be, we put beds in the corridor.

What if the malnourished children also have dermatological problems? (*We're thinking about leishmaniasis.*) Do you also treat skin diseases?

Those, too.

Who keeps the children clean?

The mothers. Otherwise our nurses wash them.

Every day?

Twice a week.

And what does the food consist of?

There are three different kinds of milk... (*Here the doctor launches enthusiastically into a lecture about diet. The problem in situations like these, where you want to see and understand everything, is that it's hard to concentrate only on words.*)

And do you provide meals for the mothers, too?

We give them what the children can't eat. Beans, rice.

(Meanwhile, a nurse goes backwards and forwards looking for Bashir's medical record.)

Well, if it's not going to take too long, I'd like to have a look at the record.

Here it is. Malnutrition, diarrhoea, vomiting. Mentally retarded.

Is Bashir mentally retarded? *(Rachel, who is the only one who's seen him, nods.)*

Yes. That may explain his physical underdevelopment.

And what are these numbers?

They correspond to his height, 70 centimetres, and his weight.

4.8…

4 kilos, 800 grams.

Bloody hell! What's the normal weight for a child of three?

15 kilos. There are also other parameters for establishing malnutrition, like the relationship between height and weight.

Excuse me, could you repeat your name again, please?

Dr Zabiullah. I'm sorry for my English.

Your English is excellent, and much better than our Dari *(which isn't saying much)*. Thank you for your help. Are you in charge of the ward?

Oh, no. *(He blushes.)* I've only just graduated. Because I can speak English, they give me the job of talking to foreign visitors. And where are you from?

We work for the UNHCR. The three of us are Norwegian, American, and Italian.

Oh, are you really American? You're so beautiful I thought you were Italian! *(He's a bit of a ladies' man, this young doctor…)*

Thank you for the compliment, on behalf of my colleague and in the name of the Italian people.

A pity Italy lost the match against Crotia.

Croatia.

I'm interested in football. I especially admire Mr Maldini.

He's a great player, Mr Maldini.

Indeed he is. Thanks again for your help, doctor…

Dr Zabiullah. I've only just graduated.

We'll be back to see you.

I have to go and find Anne, who's playing with the little girls, she always does that when she visits hospitals, nursery schools or orphanages. They laugh and take her by the hand, drawing her inside the rooms. As we're leaving, some of them follow us. Anne smiles and strokes their stringy hair. Rachel is just calling the base to find out if they've sent a car for us when we see it parked outside the hospital. The case of poor Bashir has been quite enlightening, and has given me some very clear ideas about certain things I knew before, but of which I now have a living, concrete image.

The girls who've been following Anne ask her for money as she's getting into the car.

We leave. My colleagues are dejected. R. asks me what I think of the Indira Gandhi hospital. Really not too bad. Especially when I think of what it must be like in Kandahar with ten degrees more heat and three times the number of flies.

I write a quick report, daring to add at the end that although Bashir's story saddens me, it also makes me happy because it's the perfect example we can use in discussions about what we have to do.

Women who are about to give birth or who have just given birth; elderly people with respiratory deficiencies; the chronically sick; people with tuberculosis; malnourished children. In the registration centres in Pakistan and Iran, these and other high-risk categories are supposed to be made aware of the dangers they face during their homeward journey. Of course many families decide to set out all the same, even if some members are ill or at risk (especially pregnant women and children). Other refugees, on the other hand, either develop their symptoms because of the discomforts of the journey or undergo a worsening of their conditions which may prove fatal. Although the death rate among returnees is not significantly higher than the average, it is vital that those who arrive in Kabul and the other reception centres in a critical condition be immediately taken to hospital and given specific treatment for as long as they require it. Many refugees, even when informed of their condition by the medical staff, nevertheless decide to continue their journey to their final destination because they cannot afford to pay for accommodation in the city while their family member is being treated. For this reason, in serious cases, an extra amount of money should be allotted to the families to cover the expenses they incur while their relatives are in hospital… etc. etc.

(The amount could be twenty or thirty dollars.)

(We need to find a way to allocate this money without creating a pull factor – cheating, fake illnesses, etc.)

Maybe Bashir's case will be resolved some other way in a few days. Some things are entirely in the hands of Allah – but in others, men play their part.

I spend the night of 10th to 11th June vomiting.

The following day, tossing and turning on the bed in my underpants, tormented by flies.

12th June. Visit to Chardi and District 6, Kabul. Shops selling scrap metal, piles of logs that seem to have been torn to shreds rather than cut, unmentionable pieces of meat covered with flies, buckets fashioned ingeniously out of the same black rubber as tyres (I love the smell), umbrellas over carts of bruised bananas and mangoes. An endless bazaar of hovels and prefabs overflowing with goods, most of which are indescribable.

Anyone who doesn't own a shop makes do with a cart. There are carts of different sizes, some painted in bright colours. In Dari anything that has wheels and shafts to pull it is called a 'karachi'.

I search in my memory and the word *carroccio* comes to

mind, the cart used in Italian cities in the Middle Ages.

The Barchi area, inhabited by Hazaras.

Their Chinese faces.

Administratively speaking, Kabul continues past Barchi, but it's the end of the actual city. An army barracks with long, high, broken walls, and then the countryside. The road becomes a dirt track full of holes. The villages lie on the bare plain, flat contours of mud walls. Here and there, a green patch, trees shaken by the wind, reveals the extent of the kariz irrigation system. The district governor has assured us there are no mines here, except in the area below Skort mountain, a yellow wall of rock to our left. The wheat in the fields is almost ripe. Just before we reach the main road leading to Wardak, we do a U-turn, and start up the mountain slopes. Beneath the trees, children are playing next to a little brook. They stare at us in astonishment. They have long, dirty hair and no toys. Toys don't exist here. The only one I've seen in two months was a kind of wooden scooter hanging from the roof of a shop in Kabul. What the children do have to play with is shovels. A couple of donkeys stare at us, just like the children. We leave without meeting anyone else. The wheat is almost all yellow. Apart from wheat, there's a kind of medicinal herb with little purple flowers. Little girls walk unsteadily beneath bundles of sorghum. We enter a village: according to our maps this should be Deh-alaka. But is it? There's nobody around to ask. Ten-thirty in the morning. The metal gates of the compounds are all bolted. Our two Afghans get out and knock, one going one way, one going the other. But the best thing to do is wait.

A strange phenomenon always occurs in situations like these.

You're alone, there's nobody around, and suddenly you find yourself surrounded by people you haven't seen coming. They appear as if from nowhere.

We stay by the car in the sun, in the middle of an open space overlooked by several compounds, and the phenomenon does indeed happen. By the time we've tipped our heads backwards and drunk a swig of water, three little boys have appeared.

This place isn't Deh-alaka. It has a name but isn't on any map. It's part of a larger village, Qal-eh-ye Qadzi. Are there any families who've returned from Pakistan? Of course, the boys reply with great excitement. They take us to see a one-eyed old man. We talk to him in the blazing sun, then ask him for permission to visit his house. They open the gate. The compound is on the side of the mountain and it's steep. There are half a dozen goats standing or lying on the hillside, a black ram, two little donkeys who could be Pinocchio and Lucignolo[7]. The old man's family surrounds us. There are just women and little boys. To avoid embarrassment, we prefer not to go inside the house. We stay in the yard, in the baking sun. The women wave their repatriation forms, the white one that they keep and the yellow one they'll need for getting grain: they've had only one sack so far and are due two more, though it's anybody's guess when they'll receive it, given the current shortage. The old man's family returned six days ago from Peshawar, the other two family groups arrived here on 23rd May. Fifteen people in all. I try to figure out the various relationships. The old man tells me he's the son-in-law of a woman who looks ten years younger than him. Are you the head of this household? No, my mother-in-law is. Why are you living with your mother-in-law and not in your own house? It's been destroyed, he says, which is strange because the village doesn't bear any marks of fighting. The old man soon changes his story: his brother's living in his house now, so he preferred to move to his mother-in-law's. And who among you works, who brings home money? We have to ask the question in different ways and they all want to speak their minds. But I want only one answer. The answer is: nobody. So what do you live on? The money they saved in Pakistan. The lady of the house uncovers the belly of one of the children – I have to look at the form to tell if it's her son or her nephew. It's impossible to be sure of these people's ages. The woman could be 65 or 44. Yes, it must be her son, Shamsullah. I take him by surprise by

140

calling his name. He has a white scar on his belly, the end of which is covered by his trousers. It was a mine, ten years ago. But how old is Shams now? I look at the form: twelve. Something doesn't add up: if a mine explodes between your legs when you're only two, it'll leave more than just that scar. Hypothesis: the child didn't step on a mine, the scar is from some other accident or from an operation and his mother's telling us this story because people with war wounds receive more attention (at Emergency they told me that the wounded all claim to have stepped on a mine even when they were in a car crash). Another hypothesis: the accident happened not ten years ago but much more recently. Five years ago, three years ago. The Afghans have an elastic conception of time. Third hypothesis: what the one-eyed man's mother-in-law is saying is completely true, word for word, and that ugly scar, which looks like a botched appendectomy, was caused by a piece of shrapnel while the rest of the child, his legs, his eyes (I don't know about his genitals, I don't dare ask the child to expose himself here, in the dusty yard), remained miraculously intact. I tell Shamsullah to walk and he patters away from his mother without any problem. But he looks three or four years younger than his age. He can't lift weights or make any physical exertion. So, I say, there's nobody in any of these three families who brings in any income, but it says on the forms there's a twenty-year-old. Where is he? Inside the house. They go to fetch him. Zubair appears. He's an ugly, spotty, ungainly young man with big hands. It isn't true that all Afghans are good-looking. The one-eyed man says that in Peshawar he had a karachi (see above) and did a bit of business, but here he's unemployed. But in a few days, I observe, the wheat will be harvested, and then there'll be work for everyone... Oh no, the one-eyed man cuts in, and the others, too, start shouting again. Zubair can't work, he has heart problems. They beat his chest with their hands. What exactly is wrong with your heart, we ask the boy, and he begins to mime his pains while the old one-eyed man, who should be the boy's cousin if I'm not mistaken, starts to explain, but I immediately stop him by raising my hands, palms out, saying shh, and turning to Zubair, to make it clear to everyone that I want to hear the answer only from him. Zubair touches his chest, his back, his throat, and says that it isn't the heart, it's the lungs. I can't breathe. So, is it the heart or the lungs? It's the muscles, says Zubair, through the interpreter. But do you take pills? No. Have you ever taken them? Yes, in Pakistan. But the doctors told me the problem would go away as I got older.

On Friday I attended a malnutrition screening at Pul-i-Charkhi. *Action Contre la Faim* was the agency. Every twelfth child is stopped and measured. The child is stripped naked and laid on a table and his or her head held in place. At the other end, they place a board against his or her feet and note down the measurement found on the scale: so many centimetres. The children, some of whom have only just stopped crying after the vaccination, immediately start up again. They move about on the table and kick. Then they're weighed and the percentage is calculated. There's also another parameter, obtained by measuring the height and the circumference of the arm with a kind of clamp. The percentage of malnourished children varies from 10 to 20 per cent. The families are given a letter to take to one of the institutes in the city that treat malnutrition with appropriate diets. But we know that many families don't take their children there or don't leave them there long enough for them to recover. The work is done in a brisk manner by women about forty. They seize the children gently but firmly. It's hot in the big tent even though they squirt water at us every ten minutes, and as it evaporates, the water forms a patch of tropical dampness that clings to the ceiling. I ask a young man with a number of pens in his breast pocket – which identifies him as the person in charge – what happens if they see a child passing who's clearly malnourished, maybe thinner than anyone else, but isn't actually the twelfth child, the next one to be selected for their test. Do they stop him anyway? Do they give him a letter, too? How are the eleven children who aren't in the statistics assessed?

The helicopters always fly very low. This morning one of them had a net full of cardboard boxes hanging from it, which grazed the trees as it flew overhead.

We pass a Pakistani lorry full of returnees: the wheel hubs have rostra (!) like the chariots in *Ben Hur*.

Late last night on TV, an Italian documentary from the Fifties about the profession of obstetrician.

One child in a hundred has infantile oedema. I asked the man from *Action Contre la Faim* what it is. He gave me this example: you press your thumb into the child's skin, on the arm, say. Then you lift your thumb and the hole remains.

Aid workers: the law of the three Ms: missionaries, mercenaries, misfits.

Anthony Perkins
15th June. West Kabul, district 6. The carpet factory. Beyond the usual sheet-metal gate, a dusty yard with women and children sitting on the ground, covered in flies. We enter a building which is not only unfinished, but in some places hasn't even been started. We are immediately surrounded by women. Eight hundred women and children work here. Almost all Hazaras. Their faces are uncovered, they greet us with smiles, then the older ones immediately launch into a litany of complaints. For the moment we turn a deaf ear. We climb to the first floor, then the second. The stairs are on the outside of the building, and there's no rail. There are no doors or windows either, and the skylight has a plastic sheet stretched over it, held down with a couple of beams to stop it

flying away. We pass between the looms. Dozens of girls of different ages crouch by them – along with a few wizened old women – who giggle, blush, whisper in each other's ears, hold out their hands in greeting or withdraw them, in a wave of excitement that rises and doesn't die down but continues as a constant buzz. Apart from the old women, they're all very beautiful. They either become agitated or look bewildered as we pass: a woman in a blouse with uncovered red hair and a man without a beard. With its frissons of emotion, its colours, its sly glances, the scene reminds me of Fellini's *City of Women*, while the frantic succession of images recalls the visit to the painter Titorelli in Orson Welles' film of Kafka's *The Trial*. I'm Anthony Perkins. I look around and blink, as if taking a flurry of snapshots (they'll all turn out either dark or out of focus in my mind, which is a very low-definition camera).

Through a gap in one of the many unfinished walls you can see the nearby cemetery... an expanse of dust and stones and, here and there, green flags sagging in the sultry Kabul air. Green is the colour of martyrdom.

Skirting the sea of headscarves and whispers, we're shown into a room full of sofas and invited to sit. On a wall, a stained white tapestry with a coarsely embroidered lion in the middle. An insignificant man with a goatee introduces himself as the manager of the factory. Four or five women are sitting on the sofas. They continue to talk among themselves and make signs. They seem to be arguing about what to say to us. Another woman places herself at the curtain door and holds a wooden stick against it to deter the others from coming in. Every now and again, she lets a woman in, who enters and takes the place of one of those sitting on the sofas. There's a lot of commotion beyond the door, the curtain swells and women push their hands and faces through, protesting that they want to come in, chubby faces of little Hazara girls framed by veils. The guard has her work cut out keeping the women at bay. She raises her stick to bar their way and threaten them. God knows why our arrival has caused so much excitement. We launch into the ritual questions: how many women work here, how long have they been here, how old are they, what's the minimum age, what are the criteria for taking them on, etc. Each question is repeated in at least three different versions. The manager doesn't know much and what little he does know he's hiding or telling us only part of, making it up as he goes along. In the meantime, the women continue their din, our interpreter speaks very softly (he's a shy young man who stares at the floor), we hear knocking, banging, hammering all around, all the cocks in the neighbourhood are crowing at the same time, the women downstairs are shrieking, but why? Gradually it dawns on us: this factory isn't a factory, it's a bluff...

In fact, it isn't a factory, but a centre for vocational training, opened by an Afghan 'philanthropist' hiding behind a mysterious acronym. The women and girls are supposedly being trained, and during training they should be receiving 1,200 rupees for every square metre of carpet worked on, but we discover that in three months they've never been paid – that's why they're crowding around us, protesting, they thought we were the bosses!

Poor women drawn into a trap and exploited. Their work expropriated in exchange for a little bread.

The descent into the basement. Although it should be clear by now that we're indignant and want only to leave and report the scam, the loathsome manager insists on showing us the classrooms. We go down to the cellar. Although it's blazing hot outside, it's so damp and cold here, it sends shivers down your spine. You can't see more than a metre in front of you. The floor is of beaten earth, with a few areas covered with large squares of gravel, which are not fixed but wobble when you walk on them. One of the rooms is full of stones. In another, there are skeins of wool covered in dirt. At the far end, in the largest, darkest room, we notice a small blackboard with nothing written on it.

We interview ten Afghan women for a position as UNHCR Protection Assistant. Actually nine, because one doesn't show up. It turns out to be an instructive morning. The women are very different, but all have had extraordinary careers that have led them here, to this little room. They enter in turn, clutching their purses and adjusting their headscarves. A half-hour interview, followed by a written test of their English and computer skills. Two of them are doctors, one (almost) a pharmacist, one an engineer, one a lawyer, three teachers. Their life-stories are often dramatic, and their CVs zigzag between university studies interrupted two exams before graduation by the arrival of the Taliban, jobs left to escape into exile, families dispersed, relatives killed. The father of one of them was shot when she was eight years old (we don't find this out until after the test). All that apart from the usual unsatisfying jobs, the yearning for change, the desire to earn more and gain recognition and social advancement, a desire which in poor countries is both spasmodic and perfectly legitimate. And Afghanistan is the poorest country in the world.

Our questions tackle different aspects of these women's personalities, qualifications, and aims. We need to be sure that they'll be prepared to confront problems that some may consider insoluble, defend the rights of people who've lost all hope, bargain for favours, deal with local autocrats and policemen, write legible reports, sleep outside at night in places where an Afghan woman would never ever be sent by her parents or husband. (In fact, we have to reject some of them a priori because they wouldn't be allowed to go with us on field missions outside Kabul.)

Just a few examples:

Why have you applied for this position?

Have you ever been to the rural areas of Afghanistan?

What was your last journey outside Kabul?

If you received a report that in village X abuse Y has been committed, what would be your response?

How many displaced persons are there in the country?

Which districts in Kabul have suffered the worst destruction?

How long were you in exile?

Why do you want to leave your current job?

What is the name of Dostum's party?

And what's the name of the party that used to be led by Massud?

In your opinion, what are the fundamental rights of an individual?

The name of this position is Protection Assistant: in your opinion, who in Afghanistan is most in need of protection?

Which are the areas of the country where minorities currently suffer from harassment?

Give a brief definition of 'sharia'.

What do you think you can offer UNHCR that the other candidates can't?

What does the word 'deportation' mean?

The thing that emerges is that their experience is both dramatic and limited.

On the way out, I tell my colleagues that I would never have got through the test.

Courtesy

Today I've been offered by Afghans: tea six or seven times, lunch twice, sweets or nuts three times, pieces of watermelon once.

I've shaken the hands of at least five hundred people. I've touched my heart three hundred times, and have kissed six men.

I dream that I'm in a barber's shop. Actually there are two barbers, who are arguing about the best way to cut my hair. I leave the shop with long hair on one side and short hair on the other. My motorbike is no longer parked outside, and I have to cadge a lift. We're near Follonica and I'm given a lift in a workers' minivan. The workers seem angry or worried. I realise they aren't going towards Grosseto, as I'd hoped, but north towards Cecina. It's too late now to get off. I try to make conversation. 'Where are you heading?' 'Kabul,' the driver grumbles. That's why they look so grim... 'Kabul?! I can't believe it. *I've only just got back* from Kabul!' There are five other people in the minivan wearing T-shirts, their arms are short, and their faces are grim and sad. They're all Sardinian labourers. They're going to Kabul to build a house for a rich Italian. I tell them Kabul isn't so bad after all, you can have a decent life there.

'Oh, yes?' says my neighbour, with a heavy Sardinian accent. 'So tell me one good thing about Kabul.'

'The swimming pool,' I reply.

My Australian friend, the engineer, tells me it's better not to build stair rails in Afghanistan in case they collapse in an earthquake. Is he serious or only joking?

Frauke is a WFP expert on sheep farming. I tell her my dream. 'But they'll never be allowed in the UN pool in Kabul,' she says, thinking the Italian workers are real. 'That's no problem,' I reply, 'because they don't exist.'

Or maybe they'd be allowed in precisely because they don't exist. If you don't exist, nobody can stop you, can they?

I'm hungry. I tell Wali. He goes out and brings me back some bread. He hands it to me.

There's no cheese because the goats have all died of thirst.

16th June. Another ten minutes of lucidity at six-thirty in the afternoon, reading reports on the nomads of southern Afghanistan, the poorest in the world. My mind is perfect and powerless. A very beautiful twilight over Kabul.
I go to the swimming pool to check out my dream.

The water gushes from a depth of sixty metres... a blue rectangle surrounded by girls in bikinis... in the sun or in the shade. The splash as divers enter the water, birdsong, the buzz of insects… German voices on the air… the liquid nasals of the Americans… leaves rocking on the water, blue bubbles.

There's no cheese because the goats have all been sold.

It's been the rule for a few days now. Whenever a car enters the compound, the underside of the vehicle is inspected by a security officer, using a mirror with a long handle, to check that no bombs have been attached underneath. He slides the mirror backwards and forwards between the wheels, and over the vehicle's sides, manoeuvring it carefully with a circular movement. It must be a consequence of the umpteenth bombing in Pakistan. Two or three days ago a car bomb exploded outside the US consulate in Karachi. The same method that killed a dozen Frenchmen a month ago. After the explosion, all the guests at the Marriott (five stars) rushed to check out. The force of the blast stripped the leaves from the trees all over the neighbourhood. Only five corpses in the morgue. The rest were blown to pieces and spread over a radius of 200 metres: hard to put back together.

4,000 people have died in Karachi in the past five years in acts of political or ethnic violence.

Y. was telling me how difficult it is to count bodies, even when there are eye witnesses. When he was training as a journalist, he happened to be the first reporter on the scene of a Lufthansa plane crash near Nairobi, so he counted the number of victims and phoned his newspaper, proud of his own accuracy. There were a hundred and ten. Later, Lufthansa got in touch to say that there were only sixty passengers on the plane.

What displaced persons eat
Most live on a diet of bread and black tea. Sometimes onion soup (shorba) with a little oil. Carrots, too, and very occasionally yoghurt.

Fruit is practically never eaten by displaced persons or the city poor. In Herat they eat spinach because it doesn't cost much, eight cents a kilo. Plants and wild herbs picked in the country.

Meat is eaten only by the few Kuchis who still own a flock and eat the sick or wounded animals, killing them according to halal. The others eat meat once a year after the sacrifice (qurbani) or when a cow's lungs or heart are given away free by butchers.

Qul-e-torush: grain, goat's cheese and dried tomatoes (during the winter).

Shalambe: butter diluted in water, two or three times a month.

Malnutrition causes TB, ulcers, kidney infections, blindness, scabies, migraine and nightmares.

Too much diagnosis, not enough treatment.

18th June. I watch the Korea-Italy match, not at the embassy, but at the UN guest house, in order to avoid all that whining from the Italians. I arrive just as Buffon is saving the penalty allowed by the Ecuadorean referee, and sit down on the floor beneath the TV. Almost immediately I realise that the referee's been bribed and it would have been better to be with my countrymen. All the internationals are supporting Korea, and, what's worse, they don't understand anything about football. When Korea score the golden goal at the end, they're jubilant. My two colleagues, a Scotsman and an Englishman, both telecom technicians, have teased me all through the match about my silence and my nervousness, but at least they have the good grace to offer me cans of Stella Artois out of a tub full of ice (they always know exactly what's needed to enjoy their spare time). As luck would have it, there's a party this very night at the Italian embassy. After nine, two explosions can be clearly heard, one twenty seconds after the other. The soldiers who are present are called together behind the hedgerow in a corner of the garden. I tag along but stay at a distance, and the only thing I catch is an officer telling them to 'hold yourselves in readiness'. There's nothing on the radio. The guests dance on the bottom of the empty pool.

Before I go to bed I stick a spoon down my throat and vomit, as a precautionary measure.

19th June. We talk about the explosions. Unconfirmed rumours say two rockets were fired, at the US and Pakistan embassies. Others say ISAF or the Loya Jirga were the targets.

All the fans are on.

I'm studying sheep. Fat-tailed sheep. Shepherds become farmers, farmers are transformed into nomads, nomads settle down in houses, the flock grows in size, they get someone else to put it out to pasture, and the cycle starts again, everything depending on need.

A nomad used to earn his living from selling his animals, and to a lesser extent from selling wool, milk and cheese, as well as a few other things like firewood (bramble and bushes from the plains).

The rumours are confirmed. The target of the rockets really was the US embassy, which isn't far from the Italian embassy. As they were fired from a long distance, they missed their target by at least 800 yards. Such a margin might indicate other targets in the area, such as the King's house (BBC source). But if the radius is so wide, who can say what the target was?

An update. The first rocket hit Microrayan market, about 250 metres from the US embassy. It was a BM12 rocket, like those I saw in the hen-house in Dewana. The second landed 120 metres from the embassy.

Security advice
1. All staff should make sure that they can easily find their way between their room in the guest house and the

bunker. The bunker is the safest place in the event of bombardment.

2. All staff issued with VHF radios should carry their radios with them at all times. In case of an incident – *Listen to the radio, follow instructions.*

3. Limit movements in the city to a minimum during the evenings. Avoid possible target areas, i.e. US Embassy area and other installations.

4. I strongly advise staff not to spread rumours in regards to the incident. Rumours can be much more damaging than the actual rocket attack.

(*signed:* Security officer Christer Skarp)

An Afghan girl in the office lives in the neighbourhood where the first rocket fell. She tells me that in 1992 Massud's troops fired a hundred in one night. 'And now they call him the great Massud.' Her block was hit and several people who lived on the fifth floor died (these blocks were built by the Russians, which explains the curious name Microrayan). She lives on the third floor.

'They were beautiful houses before the bombing.'

Mission to Azro, 20th–21st June
Six hours by car. After the half-deserted city of Khosh and its mosque, metal towers glittering in the sun, the plateau is split by a long ravine that sinks into it like a verdant wound, we drive high up on the left, there are water, houses and plantations down there, like damp sores beneath the dry crust of the earth. Listening to Moby and Chemical Brothers, we pass through the village of Dubandhi, which has been almost completely destroyed (I no longer remember by whom) and is surrounded by fields lush with hashish. Then our cars rise along the bed of a stream and climb into the mountains as far as Lakatur pass, where we stop for a pee. I do it standing, the Afghans squatting, as is their custom. A strong wind sweeps the summit.

On the other side of the pass, we enter a luxuriant valley that leads into another, and then another and yet another, and so on and on, one valley opening after another, like a telescope, all green with hashish (here they call both the plant and the product 'hashish'). An astonishing sight. We get out of the car to look at the plants with their small fretted leaves. The green colour vibrates, oscillating between a dusty tone and a harsh tone. There's something like an optical buzz. If you pull out a couple, the smell stays on your hands and is hard to get off: three days and fifteen washes later, some people in Kabul will still sniff and look at you in surprise. The plants are of various ages and heights. The first ones we see seem to have grown spontaneously, they're sparse and stunted, and donkeys and unattended sheep nibble them. As we get closer to the villages, though, the fields are dense and well irrigated, and the plants are one metre high and shiny. And they grow everywhere, in the yards of houses, even on the roofs. By the end we will have counted forty-six uninterrupted kilometres of cannabis alternating with bands of wheat and opium poppies, and that's only until the chief town of Azro (Babar Khel?). After that, who knows? The road bends into a gorge and continues towards Jalalabad (another six hours by car) and then who knows…

Where the dirt road forks, or loses itself in vegetation or water, the drivers have to choose at a glance which direction to take to avoid potholes or the deeper wells. They almost always get it right. Tyre tracks left by other vehicles are a help. It must be terribly tiring but the drivers clearly enjoy themselves. Even a back-breaking drive of six, eight, ten hours is a pleasure as long as they have tapes and biscuits and a bit of chat. From the driver's seat, they know when the bumps are coming, it's we passengers who get the full shock. Despite the fact that our seat belts are pulled so tight we can't breathe, we still bang our heads constantly.

(Ouch. It's only now that I realise my car doesn't have a Codan radio which is used for long-distance calls, because this was the vehicle attacked and looted on the road to Ghazni and the radio hasn't been replaced yet. They have to get it from Pakistan… and so on. This means that if the radio in the other car breaks down we'll have no means of communication and will have to turn back. When we've returned to Kabul, I'm going to have to complain: they really shouldn't send a car out on a mission without a Codan radio. On the other hand, it's my fault because I didn't check the equipment before we left.)

The purpose of our mission is to verify population movements in the area and to see what condition the projects realised in the past few years – houses, schools and clinics – are in. On some maps Azro is attributed to Logar province, on others to Paktya province. The population is 100% Pashtun. Most of them fled during the Soviet occupation, then slowly began to return, but had to flee again during the American bombing, which destroyed four hundred dwellings (a figure to be taken with a pinch of salt, like everything else). We're the first to return to these valleys since September 11th.

In the village of Musa Khan, surrounded by trees, a clinic and a school built by UNHCR. They're beautiful, their solid stone echoing the colours of the surrounding mountains. The school's open from 7:30 to 11:30 and has four teachers. The classes go from first grade to fifth. Or so we learn from a group of children who've suddenly appeared. Were they in the fields? On the paths? We hadn't seen them before. Eighty boys attend the school. What about the little girls? They go to another school some distance from here. How many of them? Thirty, in one class. We enter, escorted by the children who have managed to climb in through a half-open window and open the door from the inside. On the door, the date 27/5/02 is scrawled in chalk. The rooms are bare and clean. It's cool in here. The blackboard. Carefully wiped. A couple of the doors are padlocked. The date refers to the UNICEF anti-polio campaign.

Polio and measles. Not just war victims here. They die like

flies from measles, or from common colds. But that doesn't make the news.

The backs of the children's hands and arms are so dirty they look like elephant hide.

At Babar Khel the streams are blood red.

The meeting with the authorities takes place in a room crowded with elderly men with big white beards and shaved moustaches, and young people sitting on the floor. They immediately offer us the Afghan delicacy, watermelon sprinkled with salt, we pick at a few pieces, and leave the rest on the table, to be eyed greedily by the young men. The governor crouches barefoot on the sofa, telling his beads. He rarely answers our questions himself, but lets the prosecutor and the police chief answer for him, which is a measure of his power – and his caution.

We deal with the following subjects: repatriation – his figures – the shortage of drinking water – the maintenance of buildings – jobs – the education of girls (we're told the girls are obliged to have their classes in the open air, under the trees, but this is only because they aren't allowed to use the school attended by the boys, even if they take their turn in the afternoon…) – clashes in the border area of Parachinar between the Mangals and the Tores (Pakistani tribes, one Sunni, the other Shi'ite) which prevent the refugees returning by the shortest route.

How the old men love all this discussion! They could talk for hours more, raising their voices and then calming down and smiling through their sparse teeth (though some display a fine and robust – if yellow – row of teeth). The governor next to me remains silent, spearing pieces of watermelon with the broken point of his knife. The prosecutor, who has two pens in his breast pocket, speaks on his behalf.

Most families own a little arable land, half a jerib, which is a quarter of a hectare. The moment has come to take the plunge: my colleague asks them which crops are grown most widely.

Wheat, they reply. And apart from wheat? They list other vegetables, potatoes. Yes, of course, but what about those other green plants?... We saw so many of them in the valley. The young men sitting on the floor burst out laughing, but the old men turn quite serious. Hashish is never referred to by name, it's called 'that thing'. First they blame the Kuchis, the migrants, for growing 'that thing'. The Kuchis are the convenient explanation that people give for anything that isn't right in Afghanistan, but the excuse doesn't wash, given that there are fields of 'that thing' everywhere, in the middle of the villages, in the yards of houses: there isn't a free square metre that isn't green with hashish, how could it be the nomads who grow it and harvest it? Let's be clear about this, we aren't here to make judgements, we just want to understand how it all works.

The answer is obvious to everyone: a jerib growing wheat brings in 5,000 Pakistani rupees, while a jerib sown with 'that thing' brings in 50,000.

The governor finally opens his mouth: 'If a man is hungry he'll even eat the dead.'

The teenage guards have wrapped the butts of their Kalashnikovs with sky-blue phosphorescent tape instead of green. Everyone decorates the object that keeps him company all day. The lorry driver embellishes the doors of his lorry, the shepherd paints his sheep. So many young men in Afghanistan spend their lives with rifles around their necks. What's striking in a country that's been at war for more than twenty years is the total lack of military demeanour. They seem like the most peaceful people in the world.

When the bombing stopped, seven or eight hundred families were repatriated from Pakistan to the district of Azro, but only about sixty with the aid of the UNHCR – a curiously small percentage. We later discover that many of them are not genuine refugees but seasonal workers who come back in spring to work the fields and go to Pakistan in the winter because it's warmer. There's no escaping it: most families here derive their income from growing cannabis. The authorities declare that none of it is for personal consumption. All of it is exported to Pakistan.

At the end of the meeting we fall into a trap. We've said we'd like to see some of the houses rebuilt with materials from the UNHCR before it gets dark, and the police chief offers to take us – as chance would have it, to the village where he himself lives (we only discover that when we're already on the way there, at the same time we discover that the village is quite far and there's only one rebuilt house there – on the side of the mountain.) So he's managed to cadge a lift from us, and also takes the opportunity to let us know that his own house is damaged and needs windows. Would you like to see it? Mmmmm... maybe later, thank you. The world is an boundless Irpinia[8]. We tramp up the mountain, and the chief invites us into his house – bombed by the enemies of Afghanistan – to have some yoghurt, but if we accepted, apart from giving him the impression that we agreed to his request for windows, we'd end up going back in the dark, which is against security regulations. Thanks again, no offence meant, but we really must go. We get our reward, though: a gorgeous sunset, the fields of hashish and wheat glowing in every possible shade of green, orange and gold.

The house where we'll spend the night is even higher, above terraces that remind me of Salina in the Aeolian islands, with hashish replacing malmsey – both plants that aid oblivion. Plenary indulgence. We drink tea lying on mattresses and sleeping bags in the open air, and from tea we pass directly to dinner, while the sky becomes black and starry. Children come up from the valley in single file, carrying loaves of bread a metre long. They're silent and obedient. We stroke their shaved heads. It really is nice and cool here. In the light of the gas lamp it isn't easy to see what we're eating, as we dip the bread in the oily food. But it tastes good. The Afghans in the company tell us amusing or dramatic stories, an old driver recalls September 11th, he was here when the news came. Farid is wearing a shalwar cameez and his highly trained muscles can be seen beneath the light cotton of the shirt. Jamila sits decorously to one side and either won't or can't share the blankets with the others. For a long time we look at the sky in silence. An icy wind is blowing. We sink beneath the blankets. We're at 2,500 metres. It's 20th June.

Handshakes
Sometimes they guide you with both hands, channelling the handshake and making it easier. While you shake their right hand, they grasp your forearm with their left.

21st June. To visit a number of families who've returned from Pakistan, we have to cross the blood-red streams, walking on trees that have been thrown from one bank to the other. The trunks, stripped of their bark, are smooth and damp. Below us, the water rushes headlong. To urge us on, a swarm of little boys hop on the trunks, which has the unfortunate effect of making them shake.

The refugees lived in Pakistan for a long time and have strong Pakistani accents.

We visit other groups and families who've returned in the last few months. Some crowd into their relatives' houses, others are in their tents. Talking to them reinforces the feeling that many aren't refugees who've returned for good, but seasonal workers, who go back and forth between here and Pakistan. To confirm this, we question the children, who unwittingly tell us the truth. One of them blurts out that he went to school here in Azro last year, although his mother has stated that she spent eight years in exile – at which she gives a loud cry and shuts his mouth – but now we know.

Afghanistan is a country in which a lot of places are either too cold or too hot to endure all year. Azro is wonderful now, but I can imagine what it must be like in January. An icebox. Mule tracks blocked by snow. Nothing to eat. Quite a lot of people prefer to go away then and come back in the spring. A doctor at the clinic in Kaswal confirms this: during the winter (when there ought to be more sick people) the number of patients they treat decreases by 30–40% on average. It's physiological. They up sticks and move to Jalabad, or down to Pakistan. The common euphemism is that the border is 'porous'. In any case, everyone on both sides of the border is Pashtun. During one of the rare 'political' conversations I've had these last months, I was accused of supporting the cause of Pashtunistan. Pashtunistan! Just imagine. But if we admit that everything's the same over here and over there, then the border's a mere convention. The Afghan Pashtuns will continue to cross it as and when they feel like it, and so will the Pashtuns who live on the other side. They've moved, they move, and they will move, even without the necessities of war. We have to accept this principle.

Whodunit?
When it comes to the agents of destruction, there's a rich choice. Russian rockets? Mujaheddin? Taliban reprisals? US bombers? Militias commanded by warlords? Faced with a village that's been razed to the ground, any of these options are possible. The closer you look, the easier it is to recognise the source of the attack. Take Shaidan, an hour and a half from Bamiyan. The walls of most of the houses we enter are intact, but the roofs have been burned and have collapsed: the result of a brief but fierce Taliban reprisal, in which the houses were torched one by one, to force the people to flee. Damage not as serious as elsewhere.

Azro was very much pro-mujaheddin, then it was very much pro-Taliban, so the Russian bombers pounded it hard during the 80's, and so did the Americans last autumn. The B-52s took over from the Tupolevs. All because the valley that leads to the border at Teramangal is the umbilical cord between Pakistan and Afghanistan – a corridor for supplies of arms and men.

Today, 99% of the drugs from Azro pass that way, direct to the refineries beyond the border.

(Jamila tells us her father was killed by the Russians during the coup against Daud. She was just a little girl.)

Tapes of Indian musicals. By now, I know them by heart, I can sing the songs one after another. *Mahabat... eeeeh, Mahabat... eeeaaah.* Always with the same nasal tone.

I ask what's so appealing about these Indian films.

'They're about love,' Farid replies.

There follows a lively discussion about love affairs, both fictitious and real, in which even Jamila takes part (at last!), asking questions like: 'In Italy can you get married against your parents' wishes? At what age? How long does an engagement last?' In Afghanistan it lasts an eternity, and contrary to what I thought, people marry quite late, especially the men, who don't get married until they're about thirty. Lovers meet the usual universal obstacles: class differences, rash promises, fuddy-duddy parents, family feuds. We spend the rest of the journey back to Kabul talking about Romeo and Juliet and other famous couples of more or less cursed lovers. Then we discuss Asia, Europe and America, comparing them, and whether love can ever last forever, and what makes it last. Farid and Jamila are both young and hungry for debate, their eyes (Farid's green, Jamila's very black) glitter with curiosity. Farid laughs a lot, as if everything I say is incredible, or as if I were always exaggerating or lying. Maybe I am. Talking about Italy and its customs, I realise I have to keep making a distinction between how things were thirty or forty years ago and how they are now – although the country where housewives talk about oral sex on prime-time TV is still the same (at least a fair chunk of it is) as in the days of *Divorce Italian Style* and *Seduced and Abandoned*[9].

An English reporter has written that roads in Afghanistan 'vary from atrocious to non-existent' – and he was referring to the main roads, the ring linking the big cities, Kabul, Mazar, Herat, Kandahar, Ghazni. By the time I get out, I'm wrecked after six hours of dirt road and whining love songs in Urdu.

Bullet points (three conclusions from my report)
- The buildings built or restored with UNHCR contributions are deteriorating through neglect. The local authorities are convinced that it is up to us to maintain them: but for how long? Are they being naive or cunning? It is clear they feel more like tenants than owners.
- The education of girls is still very limited. The practical reasons given – for example, the lack of space – are unconvincing, given that school premises are not used to anywhere near their capacity. A much more serious problem is the recruitment of teachers.
- People generally have a rather passive attitude towards reintegration, little interest in getting work or even in restoring their own houses where these have been damaged by neglect. Many of those interviewed seemed to be waiting for external aid from the humanitarian and development agencies. The paradox is that the good quality of the work that was previously done seems to have created a culture of long-term dependency.

It's hot, time to get out the sandals. Along with the heat, the scorpions have arrived. Yesterday, the caretaker nailed one in the dust with a stick. It was whitish and about ten centimetres long. It shook furiously, trying to free itself. Its sting can swell the foot like a pumpkin. Worse if it stings an allergic person or a child. I think of the medical students camped on the slopes of Bibi Maharo hill, opposite our houses. It must be fifty degrees in those tents during the day.

Kabul's second orphanage, Tahya Maskan

Six huge pots in the kitchens, under two of which a fire is burning. The dining hall, with its long, gloomy benches, reminds me of Morbelli's paintings of nineteenth-century almshouses in Milan, as well as other social painters. Ten bunk beds per room. All boys. One boy's wearing a Real Madrid shirt. He's thirteen, the family also wanted the orphanage to take his two sisters but they weren't accepted. There's a third sister, too, and three other brothers.

Another boy, twelve years old, all his family are dead except his mother, who lives in the remote region of Badakshan. He's been here for three years.

I ask one of the boys if he wouldn't mind showing me his belongings. He doesn't mind at all, and pulls out a tin box from under the bed. He opens the padlock with a little key. These boxes are very common in Afghanistan, and can be as big as a trunk. The boy has his clothes and books in it, everything well folded. There's also a Russian camera his uncle gave him as a present.

On the wall there's a poster of a happy boy wearing a Manchester United shirt.

We go on to the rooms for the younger children. They have gaunt, triangular faces. Short hair. They're very polite. None of them are pestering me for a pen. I question two or three of them. They're serious at first, then smile in the most beautiful way.

What's your favourite subject?
Dari.
And apart from Dari?
Theology.
Where's your daddy?
He's dead.
How did he die?
In the war.
And your mother?
At home.

When do you see her?

On Thursdays.

On Thursday afternoons the children who have relatives in the city can go to see them. Do they come and pick them up? No, they go all on their own, even the younger ones, on foot or by public transport. The orphanage is situated in the middle of a Soviet residential neighbourhood, a hideous place, though compared to the rest it's not so bad, as is the case with many other things made by the Communists (here in Afghanistan and elsewhere).

The clinic gets about thirty patients a day. Two are being admitted at the moment. They're sitting on the beds, thin, silent. The illnesses treated: malaria, diarrhoea (watery and bloody), sore throat, eczema, scabies, leishmaniasis.

(Plain facts: the orphanage of Tahya Maskan houses between seven and eight hundred boys and young men aged between three and seventeen. Together with the Alaouddin orphanage, which we visited in April, that makes about 1,700 children, of whom 600 have no close relatives. There are 350 beds in Tahya Maskan. In some cases the children sleep two or three to a bed. The school has classes from the first to the eighth grade. All children attend in the morning, and the middle grades attend in the afternoon as well. The orphanage also used to house 300 girls, but they were expelled during the Taliban regime.

Requests for admission are usually put forward by the children's relatives. They are examined by a commission composed of representatives of the municipality, religious leaders and elders, which may take anything from three days to a month to reach a decision. Most children are admitted, but there is a shortage of places, so about a thousand requests are currently pending.)

Outside, in a vast yard, hundreds of children are playing in the dust, some on rudimentary merry-go-rounds (a gift of the Italian army), others playing football, though there seem to be no boundaries between different fields or different teams: it's as if three or four games were taking place simultaneously on the very same pitch. Groups of players battle it out in a swirl of dust. Balls emerge from the mêlée, and I'm hit a couple of times. As always happens after I've been walking in Kabul, I'm white from the waist down. Anne's heart aches from what we see.

Questions, doubts, discussions. Does the orphanage come within our mandate? Should a place like this be modernised, or else abolished? If you improve the living conditions, are you just encouraging families to send their children there? And if, on the other hand, you help the relatives and the adoptive families financially so that they can keep the children at home (it has been done by some NGOs, and indeed the reason we're here is to examine the possibility of financing a family reunification project), aren't you encouraging those with orphans in their charge to throw them out on purpose in order to get help to take them back again? In other words, aren't we going to end up making the problem we're trying to solve even worse? Discussions, doubts, questions.

24th June. By plane to Kandahar. It makes me sad to think that if I hadn't extended my mission for another month (the whole of July) I could have been home within three weeks... But I agreed to the extension, they didn't force me at all. The usual contradictions. Never a wholehearted, unambiguous decision. Among the events of the past few days: the shooting outside the Tahya Maskan orphanage, Alex T.'s fainting fit. (Meanwhile, below me, 'bitten mountains', as I read in a book by one of those adventurous English aesthetes, who travel in order to get themselves photographed on horseback with a turban and a beard, in a word, idlers). Let's start with Alex: the day before yesterday he bumped into the cement frame of the walkway between guest houses D and F, and fainted. He was alone. Nobody knew he was there. Nobody – not even Alex himself – knows how long he was unconscious. When he came to, he was very confused. He wanted to go to work, but someone picked him up and took him to the ISAF clinic. Half humorously, half as a result of his trauma, he said he'd fallen while defending one of our female colleagues from a mujaheddin attack.

To the Tahya Maskan orphanage (see above) with Anne and an Irishman who looks like a hobbit. As we were turning left from the main road, a car came shooting towards us from the opposite direction. To avoid a head-on collision it swerved, just managing to squeeze through between the front of our vehicle and a cyclist. Bastard! I shouted at him. The hobbit at the wheel only just managed to brake. A few seconds later we heard the crack of an automatic weapon and a police van appeared, on the tail of the car. That's why it had been going so fast. Then we visited the orphanage and I forgot all about the incident until that evening after dinner, when I sat down next to the new head of security, a placid-looking Swede who worked in Rwanda for a long time. He made a note of it and then (gently but firmly) reprimanded us for breaking UN rules. If we'd been wounded in the shootout, the insurance wouldn't have paid up, because we weren't travelling in our car, but in the hobbit's pick-up – a fairly clapped-out vehicle, to tell the truth.

In the little 20-seater plane, almost everyone has fallen asleep. It's nine a.m. on 24th June. I've been up since quarter to five – because of nerves. In the clefts between the arid mountains, the yellow ground is veined with streaks of vegetation. The deep valleys descend in a zigzag towards the desert – and there, a flash of green, tilled fields and houses. The canal network branches across the heath for another few hundred metres, a sign that the irrigated area used to be more extensive but retreated when the drought came.

We land. Not in Kandahar, but in Herat. It's cool and windy. We walk on the runway while waiting to take off again. The Dutch pilots joke with the Afghans. I wish I could be like these pilots. They do their work and that's it, they take the plane from one place to another and then they've finished, they don't have to worry about Tajiks and Uzbekis, war orphans, irrigation, economic recovery. It's none of their business. They pilot the plane and, hey presto, they've done their duty. I wish I could be a technician who sets off with his case of tools under his arm to repair something, puts it back in working order, and then leaves. Instead of which, I'm wrapped in words, doubts and half-knowledge.

We've arrived in Kandahar. The heat and the dusty wind hits us as we get off the plane. The air's white. The airport is an American military base. We're surrounded by tanks. We wait for an hour in the sun while well-built soldiers, both men and women, walk by endlessly, touching their caps in greeting as they pass. 'How're you doing, gents?' They have rifles slung over their shoulders or pistols strapped to their thighs and almost all of them have bottles of water, which they cradle in their arms. They drink constantly. The women soldiers wear shorts and have muscular but worn thighs. A Stars and Stripes waves from the airport tower. There are other flags around, a couple of Afghan, one Canadian, about ten US. Red and blue against the white sky. To leave the airport area, we have to zigzag around cement barriers and coils of barbed wire. The machine gun emplacements are half hidden by camouflage nets which mimic a kind of foliage that looks out of place here. The landscape around us is an overexposed photograph. Burnt and solitary trees along the roadside.

An immediate feeling of powerlessness, like retching. You can't get rid of it.

It's hard to know whether I can or can't, must or mustn't, shake the hands of the women who work in the offices and who, in theory, are emancipated. This morning at the WFP I didn't do it, and it was the woman herself who insisted on being treated equally and having her hand shaken regularly like her male colleague, which made it look as if I was the one who was trying to discriminate. Soon after, I held out my hand to another young woman, and she cried out 'Oh, no, no!' as if I was mad, pulling back her hand while my open hand remained suspended in mid-air.

A theological discussion
It's ten thirty. I want to visit the transit centre at Daman, about twenty kilometres from Kandahar. All right, they reply, but we'll have to hurry, otherwise it'll soon be too hot, in fact it's probably too late already. 'From midday till three it's hell.' I say I'd like to go anyway. The heat can be tolerated for an hour.

'You see, the real problem of hell isn't that the punishment is terrible, *but that it's eternal.*'

The sky completely white, as if it's about to snow, the trees have turned white, the walls drained of colour.

The big problem in the Kandahar area is drought and the consequent plight of the Kuchis: the nomads who've lost almost all their livestock and now don't know where to go and have stayed here, in the wrong place, or in the wrong season, depending on how you look at it. In this heat, they should be with their flocks in the pastures above 2,000 metres. But the flocks no longer exist: in four consecutive years of famine, they've all been eaten or sold, or have died. There are at least 35,000 Kuchis in the Panjway district, one hour south-west of Kandahar, as well as many others scattered in camps that have grown up spontaneously, and another 35,000 on the other side at Spin Boldak, a few minutes from Pakistan, not to mention those across the border, at least another 25,000 people dumped in Chaman, in the so-called waiting area. Waiting for what? Not all the people in Spin Boldak and Chaman are Kuchis, though a good sixty per cent are. Another fifteen per

cent are Pashtun who've fled southward to escape the persecution that followed the fall of the Taliban, and the rest are
people escaping the drought. About a month ago, I wrote that
the Kuchis are the Afghan equivalent of gypsies. It was a sug-
gestive but misleading comparison, but now it seems quite
valid: everywhere in Afghanistan the Kuchis are treated
exactly the same way gypsies are treated in Europe, with a
mixture of contempt and disgust. They're idlers, they're
dangerous, they steal other people's land, they ruin the soil –
which may be true, though it may also be true that the passage of their flocks fertilises it. Their migrations have always
been a dynamic element of the Afghan economy. The fact is
that when resources are scarce, nobody's keen on newcomers.
There have always been quarrels about grazing rights, with
the attendant feuds and vendettas, so you can imagine how
things are now that the drought has turned so much pasture
land to desert. The prejudice against the Kuchis is a strong
one, as it is against the Hazaras. They remain the pariahs of
Afghan society: at the job interviews last Sunday, one of the
Afghan women (a graduate) gave the following definition of
the Kuchis: 'They aren't very clever people.'

Talking of vendettas: In Zaranj, a policeman abused a refugee,
telling him to keep moving. The fact is, the man was a paralytic. When he didn't move, the policeman hit him in the face.
The paralytic somehow managed to get away. When he got
back to his family, he told his brother what had happened. The
brother went to see the policeman and asked him: 'Were you
the one who beat my brother? Don't you know he can't walk?'
Then he took out a gun and shot the policeman, crippling him.
(Told by the head of security in Kandahar.)

The Kuchis can still earn a lot in a good season. But it's a risky
business and the wealth they accumulate can easily 'melt like
wax'. Dependent as they are on freedom of movement – the
Kuchis cover hundreds of kilometres and their displacement

can last up to three months – any restriction can have a serious effect. The unexpected closing of borders, the danger caused to grazing land by mines, war fronts cutting across the usual routes, forcing the nomads to either choose other routes or turn back, the building of all kinds of barriers: all these things show how very fragile and susceptible the nomadic life is. In order to survive when times are hard, the nomads have to adopt a fairly flexible lifestyle. In other words, they aren't so bound to sheep rearing as their main activity that they can't take up other activities, even if the income they get from them is minimal. The nomad is always thought of as a proud, rebellious character, impatient with the restrictions of a settled life. Wrong. If necessary, he can turn his hand to anything: gathering firewood, working as a servant, weaving carpets.

Daman. Visit to the distribution and transit centre. Families in tents consisting of three crossed poles and a dust sheet. Four out of every eight who come forward are rejected. Why? They don't have any baggage with them. They have no knowledge of the area they claim to be from. They give contradictory answers. A boy of nine whose family have been in exile for ten years, which means he was born in Pakistan, says he remembers his house in Maywand well. Their sacks are filled with fufu. Their boxes contain two plates and two glasses for families of six or seven people. They have few if any mattresses. In other words, they aren't genuine refugees, or if they are their repatriation is purely practical: they'd take the money, go straight back to Pakistan, and try again. If they haven't already done so. They're recycled refugees. It isn't possible for a family to have so little. Or is it? Another family in a jeep are accepted. Three dirty, snotty-nosed children, an old man and an old woman, who are their parents. It's shameful to ask the woman to open her sack and show her possessions in front of everyone. I tell the onlookers to move away. The crowd curse and complain (these are the rejected families – a constant, insincere whimpering). A very dirty little girl with eyes of a feverish blue. Women with tattooed faces jostle me, waving papers and photographs. There's one family with practically no baggage: two boys with faces like mice, an old woman and a little girl. When they're handed back their papers with REJECTED written on them, they aren't surprised. At least they've tried. (Get Abdul Zia to show you the list of criteria for rejection.) We're handed forms with a question mark on them, which means that whoever registered them wasn't sure. It isn't hot today: 38 degrees. At the clinic I meet a nurse from Melbourne. It's her first day's work in Afghanistan. Abdul Zia has only just got married and his wife scolds him because he gets back late at night from work and sometimes has to sleep out. The traffic in recycled refugees: the border's too close... it's too easy to go back and forth and get money and food two or three times... Zia says that this is a terrible job to do if you're a good Muslim who wants to help all his fellows without distinction. But there are cheats. They're easily spotted.

(I'm determined, though, to have 'absence of baggage' deleted from the list of criteria. There's such poverty here that a family may really possess nothing.)

My assistant Karima has green eyes and a stern face. She's the only Afghan woman in the office. It's even harder for women in Kandahar than in Kabul. She wears embroidered stockings and always has her burqa ready in her bag. The women are often stern. Circumstances have made them like that. The men, on the other hand, are gentle. By Italian standards, the young men would be assumed to be homosexuals.

There's no wind today and the windows can be left open. Lars warned me never to do that: you get back to the room two hours later and find the place fit only for a camel. Everything covered in sand. Your sheets crunch.

Bazaars overflowing with goods. A real craze for motorbikes. Motorbikes and scooters everywhere. A passion for mechanics. Three or four people – all carrying jerrycans – on one saddle. Low saddles, the kind you used to find in Italy in the Sixties (the Corsarino Morini, the Motobi). Kandahar swarms with three-wheel buggies, like an even smaller Ape but with four seats, which are used as taxis. They're decorated like the allegorical floats in Viareggio[10].

The most common make is Honda – a triumph of chrome wings over tanks – followed by Yamaha and then, some way behind, the other Japanese makes. There are also various Russian models. The three-wheel taxis are called rickshaws. Who produces them? Weespa, Mirwais tells me. And where do they come from? Italy.

Rummaging in my knapsack, I find the waterproof jacket I've brought with me to Kandahar, where it hasn't rained for four years.

Maybe the jacket was meant to have magic powers and bring rain.

Driving around.
Here, as everywhere, buildings machine-gunned... shattered... crumbling...

Eyes of embarrassing depth in the children's dirty faces. It seems this race was created specially to cause unease. I'm even starting to understand the English aesthetes and their hyperboles. The most sympathetic and least rhetorical in his persistent slyness remains Robert Byron (*The Road to Oxiana*). Almost all the others go into raptures about sunsets over the Hindu Kush, ruins, young men with roses in their mouths, Russian rockets and the mujaheddin, who give them the thrill of danger.

Mirwais has classic glasses with thick frames. On one side the arm is attached to the lens with plasticine. A student of mine in the prison did the same thing. Makeshift repairs. Always makeshift repairs.

There's a man who's had to stay in Daman because he lost his papers, or at least claims to have lost them, during the repatriation journey. The others with him, including his wife and children, left again at once for Kunduz. He's 32 and has spent 15 years in Quetta. He fled during the Najibullah regime because of the fighting between government troops and those of Massud (check if the dates coincide: apparently they do, give or take a slight margin of error). He was a tailor for a while, then a labourer. He has three sons born during exile: they're 11, 8 and 2. He was part of a convoy that left Quetta on 24th June. Between Chaman and the border, there was a sandstorm, the rear door of the lorry flew open, and some of the baggage fell out. After getting out to recover the baggage, he realised that he didn't have the forms with him and couldn't find them again. He shows us the outer pocket of his waistcoat where he'd carelessly put them. He's a thin man with delicately drawn features, a straight nose, blue eyes, and a trim reddish-blond beard. He reminds me of a schoolmate of my wife's named Enrico Reggiani. My Afghan colleague, who's seen lots of recycled refugees and tends to be quite strict, thinks the man is telling the truth. All right, I say, but we still need to check with Quetta. On 24th June, only 75 families were registered there for repatriation and this man's name should crop up. If he isn't on the list, then I'm sorry, we can't believe him. I ask the man if he's prepared to wait until tomorrow, when we'll have a reply from Quetta. I tell him straight out that if he wasn't registered it's pointless for him to wait and he may as well leave right now, he won't get money or anything else. He looks at me calmly and says: 'I'll wait.'

Privilege: to have roses and grass in front of your eyes instead of sand and cement.

Visit to the displaced persons camp at Panjway (27th June)
In the tents: a teapot, two or three motor-oil jerrycans, a bundle of rags and (where food has been distributed) one or

two sacks of wheatflour mixed with soya. The people in the tents complain that they can't make bread with this flour. They show us the results: a crumbly black pizza.

Three elders whip the children to keep them at a distance.

An old woman is spinning a rope to support the poles of the tent. The floor is strewn with dried shit. The old woman has only one sheep left and it'll take her months to make a rope.

We've said often enough that aid should go by priority to the most vulnerable individuals (see categories), so in the second village we visit we're taken to see the most wretched of the wretched. It's like a treasure hunt to find the most deformed person. Flanked by children, we're dragged from one ragged tent to another, and shown an old madwoman, a cripple, a phocomelic, a blind man. The ones who can't move are carried out of their tents and set down in the dust so that we can get a better look at their sores and stumps. For God's sake, there's no need! Take them back in the shade! But they continue to prod the village freaks, forcing them to walk like lame ducks. The madwoman's eyes are covered with white cataracts, and her muttering makes the children split their sides with laughter.

If it's all an act, congratulations, it's very impressive, we'll put the old woman at the top of the list.

Hard luck for the families who don't have their monster!

Why, why, why? I ask myself as I walk, blinded by the light. White sky, dusty wind. The tents stretch in all directions. The camp seems infinite.

I use the radio to call for a car, but there's no answer.

Why what?

I don't know.

I'm glad to have Alia with me. She's an ironic, energetic girl, who can outguess me or follow me as need be. She never loses her temper, but she can be abrupt when she wants to be. I predict she'll go far in this fucking job. She's good.

Yesterday I received a message from Italy that said: But what on earth are you doing in Kandahar?

There are camels in the freaks' camp (a sign that they're doing quite well, comparatively speaking). Among the activities: gathering the camel droppings to make fire. Once they're dry, they're light and almost odourless, they look like those plant balls you find on the beach and little boys throw at each other. Now I realise where the camp is: we're in the middle of the river bed. When the evacuees arrived in Panjway three years ago they settled on the bank, then the Arghandab dried up and they went down into the bed. If one day the river starts flowing again, they'll be submerged. I wish to heaven it happens – just the first of those two things.

28th June. I wake up early as usual, and there's an emergency: rockets have been fired at a UNHCR office in Spin Boldak, a hundred kilometres south-east of Kandahar, on the border with Pakistan. 35,000 evacuees live in the camps around Spin Boldak, while ten minutes' car ride from there, in Chaman, another 25,000 are stuck in the no man's land between Afghanistan and Pakistan known as the waiting area, unable to move because Pakistan won't let them in and they have nowhere to go in Afghanistan.

We get in the car with our chief who, as today was supposed to be a rest day, is dressed comfortably in an immaculate shalwar kameez and a beret from Tanzania. We load up with bread and bottles of frozen water. The whole six-hour journey sitting between a robust Canadian policeman and a wiry Danish policeman (who tells me later that he's lost fourteen kilos since he's been in Afghanistan). We know now that the rockets that fell on the office came from an arms depot that blew up. After a few kilometres of asphalt the road becomes a dirt road, but it's still possible to do sixty an hour. We cross bridges over rivers that no longer exist. We can see they're rivers because of the banks, but the beds are as dry and yellow as the rest of the flat country around us. The red and black mountains in the distance seem unattainable. One of the bridges, bombed by the Americans, is in a precarious condition, all uneven and bent and broken, in some places the cement has crumbled revealing the iron structure, sooner or later the bridge will collapse, and yet fully laden lorries pass over it, zigzagging around the chasm, and the whole structure shakes and sways, unless that's just my impression. There's an alternative track, which descends and crosses the dry river bed, but it's too late to tell Bismillah to choose that one, we've started across the bridge and it would be more dangerous to try and reverse now than to go forward.

'Let's remember on the way back,' I whisper in the Danish policeman's ear.

We resume our journey across the desert, where there used to be vineyards and fields of pomegranates celebrated by sensual poets. A car appears, signalling with its headlights. We stop. It's on its way from Spin Boldak, with a wounded man on board. He's an old driver hit in the head by shrapnel. He was sleeping on a mattress on the veranda when the shells started raining down. His forehead is bandaged and his beard is red, his shirt and waistcoat are spattered with blood. The wound has been stitched up and he can't wait to get back to Kandahar. The man with him warns us not to go anywhere near the arms depot when we get to Spin Boldak because it's still burning and the explosions haven't stopped. We set off again. As we cross the desert, red and grey peaks in the distance, I have flashes where I imagine I've been invited to talk about one of my books at a literary gathering in some carefree seaside town, and for a couple of days I'm living the life of Riley in a beautiful hotel with my wife.

Meanwhile I unconsciously whistle songs by Prince, like *Raspberry Beret*.

Very young children appear at the sides of the track and hail the lorries which brush past them without slowing down and cover them with dust. They're so dirty that their faces and hair and clothes are all one colour. They either join their hands as if in prayer or make threatening gestures with their fingers. I haven't seen anyone stop. Lord knows where these little beggars come from, as there are no houses to be seen between here and the horizon.

To enter Spin Boldak we have to pass a roadblock. The village is shrouded in smoke, which mingles with the dust carried on the wind. It's hard to speak because your mouth immediately fills with sand. Despite the danger and the presence of police, there are a lot of people walking around outside the burning depot, dragging their feet in the dust. Fine and grey, like volcanic ash. The last explosion happened five minutes ago but the onlookers aren't afraid. Apparently there are still many unexploded missiles inside, which they're trying to cool down with hoses. Almost impossible to breathe because of the stench and the gusts of smoke, anyone with a handkerchief puts it over his mouth, men with turbans have loosened them and stuck the flap between their teeth. The UNHCR office is just opposite the arms depot, at a distance of about 150 metres. The explosion tore off the gate. The projected material has made holes at several points in the perimeter wall or rained down from above, and the whole courtyard is covered with contorted pieces of metal. Scattered in the dust are thousands of exploded and unexploded shell cases, fused missile cones, fragments of grenades, ailerons and tails from munitions of all kinds. The windows of the vehicles have been blown out and their roofs completely collapsed, a sign that something very heavy must have fallen on them. The guards have tried to clean up, collecting shells and stacking them against the wall, but as many are still unexploded, and there are also a number of intact mortar grenades, we tell them to leave them where they are: better to wait for the bomb disposal squad. Something very powerful has broken through the perimeter wall, leaving a hole half a metre wide, then the wall of the building, gutted the admin office and blown two doors to pieces before ending up in the toilet. Anyone finding himself in its path would have been cut in two. The staff have spent all night flat on their stomachs on the floor while fragments of glass and debris rained down on them. The first explosion took place at a quarter-past midnight, and then it went on without respite until the morning. Here's the bloody mattress on which the driver, Ismail Jan, was sleeping.

The staff are so exhausted after the night of fires that some are lying on mattresses in the middle of the wreckage, trying to sleep. We step over them during our inspection.

Accounts of the incident vary greatly. Two soldiers dead, plus six or seven civilians, including a child, says the district administrator. Four soldiers missing. The estimate this afternoon from the Pakistani authorities on the border will be three times bigger. According to the district commissioner, someone was seen throwing a grenade or a Molotov cocktail into the arms depot just before the chain of explosions started. The identity of the saboteur is not known. There's another completely nonsensical version, saying that a bomb was dropped on the arms depot from a low-flying plane. The rumour immediately spread that it was an attack by Mullah Omar's men. It's also possible the accident was caused by simple negligence. Operating the hand-pump, I wash my head at the well in the courtyard, but the layer of dust remains. Our man in Spin Boldak takes me aside. We walk in circles, the munitions clattering between our feet. This area is a sanctuary. Hard to determine where 'the enemy' is hiding. The border between Afghanistan and Pakistan is an abstract line, people come and go, and so do money and arms. On the other side of the border, at Chaman in Pakistan, in the bazaar where money is raised to finance the Taliban resistance, there's one area that consists almost entirely of dressmakers' shops, and on the doors someone has put up posters saying:

WOMEN WHO SPEND MORE
THAN 5 MINUTES AT THE DRESSMAKERS
WILL BE REPORTED TO THEIR HUSBANDS
AND SEVERELY PUNISHED UNDER ISLAMIC LAW

An hour later I cross the border. My Pakistani visa has expired but it doesn't matter, I don't even need a piece of paper. To get across, you go along a winding corridor that cuts through the bazaar. Although today's a rest day, the bazaar is packed and very busy. Children with jerrycans, Yamaha motorbikes, three-wheel buggies – Pakistani-style, with the rear seat facing backwards – lorries unloading an enormous variety of goods in filthy plastic wrapping. Most of all, tyres. The border is one huge tyre shop. Impossible to find my bearings. I only realise I'm in Pakistan when our car moves to the left-hand side of the road, which isn't a road but a track over the dust dunes. It's hard for the wheels of the Landcruiser to get a grip on the slopes. A few hundred metres from here, beyond the shops converted from old containers, beneath the high watchtowers built by the Pakistanis, are the 25,000 desperate people in the waiting area.

The doctors look sleepy. The explosion was so big, they thought it was an earthquake. The sheet-metal roof of the clinic shifted. And we're at least twelve kilometres from the arms depot here. The woman doctor has tired but beautiful blue eyes. Her exhausted colleague says you could see the flashes and the trails of the rockets high in the sky.

At the Chaman base, the UNHCR officer (a Bosnian woman from Tuzla) manages to wangle us some very spicy food and tea with milk in the Pakistani style. I scratch away the dust from my forehead.

Voglio andare a casa / la casa dov'è?[11]

We drive back through an uninterrupted cloud of sand creeping slowly over the road. When it clears, we see funnels of wind lifting the sand from the desolate heath and up into the sky. Twisters. They dart about for a long time and then dissolve. The air is white with fine dust and the tangles of rocks are faded in the diffuse light. In the middle of the desert, we pass tubs in which dozens of boys are bathing, many of them with their trousers and shirts on.

The UNHCR distribution centre at Tak-ta-Pul is soon to be closed and moved to Daman, further from the border, to discourage the recycling of refugees. The journey will cost more, which will make fake repatriation less profitable. I imagine they'll also close the drinks stalls outside. All they sell is orangeade. The bottles hang on threads from the roofs of the stalls to attract customers.

Crossing the desert, the two security people have been listening patiently for hours to music chosen by Bismillah. The same cassettes over and over again. In the hierarchy, the driver occupies the bottom rung of the ladder, but in some ways he's also the chief. His music gives him supremacy over the ears, and by extension the thoughts, of his passengers. A plaintive voice with a tabla backing has kept us company all the way to Chaman and then all the way back. Even I – 'open' to other cultures as I am – thought it sounded like someone complaining about a stomach ache, so I can imagine what the two policemen must have felt. Half an hour from Kandahar, the Canadian does in fact lose patience and get Bismillah to turn it off.

29th June. I was supposed to be present at a food distribution in a district of Kandahar, but I've been kept here by an attack of dysentery.

30th June. The problem in Spin Boldak is that, despite the danger, the authorities don't want to close the area around the arms depot. There are still three hundred missiles inside, along with other stuff. The firemen say they've put out the flames and eliminated any residue that could be a source of risk, but a blast this morning, which released white phosphorus, has given them the lie. If the depot catches fire again, the radius of destruction could be three kilometres. A mine-clearing organisation has said it's prepared to assist the authorities in moving the unexploded munitions to an appropriate place, where they can be detonated in safe conditions, but the administrators seem reluctant, and are waiting for authorisation from the governor of Kandahar, as if they thought those three hundred missiles could still be used. But it's clear that the unexploded munitions will be destroyed anyway. An information campaign has been started to prevent children from picking up any devices. Two little boys have been injured by unexploded shells while playing near the depot. Only yesterday, three thousand were recovered from the ground.

We're watching Brazil-Germany, maybe the most boring final of all time, when the representative of the Minister for Repatriation arrives. Alia and I have to go out and talk to him. (Alia's mother is German and so she's the only one out of the fifty people present to support her national team.) There's an important matter to discuss: the distribution of tents and blankets at Panjway to the most deprived group of all, the Kuchis. As we leave the room, a roar goes up, followed by applause: Ronaldo's first goal. Our bargaining continues for quite a while: we have to make it clear to the man that the list of 6,249 families he's brought us is useless, he has to select 1,000 from it, just 1,000, no more than 1,000, the poorest, most destitute families of all, those with rags for tents, the widows, the families without able-bodied males, those who don't have a single sheep, only 1,000, understand? 1,000 out of 6,249, because we only have a thousand tents and we can't give any more. It's an extremely difficult negotiation and our Afghan is frightened because instead of being thought of as a benefactor, a title he thought he'd earned by collecting the names of people in Panjway and promising to help them, like a Christian Democrat of the old school, he's now likely to be a figure of hate for all those he'll have to exclude, which is five out of every six families. A thousand tents, understand, we only have a thousand tents. I do him a drawing to make it crystal clear: a circle full of little dots and a smaller circle inside it. He has to choose the poorest, the truly needy, with the help of the camp elders, who know their people and know who's worst-off. The first few times I was dubious about this system of letting the old men do the selection. I thought there'd be favouritism. I found the very term 'village leader' suspicious, thinking of the usual local notable who finds jobs for his nephews and makes a fortune out of state-owned land. But the shuras work. They're traditional popular institutions. It's an aspect of Islam that has a lead over other societies. Without this solid distribution network behind them, a good many Afghans wouldn't have survived the emergency.

It's reported on TV that the Americans have bombed a marriage ceremony by mistake in the province of Uruzgan, north of Kandahar – at least forty dead, maybe a hundred.

JULY

We go to the waiting area at Chaman. It's a no man's land, even though officially it's in Pakistan. A thorn between the two states, an infected blister. Images like these have probably already been used in the press, where the place is usually referred to as 'the hell of Chaman'. Since the border was closed in October 2001 to stem the tide of people fleeing the bombing, tens of thousands of refugees have gathered in this pocket, creating a camp the Pakistani authorities are now fully determined to close. It's the foulest place I've ever been to, and yet people are reluctant to leave. They have nowhere better to go and they think that as long as they stay there, they'll get some kind of help. They all live in abject poverty, crammed into a city of tents surrounded by dust dunes and swept by constant storms. The border is a joke, a mirage, a huge country fair. I understand now why, in spite of everything, all displaced persons gravitate to this chaotic bazaar. All kinds of business are carried on there: underhand, illegal – and profitable. The perfect place to write a Marxist ballad about. What keeps mankind alive[12]... Left-wing bards, forget Berlusconi for a while and make a beeline for this place, where goods and the movement of goods are sold for a profit. The road between Chaman and Spin Boldak (six or seven kilometres in all) must, I think, be the largest tyre market in the world...

In the tents of the Kuchis. We have to shield our eyes from the dust. Before you open your mouth, you take a swig of water and spit it out. Under the carpet.

...it's almost impossible to carry on. My Afghan colleague asks me if we've finished, or if we should keep on moving from tent to tent. He's been going along with me politely but now he throws me a questioning look, as if to say: We can carry on, but what's the point? All right, I say. Let's finish now. There's no way to talk or to understand anything with all this wind and dust.

I climb on to a low wall and take a couple of documentary photographs, but when I look at them on the display they're just blurred spots. It seems even a camera can't record the reality of this place. I put it in my pocket to stop the shutter getting clogged with dust, which has been chafing us relentlessly since we arrived. Even the microphone of the radio at my waist is full of sand, I have to blow it away before calling the driver and signalling our position. Please come to pick us up at the camp watchtowers – pick us up at the camp watchtowers – over *(bleep)*. We're beneath the blockhouse from where the Pakistani police keep an eye on movements in the waiting area. The camp is huge and shapeless, the rows of shelters extend as far as the eye can see. There are the traditional black woollen tents of the Kuchis, blue and white UNHCR plastic sheets, shelters that are just patchworks of rags, and a few good tents from previous emergency distributions – which may have been bought in the market, because that's where a certain percentage of humanitarian aid always ends up. We can't see the car. We wait in the sandstorm. The Afghan asks the policemen for permission to drink from the well. They give him a ladle full of water.

Finishing my inquiries, I rejoin my colleagues, who are having a boundary meeting with the authorities and the camp leaders, each of whom represents hundreds of families. The meeting is taking place in a wicker hut, which doesn't really give much shelter because the gaps between the canes are very wide and let the sun and the dusty wind in. When the gusts blow in, all the participants have to cover their faces with their handkerchiefs or turbans. It's at least 45 degrees in here, but the discussion is calm and unhurried. It's three in the afternoon, Pakistani time. The population of the waiting area currently consists of: a) nomads who have lost their flocks and have no other means of sustenance; b) peasants and other victims of the drought; c) Pashtuns who fled from the northern and eastern provinces because of ethnic persecution. I am on my feet leaning against a post, next to a girl who, when the wind blows stronger, covers her mouth with her long hair. It's an effective shield, as she has a lot of hair: black, with bluish highlights. I talk to her later, at the Pakistani officers' club, in front of a stuffed buck's head with a surprised look on its face as if it had been killed by trickery. She has a Danish passport, but from her features I'd guess she was Inuit. One of the Pakistani officers tells me that in this dry heat he has to put vaseline on his two-year-old son's mouth and nostrils several times a day, otherwise he'd start to bleed. After lunch I go to the smoking room, where I beg the last puffs of the cigarettes lit by the Eskimo girl, and I'm reluctant to say goodbye to her when she asks me if I like Palladio's theatre in Vicenza.

On the way back we stop in Spin Boldak. The office has been cleaned, plastic sheets stretched over the windows, and the yard cleared of shells, which are now heaped beneath the perimeter wall. Tons of contorted iron. There's still the problem of the unexploded munitions inside the depot. There's a rumour going round that there are – or were – fifty thousand kilos of hashish in the depot and that this may have been one of the reasons for the sabotage: to get rid of some awkward merchandise.

In the office, one of the computers, which they're still using, has an unexploded shell inside it. I bend and look through the slot at the back. It went through that slot and now it's jammed next to the hard disk.

Germany
A colleague has gone to visit the people wounded by the American bombing who are in hospital in Kandahar. The celebration was for the wedding of the nephew of Mohammed Anwar, a Taliban boss. 160 people were killed, according to

the witnesses, as against the forty reported by the BBC. Almost all were women and children, because the men escaped immediately while the women stayed behind, waiting to be rescued, and the bombing went on for four hours (others say seven). Most of those in hospital in Kandahar have suffered burns and fractures. Anwar's wife was killed. His son, who is one or two, is in the hospital with his relatives in attendance. Anwar himself has disappeared. Another child of seven has a piece of shrapnel in his thorax that can't be operated on: he'll probably die. Some of the most seriously wounded have been taken by helicopter to Germany. What? Germany? This curious statement could mean that they were taken to the ISAF German Clinic in Kabul, which has a specialised surgical ward. The village, in the district of Torin Kowt, had been under American surveillance for quite a while. The guests were firing in the air with Kalashnikovs to celebrate the wedding, the Americans say they thought they were under attack.

The final official death toll is estimated at 44.

On a mission. The driver, Mirwais, buys eight packs of biscuits. Filled biscuits, like Wagon Wheels. They can give up bread and butter, but not biscuits. It's the same with watermelon. Faced with a sliced watermelon, they forget every other need. Food infantilism. It happens on almost every mission: after hours of nerve-wracking work and travel without anything to eat or drink, we stop at a bazaar to buy... what?

It's after eight in the evening, and we should be going home, but various questions have arisen about tomorrow's distribution of tents in Panjway. How big should the lorries be? Where do we unload and distribute the things? None of us know the place or have ever been there in person. Who has the lists of beneficiaries? Not us, or the GTZ. Only the guy from the MOR (Ministry of Repatriation) has them, and he'll be waiting for us in Panjway tomorrow, but where, since he's the only one who knows the place? We have no idea. There's a lot of tension, the argument becomes heated, and the chief has to intervene to pick up the pieces. 'Do your best tomorrow,' he concludes. We commit ourselves to trying. I still go to bed worried.

2nd July. What follows is an account of a day spent distributing aid in the camps of Panjway, less than an hour from Kandahar. It used to be a verdant area, famous for grapes and watermelons. After four consecutive years of drought the river Arghandab is dry, and the people who sought refuge here now find themselves in the same situation from which they fled. The Taliban government organised a massive salvage operation with planes and lorries, transporting even donkeys and camels by helicopter. But the desert kept advancing and caught up with those it had previously displaced. Now they have nowhere else to go.

Kandahar is a burning oven, even at night.

There are half a million displaced persons in southern Afghanistan alone. The vast majority of them are nomadic shepherds, Kuchis. They used to have impressive flocks, five hundred sheep per family. Nothing remains of the good times except a few living animals and a little yoghurt diluted with water – the shalambe – the food most of the displaced persons eat.

We have two hundred numbered tents to distribute in the Panjway camps. Another eight hundred in the next few days. There are blankets, too, and jerrycans so that the women and children can beg for water in the nearest villages – if they can still get it. Lately, the owners of the wells have been refusing them access. They say the water is running out and they need it to irrigate their vineyards.

The vehicles in the convoy, which left at different times, meet up again on the western carriage road. One big lorry and two smaller ones, the GTZ minibus, two UNHCR Pajeros. As we go through the villages of Panjway the column comes to a standstill, we have to make the people perching on the roofs of the lorries get down because they can see into the yards of the houses. Squeezing together, we find room for them in our car. Later on, when the minibus gets stuck and can't move forward unless everyone gets out except the driver, we have to squeeze together even more.

There are eleven displaced persons' camps to be reached today, scattered along the banks or in the middle of the dried-up river bed. The minister's representative insists we can unload and distribute everything in one place, and let the people fend for themselves transporting the tent. I ask him to show me where exactly the camps are. He keeps repeating, through the interpreter: 'The people will be quite happy to collect their tents in one spot…' until I lose my cool and raise my voice. But it has no effect on him: it's as if I hadn't opened my mouth. Many of the tents are supposed to be distributed to widows with little children, and how can a woman on her own drag a tent weighing 85 kilos, plus the other things, across the desert in a temperature of 50 degrees?

It'll need more time, and there's a risk the lorries won't make it (we've already had to leave the biggest one behind because it was buried up to the wheel hubs in the sand), but it doesn't matter, I refuse to just dump the tents and force people to walk several kilometres to get them. I want to see with my own eyes where the tents are being distributed, and above all I want to get as close as possible to the camps, or at least to a small group of camps, two or three, let's say, and choose a halfway point to unload. It takes me an hour to get this elementary logistical principle into the head of the man from Kandahar, helped with great patience by Evelyne, the girl from GTZ who I thought was German and is in fact Belgian. We end up with four distribution points: first the villages marked with the letters E, C and G (23 + 20 + 20 tents) – then A, B and D – K, F and H – and finally the furthest two, J and I, the inhabitants of which would never ever have been able to collect their tents from the place where the minister's representative suggested we unload them.

Our lorries advance with difficulty along what used to be the river bed. The heaviest one gets stuck in the sand, which means we have to go backwards and forwards, unloading the tents and reloading them on the two smaller and more manoeuvrable lorries. By the time we start the distribution it's already so hot that it's hard to talk, a sandstorm is blowing, and our tongues dry up in our mouths. In the course of the day, the temperature will reach 54 degrees. My interpreter, Sultan, a handsome young man of twenty-five, has forgotten his turban and an old man unrolls his own and puts it around his head. Without it, it's impossible to survive.

Hopeful crowds follow us wherever we move the lorries, but only a few have the tickets they need to receive the tents. Meanwhile I go around the camps, putting my head inside the huts to check if the selection has been properly carried out.

Conditions in general are very poor, but the children are in a particularly dreadful state. Many seem, and in fact are, sick. They're covered in blisters. Eyes burning with fever and no medical assistance. They lie in the dust, they're the same colour as the dust and don't bother to drive away the flies. In many tents they sleep on the ground, with their faces in the sand, while I talk to their parents, who look like their grandparents.

Their immediate needs: food, water, shelter.

Their diseases: diarrhoea, malaria, skin that blisters.

I don't know how people can live in Panjway. We manage to stand it for a few hours – hours we'll never forget – but what about those who've been living here for months, for years?

…by the time we reach the last of the camps, it's about four. The sun is still blazing. Here things seem to be even worse if that's possible. One out of every two tents is just a heap of rags swaying in the wind, which is no protection from the sun or the sand. Motionless figures crouch under these scraps of cloth. The children's eyes shine out of their dirty faces. There are women with one eye, or tattoos on their foreheads, the rest are veiled. While the others in the team prepare for the distribution down in the old river bed (the lorries can't go any further without getting completely bogged down), I go looking for someone to talk to and the camp leader totters towards me. He's a tall and very thin old man with hollow cheeks and not many teeth. It's difficult for us to understand each other because he's half deaf and the fatigue is making me dizzy, the wind is blowing sand in our faces, and most of the time he has to hold a turban in front of his mouth as he speaks and I have to hold a handkerchief in front of mine. We shelter inside his tent, which is extremely poor. On the ground, a couple of pieces of thin, ragged quilt and something wrapped in patched cloth. We're soon joined by other old men, who enter, bow silently and squat in the dust. They are Kuchis from the Reg. They've lost all their possessions through the drought. They've been in Panjway for six months. They used their remaining donkeys and camels to get here, then sold them for food. Now, out of 240 families, not one owns a single sheep. The mullah says he used to have a flock of six hundred. He may be exaggerating a bit, but it would mean that this emaciated old man was once rich. I ask him: 'Where did your flocks graze in the summer?' and all the old men start rattling off names and waving their arms. My pen squeaks as I write and I have to wipe the pages of the notebook to clear away the dust that keeps blowing in through the gaps in the tent. The old men all keep answering my questions at the same time, and Sultan struggles to translate. I lose patience and dare to tell them off. We need this information to help us to help them, so it has to be specific. They should keep their answers short: just yes and no, numbers not speeches. (When you ask an Afghan how many children he has, what job he does, how many years he's been in exile, instead of answering 'five' and 'shepherd' and 'thirteen', he usually launches into a half-hour lecture. And he thinks that the louder he yells, the more weight his words will have.) This time, the old men understand and cut things short. I still have to repeat the same questions several times, but that's because I'm getting confused and my mouth is dry and Sultan is having difficulty understanding me. I get him to ask them if they're prepared to abandon the nomadic life, to forget their Kuchi customs, maybe forever. There's a preconceived idea (very politically correct) that the Kuchis should never adapt, never do anything other than graze their flocks, because they're migrants by nature and can't bear to settle down in one place. The aid agencies are reluctant to interfere with this natural cycle, after all, nobody wants – good heavens – to be accused of destroying the traditions of a people, blah-blah-blah... But that's just idle talk or romantic nonsense. The Kuchis say they're perfectly prepared to do any kind of work they can to make a living. At the moment they have nothing and are starving.

Food, food, food, that's the refrain.

Then one of the old men grabs a dusty little bundle. He unrolls it carefully, as if there's something precious inside. What it turns out to be is two small pieces of dry bread, one of them already half eaten. That's all his family possess. They have nothing else for dinner or for the next day or the days to come, and no money to buy anything else.

Instead of the usual commotion, nobody else says a word as the old mullah tells me this, everyone falls silent and stares into space. I feel as though I've understood the last sentence *before* Sultan has translated it from Pashto: 'This is all we have to eat.' My heart doesn't skip a beat at the sight of the two wretched objects, the two pieces of dry bread wrapped in a rag, and I ask Sultan to please translate to the head of the village: 'I'm very sorry, genuinely sorry, my organisation is doing and will do everything it can within the limits... the limits of the available... the limits of our resources...' but I have to stop, Sultan can't translate, at the sight of the bread his eyes have filled with tears, he tries to restrain himself but he can't and he bursts out crying. He turns his head away, bends down, and covers his face with his hand.

The sight of that dry bread. A mixture of pity and shame. For two minutes, maybe more, there's silence. Nobody speaks.

Two or three of the old men also have tears in their eyes. They hide them with their turbans.

I go up to Sultan, stroke his beard, and wipe his cheeks with my thumb. I tell him he must help me to talk to these people. Maybe the demands of the job can purge him of his emotions. My own emotions remain locked inside me. They have no outlet.

On the way back, I don't say a word. Sultan is calm and chats and laughs with Mirwais. We stop at a bazaar and I offer to buy them Pepsis. Sultan accepts, Mirwais doesn't.

All he likes is biscuits.

The meal of the day was a third of a sandwich, two cucumbers and a bunch of grapes. Two litres of frozen water.

The plasticine has come loose in the heat and the arm of Mirwais' glasses has come away. Now he's driving with his glasses askew.

The day, which began at 6:45, finishes at 19:30.

I sit in the near-dark and type up a short report.

More explosions in Spin Boldak. Our representative hurriedly closed the office, which had only just got back on its feet, and has gone to Pakistan with all the staff. It seems, though, that the explosions were controlled ones carried out by the mine clearance people. They've started to empty the depot and destroy the munitions. The trouble is, our official had some cases of beer in the boot of his car, which he was supposed to bring to Kandahar, and now the beer has gone back with him to Pakistan. We could have done with it right now. The wind is still very hot, even at night.

(Next morning, the after-effects of working in the Valley of Death. I feel as if I've been beaten up. My thighs, my face and my back hurt and my hands are shaking. I was supposed to go on a mission to Laskar Gah, but luckily there was a shortage of cars and drivers, and the mission has been cancelled.)

Kabul, Friday 5th July

When I arrived in Kabul in April, the international staff even worked on public holidays, eight days a week, like the song says. Now it's July, and the office is almost empty on Fridays. People can't take any more, they need a break at least once a week. The obsessive drive of the first months of the operation has fizzled out, or rather, the mental and physical needs of even the most compulsive workers have become priority – and that's good, otherwise the stress would eat your soul. Now I understand why Our Lord invented the seventh day. It's the right pause. The only reason I don't respect it and continue to work is that I feel I'm on the downward slope – I'm less than twenty-five days from the end of my mission, twenty-four to go (not for you, new boys!) – and I can cruise home, like a swimmer making a final spurt to the finishing line without taking a breath, or a cyclist after the last kilometre has been signalled.

As soon as I set foot back in Kabul (la ville-lumière), a lovely ICRC party: feet in the water, a cool evening, girls and boys dancing on the grass. I get drunk too quickly. Kandaharian thirst + tiredness + the desire to enjoy myself. I misjudge the doses. I stagger back to the guest house. Can't get onto the stairs.

Big trouble in Pul-i-Charkhi

I'm only here because I'm showing a colleague called Bernadette around. She's just arrived from Quetta, Pakistan. I've told her that our encashment centre is a gem, that it works like a well-oiled machine. Saturday's a quiet day, not many people arrive on Saturday, but if she wants to visit it I'll go with her.

It's obvious as soon as we get there that something's wrong. We enter the big tent where the money is distributed: it's full of people sitting on the ground grumbling loudly. There may be four or five hundred men. Another hundred are waiting outside. What the hell is happening? The cashiers have run out of money and have gone back to the city to stock up. It's happened before, but on those occasions the queues were small. These blessed cashiers still haven't grasped that they have to send someone to Kabul to stock up with money *before* they run out in Pul-i-Charkhi. Instead, they wait until they've given away the last banknote and then announce that they don't have any more. And the distribution chain grinds to a halt. It's fine if it's only a question of waiting for half an hour. Even the perfect engine of Pul-i-Charkhi sometimes gets flooded.

The men have been made to crouch inside the big tent because it's too cold outside.

The trouble is, when the cashiers come back they've only scraped together 20,000 dollars. It seems there are no dollars to be found anywhere in Kabul today, and it's too complicated to pay in Pakistani rupees. Don't even think about Afghan currency – you'd need a wheelbarrow. We make a quick calculation: as every family has to receive on average between 80 and 160 dollars, sometimes more (we give 20 dollars a head now, with no ceiling), we have just about enough to cover 150 families. I start to get worried. We have two alternatives: either we send everyone away and tell them to come back tomorrow (a disaster, because many people don't have enough to pay the lorry drivers, and they weren't anticipating having to stop in Kabul) or else we try to distribute the money which is in the till in a consistent way. We choose the second alternative: we'll give the money to just one family per lorry. Just one family. Generally there are between four and six families in a lorry. This will help towards their transport expenses, then the other heads of families can come back tomorrow to get the rest. In the meantime, I send one of the cashiers back to Kabul to look for more dollars.

Taking heart, three of us – Bashir, Anne and I – enter the big tent. Everyone's on their feet, yelling excitedly. We elbow our way through. Using the megaphone I apologise for the discomfort, we're very sorry but it isn't our fault, and I outline our plan for distributing the money. If they agree to it, at least one family per lorry will receive money, otherwise we close. I spell out short, clear sentences in basic English, and Bashir translates. He could speak to them directly, but I know that I must take advantage of the effect that being a foreigner always has. The words take on a halo of authority (based on nothing). It's like a circus act, but it works. As I speak, I start to realise the shortcomings of this plan. How do we know that families or friends are all together in the same lorry? How will it be decided who gets the money and who doesn't? And it's always better to grab money and food *immediately*, without waiting for tomorrow, that's something the refugees have learned well…

They're a bit puzzled, they shout and demand explanations, but then the proposal is accepted with a kind of standing ovation. Better than nothing. Anne explains that if anyone wants to spend the night in the transit centre, they can. At this point the Five Hundred start getting excited again and shouting, and I fear the worst. I have the impression the tent is swelling. We have to push them together and divide them, we're losing our Afghan colleagues in the crowd, there's a risk we'll be crushed, where's Anne got to? Go, go away, for fuck's sake, but of course, instead of leaving the tent in an orderly manner and assembling outside in groups, the heads of families turn round and throw themselves at us again, waving their forms. The agreement – one family per lorry – has gone out the window, I want to be that family! I need that money right now! Some beg, some threaten, one of them shows me his wooden leg, another a swollen eye, a disfigured face, some women hold their little children up in the air in a Biblical gesture.

We want our money today!!

There's nothing we can do about it, we internationals attract them like flies.

Engineer, engineer! they all call me.

Out, out! I shout, out! Out! Bro! Bro! And we start pushing them, Harun and Bashir and I, as well as the guards (who are completely useless in spite of the Kalashnikovs over their shoulders), we keep pushing, like those officials in the Tokyo underground rush hour, until at last they're all out of the tent. But once outside it's worse. Despite all our shoving and all our orders shouted through megaphones, they refuse to regroup. The individual cases return to the attack. We're surrounded, we have no room to breathe, again we have to push away women in burqas and old men in order not to be crushed. I stroke the beards of some of them to make them understand that deep down I like them and respect them, it's just that they mustn't scream in my ears, but fuck it, they have to round up the other families from their lorries and collect all their forms! HARUN! HARUN! WHERE THE FUCK WERE YOU??? Will you explain to these people?

Oh, God, is it possible they don't understand? They all seemed to agree...

(Sorry about the bad language. All this screaming is done in Dari, Pashto and English, but my swearing is in Italian and I'm the only one who understands it. It's self-referential. I've sworn so much today, but this time I've shouted my curses instead of just thinking them. For days now, mental swearing and a few verses of the *Purgatorio* have been my only contact with my own language.)

At a certain point I think: things are looking bad. We have to contact the base and ask for reinforcements. The colleague who arrived this morning from Quetta (the one I told that our encashment centre works like a Swiss watch...) asks me if she can help in any way. She's looking pale. She hadn't expected her first day in Kabul to be like this. I tell her to go to the car and call for help. A couple of months ago I saw a TV report about a food distribution in Africa. It ended badly. Depots were looted, people were beaten or shot. Something like that could even happen here. The situation is out of control. We're submerged by the crowd. The guards try to pacify them with whips. Our local team leader, a muscular young man with a friendly face, screams at the Afghans through the megaphone, I scream at him what he has to say, the Afghans scream at me, I ask the team leader what the fuck they're screaming. I've lost Anne in the crowd again. Jesus. Where's Anne? Where's Bernadette? *Calm down, calm down, keep cool, act the way you usually do, act as if you didn't care. Act as if you were in your world: an Italian prison.* But here, I don't have my tool: words. All I have is my body. We push forward, heads down, like a rugby scrum. I grab hold of the megaphone again and tell them that if they don't calm down and split up into groups, they won't get any money at all and we'll evacuate the camp. Understood? Nobody will get any money! Please translate. *But don't shout at them, please, Bashir, be cool, OK?*

I don't know how Bashir does it, but he gets them to sit down.

It's a surprising phenomenon. They squat. Afghans naturally squat with their arms clamped under their knees: it's their 'at ease' position.

Half an hour later, things have calmed down, relatively speaking. A lot of people have understood what to do: they've collected the forms and given them to their representatives. The chosen ones are squatting in a queue outside the tent. Each of them represents five or six families. We're inside, ready to start again. The cashiers have brought another 10,000 dollars from Kabul. I've had to clear the tent of those who sneaked in or have been hiding from the start. They were seized by the scruff of the neck like little boys and dragged out. The only ones still inside are the women and the genuinely sick, or at least those who put on the best act, there's no time to check right now, and we couldn't face any more displays of sores and plastic legs. Let's give them the money and off with them, out to the lorries. Right to the end, a few try to slip inside with their one form in their hands, or roll on the ground or try to get through the barbed wire, mindless of the guards' whips. It's tragic, and at the same time comic: when a refugee gets a lashing from the guards, the others laugh, and often he laughs, too. Although it's devilishly hot in the tent, we open it only a crack so that one person at a time can pass. Even so, we have to push people away, scream at them, chase them off…

Two hours later, the money's almost gone and we've dealt with all the people waiting. Never mind how it went. Totally ridiculous, but at least there wasn't any damage. Were we good? I wonder. Were we crap? I don't know. They'll come back tomorrow to get the rest. As there was still a bit left in the till, we allowed the last heads of families, who'd collected a lot of forms, to take money for two families instead of one. But as we could only give the money directly into the hands of those whose names were on the forms, we had to track down the other lucky ones over the megaphone and call them back – having thrown them out with such difficulty only a little while earlier. It was like a lottery. The winners were so excited, they tried to slip back in under the barbed wire instead of going through the gate, and several times I had to go and stop the guards who were trying to beat them off and explain that we'd called the poor wretches back ourselves.

No more money. Stop. We're closing for the day. Let's go, Anne.

Anne and Bernadette have been great. Bashir got through his ordeal of fire.

As we walk along the edges of the camp, arms continue to wave, holding out forms through the barbed wire…

Imploring faces…

No money. Finished. To show there's no more money, I pull the lining out of my trouser pockets.

It's a universal gesture. The people behind the barbed wire laugh. A cruel game that the poor understand.

When we get back to Kabul, we find the streets in the centre blocked. For a long time we can't move. Cars and armoured vehicles pass.

Later, the explanation: the streets were closed because there was a shooting, a politician was killed.

I call on the radio, trying to find out more. Some say it was the Minister for Repatriation, others the Minister for Reconstruction.

After dinner I walk home slowly. It's five to ten, the air is cool and the street empty and dark. The politician killed today was Hagi Abdul Kadir, Vice President and Minister of Public Works. From the handset I have on my belt comes a mournful Afghan voice repeating: 'I love you I love you I love you I love you... darling.'

7th July. I'm just going out into the street when I take a good look at my watch and realise that it isn't twenty past six but twenty past five.

I don't know why but it reminds me of coming out of the sea after a bathe and sucking the salt from my baptism chain.

I go with Anne to see the medical students camped opposite our houses. They come from every province of Afghanistan. Not all of them are very young, some are over thirty. The hospital gives them two meals a day, but food is scarce. They don't receive a salary: some are helped financially by their families, others work part-time in the bazaars, or as labourers or delivery men. Their living conditions are precarious. Their lessons last from 8:00 to 12:45 and after that they have nowhere else to go except the camp. The tents are overcrowded, hygiene is not what it should be, there's no space, the conditions aren't right for studying. The insects, the dust and the heat plague them through the day.

(The paramedics have been eating bread and rice with

lentils from a pot placed on blankets on the ground. There are so many flies they don't even try to chase them away. Apart from a couple who are more serious and aware, and who turn out to be the chiefs, the others have innocent open faces. When we entered the tent there were five of them, but now, a few minutes later, there are about twenty. Sitting on the ground, lying on the camp beds or squatting on their heels. They've crept in from all sides, some springing up from behind the camp bed where they've kindly made room for us. And there are others outside the tent, poking their heads in, crowding around, it's the same thing that happens when you take a photograph, they manage to fill the whole space with their faces, there are at least ten faces in a square metre, now there must be thirty or forty in the opening of the tent, arranged in rows: eyes, hair, boils, smiles.

By the time I leave the tent I'm completely bathed in sweat.)

Only now, with three weeks to go to the end of my mission, I've started to stick maps and photos on the wall.

Maybe it's a result of the work, but I can't form complex thoughts in my mind, only short sentences.

11th July. The journey to Kandahar is quite smooth this time. When my case is opened at the airport and they see the three bottles, they want to seize them, but Sayid defends me.

The air today is strangely clean and the jagged mountains that break up the city, as in Kabul, are clearly visible.

We're given a security briefing by the new officer (an Australian) who paints a frightening picture of the risks we face. Kandahar and the south are bristling with dangers: internal clashes between factions trying to control the drug trade, attacks against foreigners, mines, and all that jazz. There's been a campaign to disarm the population, but it's produced a paradoxical result: the common people have handed in their weapons, but the militias obviously haven't, which means that the former are now even more at the mercy of the latter than they were before. And talking of physical safety, there are many different ways to get hurt. The last piece of advice is to be careful not to slip while taking a shower. It's true: bath tiles are slippery – you feel wrecked in the evening, your legs are shaking with tiredness – you can easily fall and break your head.

A frustrating afternoon talking to people who claim to be good, to be in the right, to have the best interests of the women and children at heart, while you're bad and want to let them die. At last, evening comes and I'm relaxing with a beer, when I hear several bursts of automatic weapons fire outside the window. A fat Canadian grabs the radio and calls: 'Zulu One, Zulu One.' I look at him questioningly and he murmurs 'AK-47', then as he can't get anything over the radio, he goes out of the room to try again.

He comes back. False alarm. They were firing into the air at a wedding ceremony.

'Oh, no, not another wedding ceremony! Now the Americans will bomb us.'

Lorenzo's breakfast
I sent a friend in Italy the notes I made last week in Kandahar. This was his reply: 'Hi, Edoardo, I read your notes last night... and still managed to have breakfast this morning, with butter and jam... the fact that it's a person I know who's bearing witness to this suffering gives me an even greater "sense of guilt", but being powerless to do anything (doubly so in my case) doesn't even make me retch, it has no effect on me... the story of the Kuchis, those two pieces of dry bread (objects, not food), the tears dried with the thumb, your enlightened efforts to "gather information to help them"... what can I say?'

I wrote back that he shouldn't worry, because I, too, have carefree breakfasts of poached eggs, French toast and fruit jam imported from Dubai. Of the nine dollars a day I spend at the canteen in Kabul (enough for a small Afghan family to live on for a week) most in fact goes on breakfast, which is very varied in order to cater for international tastes (for example, the Australians can't resist that awful Vegemite – the English put HP sauce on their omelettes), whereas lunch and dinner are plain and repetitive. There's no point in hiding the fact that the internationals lead a decent life here in Afghanistan, or rather, they lead an absurd life which is compensated for by little luxuries. I think these substantial breakfasts are an aspect of work psychology: they're intended to give the staff, who wake up every morning ten thousand kilometres from home (breakfast being the domestic meal par excellence) a certain consolation, or at least a rush of calories to keep the chronic depression of the expatriate at bay. To tell the truth, they just make me feel as if I'm in a hotel. I wake up with a sense of absurdity that I can't escape, and seeing twenty different boxes of cereal on the table doesn't bring me back to earth at all. It looks like a spoof advertisement of the Western way of life. Those few of my colleagues who are up at that hour (early birds or people about to leave on a mission, with their rucksacks and thermoses ready) dip their spoons into their muesli in silence. You try to keep out the images of poverty and danger you've accumulated at work, or at least on the edges of your field of vision. They're reduced to icons at the bottom of the screen. If you touch them they spring up and fill the whole space. In the UNHCR emergency manual there's a whole chapter on how to deal with stress. Cumulative stress and traumatic stress.

'Between consoling the afflicted and afflicting the consoled there is a virtuous circle (or so we like to think)...'

Yellow desert
I go with the engineers to visit a site called Zharay Dasht.

60,000 people are supposed to be coming to live there by October.

There are four of us: an Australian, an Afghan (who's been here for six months but whose normal residence is in Toronto), a Swiss and I. After about thirty kilometres of a rather crazy journey on the Kandahar-Herat road, with motorbikes zigzagging in front of us and an accident in which a trailer overturned and crushed the passenger compartment of a pick-up, we steer left into the desert. In this bare yellow terrain, jagged mountains on the horizon, the Soviet tanks used to manoeuvre into position to bomb Panjway, from the other side of the former River Arghandab. The mujaheddin mined it at random, under cover of darkness, without leaving any maps of the area. Now we have to rely on memories. Stones at the side of the road indicate the limits of the mine clearing operation. A thirteen-kilometre ride across a red zone *(mined)*, then a yellow zone *(suspected)*, and finally a green zone *(safe)*, will take us to the site selected for the new settlements. The anti-tank mines are buried twenty centimetres below the surface, which is a stony crust. They use metal detectors and Alsatian dogs to find them. The dogs are able to sniff out the explosive but only when it's not too hot yet, in the early hours of the morning, otherwise their sense of smell disappears. That's why they keep the dogs wet inside tubs full of water and ice. To cool them down. Far away on the plain, we can see the usual swirls of dust. We follow the tyre tracks. Beyond the row of stones, you can still see the deep tracks of the Russian tracked vehicles. At a certain point the engineers all cry in unison 'STOP! STOP! STOP!!' and the driver slams on the brakes, raising clouds of dust, because without realising it he's continued to follow the tyre tracks and not the stones left by the mine clearance people. The tracks went right, the stones left. We make him reverse carefully (twenty seconds of suspense, waiting for the bang, the end, the blackness, goodbye, it's been a good life) and return to the point where he made the mistake. The engineers get out and collect stones to delimit the road more clearly. In theory, the weight of a standing man is not enough to set off an anti-tank mine, but I hesitate to get out of the Landcruiser. I don't want to seem chicken, though, so I join in, searching for milestones and setting them in place by the road. Tomorrow, the mine clearance people will mark it more clearly. We dash off again across the desert. There's supposed to be water under the crust. They're drilling twenty wells – I'm starting to see them now. By the time the work is finished, there'll be two hundred of them. At last we enter the green zone. Here they're going to put the reception area. A thousand arrivals a day for three months. Young men crouched in the holes are digging with picks. I take a photo of them down there. They laugh, then wriggle out to see themselves on the display. I lift the lids of the tanks: they're full of cold, transparent water. The sky is bluer than I've ever seen it. It's time to head east, to what will be settlement number 4. Here, things are going less well: they've drilled three wells, but not one has reached water. One of them has reached fifteen metres, the second sixteen, the third twenty-one metres, and still there's no water. This is because we're on a slight slope. I ask Chris how far they dig before they give up, 'Let's say forty metres,' he replies. I think of my own well which is eighty metres deep, but that's because we live on the top of a hill. Beneath the gravel there's hard stone, very hard, the Afghan repeats. The generators splutter. We take shelter in a tent to eat watermelon, not in slices but in little chunks.

In the car we talk about the future site, about Australia, about heavenly constellations and about scorpions. All of them have been stung except me. Dante says the northern hemisphere is 'widowed' because you can't see the stars of the Southern Cross from it. But the Australian says they're nothing special. There's a constellation called the Seven Sisters, the Afghan hydraulic engineer insists it's the Seven Brothers. It turns out they mean Ursa Major.

After visiting the wells, we climb a little mountain on our hands and feet. The Afghan and I stay behind, he because of his belly, me because of my vertigo. The rocks are sharp.

Returning at twilight, the road to Kandahar is crowded: subdued excitement, cars parked in double lines, side lights on. In the Senjeray bazaar they sell nothing but tyres and cans of oil. Countless shops piled high with cans of motor oil. We pass the former river and the Russian silo, which is like the one in Kabul, only a little smaller and with less bomb damage. The villages outside Kandahar look peaceful before dinner. Pick-ups speed by, their backs crammed with little boys, some sitting on seats uprooted from elsewhere, goats leap from rock to rock, evening falls, people have carried netting from their beds up onto the roofs of their houses to get some fresh air and watch the car lights passing, turbaned men squat over picnics in the already dark fields, by the canals, others are stretched out on carpets, praying. Only men, there isn't a woman to be seen, they're all at home making dinner. Ghulam says the people here lead a peaceful, stress-free life (if they survive), the only problem is finding food, but if there's something to eat life is easy, they don't care who's in power, they're simple, unpretentious people, they lead a relaxed life, the one problem is survival…

I've asked Evelyne from GTZ if there's a relatively uncomplicated way to mark the eight hundred tents that still have to be distributed in Panjway. They're of excellent quality, with double lining and reinforced seams, and can be used even in winter (which is why they weigh so much), but they're completely anonymous. If we can put a mark on them (it could be the Red Cross – they're the donors – or it could be anything, even a big question mark…) it'll be easier to recognise them later, when we return to the same camps, or even spot them on the market, after they've changed owners, given that the beneficiaries are free to do whatever they want with them, even resell them immediately. They get cash for them, to buy food or other things, and at the next distribution, done by a different organisation, they'll be in the front row with their hut of rags.

It's impossible to control this business, and anyway only the very poor do it.

There's nothing scandalous about it.

Ultimately, the important thing is that the tent (or its equivalent in money) ends up with whoever needs it most.

Then it will be up to him to decide if he prefers shade or bread.

I've been told that a tent can be bought for thirty dollars, although the real value is higher.

The last time, I followed a smart aleck who was taking a tent away on his wheelbarrow. He was from the city and I don't know how he'd managed to get himself on the list and receive a distribution ticket. He made his getaway before we'd even finished. I followed him between the dunes. His accomplices dropped the tent and scuttled off, leaving him alone with his barrow, which had sunk into the sand and couldn't move. He told me a heap of nonsense about taking the tent to a certain house in the nearby village, after which he was going to bring it back and put it up. Oh, yes, of course, the temperature's 50 degrees, so you go for a stroll in the desert carrying eighty kilos. He said that the tent had been assigned to his family. Where is your family? He led us to one of the ragged huts. Keeping our voices low, we asked the man for his name. Then Sultan, through the tent material, asked a woman who was squatting inside, what's your husband's name? She said a name, not the one he'd told us. The head of the village arrived and started hitting the man rather melodramatically and calling him a thief, even though it was clear they were in cahoots and the man's name had been slipped onto the list by the head of the village himself. Get out of here, you city vampire, I thought, and you, you old crook, look after your people instead...

I was furious but calm.

All I said to him – coldly – was that we were taking back the tent. Come on, carry it back to the lorry. I'm not listening to any more stories.

Now we have not eight hundred, but eight hundred and one tents to distribute.

Every time we take from someone bogus to give to someone genuine there's a sense of triumph.

The terror of making a mistake.

I meet Evelyne again at the farewell ceremony for the Swedish Taliban, who's leaving Kandahar for Kabul. He's a little man, as red as a carrot, and his friends call him the Swedish Taliban because he's lived here a long time and has an orange beard down to his chest and wears a fur cap. I ask him if I can stroke his beard, but he refuses, saying I might pull it and find out it's false, ha, ha, only joking. When he talks, the beard moves up and down and brushes his shirt.

(There are constant power cuts as we work. The generator goes beep beep beep. The ceiling fan slows down, then speeds up again with a jolt. Reading the UNHCR manual on how to recognise stress, I've discovered I have eight out of the ten symptoms they list. I'm struck by the mention of 'invasive memories'. I'm tormented by them. Actually, they're very beautiful memories, not nightmares, yet they leave me feeling drained. I often have visions of Italian landscapes, glimpses of cities, like the black and white images you used to see on TV with the word INTERVAL over them. Vicenza, Otranto, Orvieto cathedral, Massa Marittima, Mantua, the Maremma, the Zisa of Palermo, the abbey of Fossanova, Stromboli.)

The French bomb disposal expert was explaining yesterday why they used to mine the sides of the roads. It was so that the convoys were forced to proceed in single file, thus becoming an easy target. One by one, said the Frenchman, miming the arrival of the vehicles with one hand, and firing at them with the other hand: pow, pow, pow.

Tents in the sheep market
14th July. Eight families are ready to return from Kandahar
to Badghis, in the north-west, from where they fled during the
winter to escape the anti-Pashtun persecution that followed
the fall of the Taliban. As the Taliban were mostly Pashtun,
when their regime collapsed in the north, the Pashtun became
the favourite targets of the Uzbekis and the Hazaras, who
wanted revenge, as well as bandits seizing on a political
excuse for their looting. The Northern Alliance militias – to
what extent with the knowledge of their commanders isn't
clear – repeatedly sacked the villages, raped the women and
killed a large number of people, shooting them with their
Kalashnikovs or beating them to death. Where they didn't kill
them, they would extort money and other things from them.
As a consequence, many fled to the south where the Pashtun
are the overwhelming majority, jumping out of the frying pan
of ethnic persecution into the fire of drought. Now the situation has improved in the province of Badghis – there's still
violence in other places, but they can return to Badghis.

A.Q. tells us stories at lunch about when he was working in
Tanzania and the camps were closed from one day to the next
and the Rwandan refugees had to return home: forced
marches, day and night, walking as much as sixty or seventy
kilometres, with thousands of soldiers hard on their heels.
Women gave birth at the side of the road, in the pouring rain.
400,000 people were forced out in this way, after the
Americans suddenly cut the funds. 'Listen, son,' an elderly
Senator told A.Q., 'the equation is simple: we support the government of Rwanda, and these people have to return home,
otherwise who's there to rebuild the country? So from tomorrow your camp won't receive another dollar in aid.' In A.Q.'s
camp there were 160,000 people. All forced out.
    After two months of this, A.Q. went to the doctor because he
was getting dizzy spells, there was a strange humming noise
in his head, he heard voices talking to him, he couldn't sleep.

The Pearl of Kandahar has returned from her holiday. She's very thin. One evening we drink something with ice in it. Is this ice safe? Yes, yes, it's made with mineral water. I spend the night vomiting and having attacks of diarrhoea. So does the Pearl.

The next day: Are you sure the ice was clean?...

Well, yes, I think so...

Diarrhoea is one of the most common subjects of discussion.

15th July. Feeling ill. My mission to Laskar Gah is cancelled. I try to get up and dress, but it's impossible. I only manage to inform the team leader and go back to bed. I feel dizzy and nauseous. That damned ice last night... it wasn't from clean water. I spend the morning on the lavatory bowl, leafing through the fashion magazines I've found in the bedroom: *Tatler*, *Cosmopolitan*, with its 75 infallible ways to excite your partner in bed. There are other books and magazines left by previous inhabitants of the room. Essays about Central Asia, Islamic jihad, and gloomy articles written at the beginning of the American bombing last October saying the Taliban will never fall. I gladly turn back to *Cosmopolitan*, which is full of career girls eager for explosive sexual encounters. I'm amused and intrigued by their adventures, but at the same time they make me see our world and its famous values from a very Taliban perspective.

16th July, Panjway, an inspection in order to select beneficiaries from four camps: Abdul Habib, Al Anazar, Salih Mohd Pashtun and Wali Jan (the camps are named after their elders). 710 families registered. While we are inside a wicker hut, children sprinkle it with water from outside, to cool us down. We like it but tell them to stop and not waste water. The weather's extremely hot again.

17th July. Still feeling a bit under the weather. Mission to Laskar Gah. We leave from the office at 8:40. I think that on a day as hot as this we should have left at 6:30, but working patterns in Kandahar are very Southern Italian: you never see the local staff before eight o'clock, they arrive in dribs and drabs and spend ages salaaming and hugging and smooching, then they start getting the water and provisions together, they say they'll take five minutes to do a few little things and twenty minutes pass, you find the driver and in the meantime the interpreter has disappeared, here's the interpreter but the driver's missing, he's gone to refuel. They're quite philosophical about it all. The boy who's going to be my interpreter today, whose name is Nawabi (Nawab, nabob, very rich man) turns up at half-past eight and tells us straight out that he had to take some medicine to his uncle first. 'He's sick and I have to look after him.' 'Fine, but next time get up early and take it to him at seven, is that clear?'

It's like setting off on an outing. (To the sea, not the desert.)

On the way, we buy biscuits and cucumbers.

Other makes of motorbike: Jawa, Simpson, Minsk.

The air very hot and white.

Nawabi tells me he's related to King Zahir. He's an alert, ambitious young man. He tries to regain ground after this morning's false start. He tells me that he's working with UNHCR to help his people. Oh, yes? And next year he's flying to London to study. He's eighteen. He wants to help his nation but he's leaving for Europe. That's the destiny of the cleverest and most qualified people in Afghanistan: to emigrate. And if they've already emigrated, to stay abroad. The country needs them, but does it really suit them to return? If I were a successful professional, a scientist, an artist, an entrepreneur wanting to invest his money, I can say in all honesty that I'd think about it very carefully and maybe in the end I'd decide not to return, even if they made me a minister. I'd stay in London or Sydney or Toronto or Paris... with the diaspora...

(A dangerous attitude common among the youngest/ brightest/more educated/more westernised Afghans: they become a little arrogant, and think they're superior to the

212

others, and in a way they are, which is why they feel indispensable at their jobs and use their fluent English as a weapon. Sometimes, when we're interviewing some of their poor compatriots, they start laughing contemptuously and don't want to translate the replies for me, thinking them too stupid. I have to be very firm with them. 'I'll decide what's important, all right? Translate everything, thank you.' The more mature men are quite different: they're always kind, considerate and open towards their own people.)

(The other day, driving to the Zharay Dasht site, the engineers pointed out a patch of green on the edge of the desert, beneath the mountains. 'See? That's where we're building the new camp.' I squinted. 'Yes, of course, right over there…' 'Can you see it?' 'Yes, yes… I can see the trees…' At which they all burst out laughing because in fact there wasn't anything there, just desert and heat.

The strip of vegetation was a mirage.)

The Laskar Gah bazaar is immense, with an impressive range of goods on display outside the shops, from aubergines to tar. I've only just realised that one of our drivers is the same one who was injured two weeks ago in the explosion of the arms depot in Spin Boldak. Everything's fine, though he still has scars on his head, and scabs on his arms and legs. He shows them and laughs. He describes the rain of shells that night. The experience wasn't a novelty, it happened to him once before, when he was young (they all burst out laughing and slap him on the back…) and he was fighting with the mujaheddin against the government.

In the Mukhtar camp there's a community of displaced persons led by a sixty-year-old woman from Herat, named Malika. She represents 360 families who arrived here last April. Half are nomads who no longer have flocks. We don't have time to enquire how a woman was able to become their head: a pity, it might be very interesting. She complains about an accident that took place only yesterday. We follow her to the banks of the Helmand. Two boys of fifteen and thirteen drowned while bathing in the river. She shows us where they were found, three hundred metres downstream.

We meet the district administrator of Laskar Gah in a large room. The windows are obstructed with bundles of dry brambles, which keep out the heat and dust as best they can. He sits on the floor amid piles of documents. They offer us orangeade. Several young men are present, sitting silently in various parts of the room.

Another man comes in and is introduced to us: his claim to fame is that he had the current President Karzai as a teacher during his exile in Peshawar.

At the end of the meeting he shakes my hand warmly. 'I have an uncle who lives in Washington,' he says. I feel I have to compliment him on his American uncle (who probably sends money home, I imagine, the way Italians used to). Then he bends and whispers in my ear: 'I'm a friend of yours,' meaning: I'm on your side. On whose side? Obviously, the Americans. In southern Afghanistan, such a statement can only mean one thing. Maybe he hasn't grasped exactly who we are. Or maybe he bundles all internationals together: American, of course. To what extent it's a mistake or an understandable approximation I'll let others judge. My UNHCR colleague is black, Sudanese I think, and his name is Mohammed. There's nothing American about me except the Nikes on my feet and my Ray-Bans, which are stuck together with Super Glue (it works better than plasticine). At a pinch, we could pass for one of those odd couples – one white and one black – in American police movies: *Beverly Hills Cop*, *48 Hours*, *Lethal Weapon*, etc.

We follow the River Helmand, which compared with the Arghandab is still alive, in other words, is still a river, but when we cross it on a very long bridge, watched at the other end by soldiers behind the usual chain fence stretched between sentry boxes, we realise that the water only runs in stretches of a dozen metres, or even less. Swarms of little boys are bathing in it, playing with lorry tyres. The rest of the river consists of islands run dry.

Beyond the bridge: eighteen Kuchi families from Badghis camped in a field.

The usual question: why are you here and not there? They're here because there's water here, and work, too.

Who owns the field? Don't know. What if he arrives? We'll leave.

In the villages and fields, many young men come up to you just to shake your hand, shaking your hand fills them with satisfaction and pride, if you haven't shaken a foreigner's hand it's as if you haven't met him, but they don't really shake your hand, they just hold their hand out, stiffly, like the hand of a wooden doll. The old people encourage the young. It's like a miraculous touch. They feel embarrassed and happy.

Back on asphalt. Every ten kilometres there's a stationary lorry, with flat tyres or a smashed axle-shaft. Others are lying peacefully off the road. They've piled up to an improbable degree and then turned over on their sides. Among the victims of the Herat-Kandahar road, a coach whose driver had the brilliant idea of loading on its roof, not baggage, but another car and a minivan. Result: the coach collapsed and the wheels were knocked out sideways, like in a TV cartoon.

The lorries transport only basic goods. Wool, cement, firewood, wheelbarrows, wheat, tyres. Everything bundled together with lengths of yellow and blue string to form a net.

Meanwhile, what's happening in Italy?
WHAT TO PUT IN YOUR SUITCASE THIS SUMMER?
THESE ARE THE MUST-HAVE ITEMS FOR THE
HOLIDAY SEASON: FROM ETHNO-CHIC SARONGS
TO FLIP-FLOP SANDALS, FROM LONSDALE PURSES
TO SNORKELLING MASKS

The news that has filtered through from my country in the
last few months: the madman who crashed his plane into the
Pirelli tower in Milan, the ferocious attacks on the referees
after Italy's elimination from the World Cup.

There are lots of anecdotes about life under the Taliban, told
by those who were here at the time, both Afghans and foreigners. I'm always curious to hear them, and always amazed.
It seems that nobody really liked the Taliban. The one
advantage of their dictatorship was that you were relatively
safe – but safe to do what, given that practically everything
was forbidden? The only people who really benefited were the
lorry drivers, who were free to run from India to Iran. Come
on, nobody likes to be whipped at the slightest infringement
of the rules. Christian tells us about the time the Afghans in
his office rushed to him and begged him to call a work meeting: they all sat down in a circle as if they'd all been having a
discussion and taking notes for a while. At that moment the
Taliban guards burst in to check if everyone was praying
according to the rules. The employees excused themselves on
the grounds that their boss had called a very important meeting, they would pray soon, once the meeting was over, and this
time they were let off the hook. Otherwise, it would have been
lashes for everybody.
    People get tired of lashes.

Before going to sleep, I stick the handle of the toothbrush in
my throat and vomit up my dinner.

18th July. Kandahar airport. Security checks. The soldiers order us off the minibus. The dogs arrive to sniff out explosives. I thought they were pure Alsatians, but in fact they're mongrels, long and low with straight ears. They smell the seats, in front of the engine and underneath. They manage to sniff the petrol tank by standing up on their hind legs. Their trainers are massively built soldiers, human cubes. They allow us back on board but only to zigzag another twenty metres between the cement barriers, after which we have to get out again and walk along a trench lined on both sides by very sharp barbed wire, with spines like tiny two-edged axes. The men are carefully frisked, then we have to wait for a woman soldier to arrive to body-search the four female passengers. She, too, is well-built and blank-faced. The thick strap keeping her holster in place accentuates the enormous girth of her thigh. She frisks the women more thoroughly than we were frisked. She uses both the palm and the back of her hands. I assume at first that she's using the back of her hand to be more discreet when feeling the passengers' breasts and genitals, but she does the same to feel their backs. At last we're allowed back in our vehicles, and slowly, like cable cars in a theme park, we advance into Kandahar airport.

19th July. In Kabul, at the house of friends, I stay behind after dinner to watch Disney's *Jungle Book*. I hum the Italian version of the song *The Bare Necessities* to myself.

(From TDH survey on street children of Kabul)
There are about 50,000 street children in Kabul. Eight out of ten are boys. About half are between twelve and fourteen years old. At that age, a boy is considered an adult and capable of looking after himself. The girls are usually between eight and ten. Above that, they would not be allowed out.

Contrary to what many might suppose, these children are not orphans, except in very rare cases. Almost all of them have families, and indeed it is their families (generally they have between four and seven siblings) who depend on their working in the street. They earn up to a dollar a day. Cigarette sellers and drink sellers earn more: as much as a dollar and a half.

Almost all work seven days a week and more than eight hours a day. The girls work less because they are not allowed to stay in the street until evening. They collect firewood and sweep refuse. They do not usually work as vendors, in order to avoid contact with males. It has been assumed (I don't know by whom) that the children are happy to work, as it gives them the freedom to go around the city as they please. Wrong: they hate working, they find it difficult and dangerous. It might also be supposed that they are all illiterate. Wrong again: 60% have been to school and 30% are still going, which for Afghanistan is somewhat above average.

To sum up, then: street children in Kabul have families, support them with their work, have an education, and earn as much as adults.

A survey carried out six years ago came up with almost the same findings. This is a relatively stable class, a social institution.

One child out of ten is sick. What they want more than anything else is to play.

Bettina and Jeddy

For a month now, I've been trying in vain to organise a mission to Ghazni. It's only three hours' drive from Kabul. There are two very good officers there, Bettina and Jeddy. Jeddy is the one who was shot at on the way to Kabul: one of the tyres of his jeep was hit. But first the road is closed for security reasons, the usual kind – tribal clashes, rockets, looting, etc. Then I have to go to Kandahar, and you can't travel between Kandahar and Ghazni (the Americans are bombing in that area). Finally, two missions from Kabul to Ghazni and back have already been approved, one of six days (too long for me, unfortunately), the other of twenty-four hours (useless) and there's no way I can set up a third. I don't have much time left to finish my report on the nomads, I have to choose, so I choose to go to Herat by plane. Preparing a mission is more stressful than actually doing it. You spend hours moving between the radio room, sending messages and getting only whistles and disturbance in reply, the security room, checking to see if the signed permits have come back, and the prefab, where flights are booked and names are written up on the whiteboard and rubbed out as they go along. You never know the time of your flight. You can get to Herat all right: the problem comes when you try to get away. Flights are often cancelled, or else you are 'cancelled' at the last moment to make way for some VIP. I know people who've tried to leave Herat three or four times without being able to get on a plane. Getting from Herat to Kabul by car is out of the question, even for matters of life and death. If I miss the Saturday return flight I'm screwed. That's why I'm forced to fight for a place on Wednesday. But that means I'll only be in Herat for two days, or rather a day and a half. Doing what? And how can I ask for the security clearance for my missions, which requires 48 hours' notice? That means I'll get clearance to leave for my missions outside Herat the same day I'm supposed to be coming back to Kabul... You can't email to Herat, there's no telephone line even now, and I don't have a satellite phone to get in touch with them. I ask in administration if they'll give me one for a couple of days while I'm there, just as a loan, but they turn me down. Maybe I should have insisted more, then they wouldn't have said no.

It seems every Tom, Dick and Harry's got a satellite phone except me. I've never even had the Ericsson everyone's been using in the past few months to phone home. I haven't made a single private call, damn it, while there are people who...

(These reactions not only show that there are some real difficulties, but also that the stress has reached danger point. But foolishly I think: I don't have long...)

To date, 1,316,000 Afghans have been repatriated with the help of the UNHCR. 1,200,000 from Pakistan, about 100,000 from Iran. Another 200,000 have returned under their own steam. More than half a million in the province of Kabul alone. The UNHCR had anticipated that 1,200,000 people would return by the end of the year: a figure that was reached and surpassed in only fifteen weeks. The anticipated figure has therefore been increased to about two million returnees during 2002.

Mission to Herat, 22nd-24th July
Kabul airport, waiting for the flight to Herat. A frustrating day yesterday, doing exhaustingly trivial things: forms, permits, visas, tidying, plans, reports. I met an Afghan girl who learned Italian as a child from De Gregori[13] records. Her father, a politician, bought them for her when he went to Italy to meet Aldo Moro. Who is Aldo Moro? 'An Italian statesman kidnapped and killed by the Red Brigades.' I feel infinitely tired. I keep having to take deep breaths. I'm losing blood from my nose and my arse.

Herat, a clean, orderly city, very strong wind and blue sky. Visit to the Shaiday camp. It's difficult to stand and walk in the wind. Talk to old Kuchis in the mosque. Patches of light in the darkness. Crowds outside, a rarefied atmosphere inside. Then we talk to the women, who screech like eagles. Eggs: never eaten them. Sugar: they don't even know what it tastes like. Meat: a few say they ate some three or four months ago. Then the magical sight of the Friday mosque (a big complex I can't begin to describe) at sunset. A huge, silent marvel. An enchanted hour in the enclosure. It's the first time something man-made has impressed me here. Man-made, even if not made for man. Inside, a long unrolled carpet that cuts the space in half. Old men squat or kneel on it. Visible from close range, arabesques on the walls. On the other side of the street, I buy some blue glasses, a silk shawl, then two identical little rings, for which I offer three dollars, but he doesn't have change for a five-dollar bill, so I have to take a third little ring, exactly the same as the other two. Now I have three identical rings, like the story from the *Decameron*.

The Shaiday camp (10 km south of Herat, opened in 1996) has a population of 21,563 (estimate of 1st July 2002). They live in mud houses. We visit and interview a group representing about 450 Kuchi families. 300 come from the village of Chepchel, in Murghab district, Badghis province. Another 150 are from Gormash, also in Badghis province. They are all Pashtun. They arrived at Shaiday two years ago. When they were still leading a normal nomadic life, they would spend at least two summer months in Ghor and six months in Badghis during the cold season. Their migration would take between twenty and forty days.

Their way of life was shattered by violence and looting, the work of Uzbeki militias generally thought to owe allegiance to General Malik. The soldiers plundered all their possessions and all the flocks. At the moment, none of them own a single animal. At one time, every family owned a minimum of between ten and a hundred sheep, but there were some who owned as many as 1,400. At Shaiday they live in mud houses which they built using materials (wooden beams, etc.) supplied by DACAAR. Out of 450 families, 100 are registered with IOM for transport to Chepchel. The convoy is leaving next week. Only ten people in the community have an income from casual work. They earn about 30,000 afghans a day: about a dollar.

The Kuchis used to cultivate the land where possible and the women wove carpets, but in their present state they have neither wool nor looms. The collecting of firewood is exclusively for personal use. While there are no worries about the safety of their place of origin (no minefields, not even any persecution from other ethnic groups), the main reason not to return there is the lack of drinking water (there are no wells in Chepchel) as well as the lack of work and schools.

There used to be a UNICEF school in the camp, but it was closed when the bombing campaign against the Taliban started. Which means that none of the children have been to school this year.

Next, we interview a group of some twenty women and girls about living conditions in the camp. One small source of income is spinning wool. Both the wool and the little looms are supplied by the employers, who pay 40,000 afghans for every four kilos of spun wool. As it takes four days to spin four kilos, the workers receive on average 10,000 afghans (thirty cents) a day.

Meals consist of bread and green tea. Those who have some income eat meat once every three months. The families have between six and ten children. The Kuchi women's main requirements are, in order of priority: food, lodging, and shoes for the children.

23rd July, morning in the Maslakh camps.
A whole morning asking questions, I ask about three hundred questions – did they, do you, would you, would they, should he, what if, how many more, how much?

Maslakh has been in existence since 1999. Up to 120,000 people have lived here, but currently there are half that number. Most come from the provinces of Ghor, Faryab, Badghis and Herat. Their problems? Lack of personal safety, lack of drinking water, they have no tools to work the land, they don't have seeds, they don't have land, there's no work, they don't have livestock, they have lots of debts.

Hard work. We leave Maslakh and carry on towards Iran. The villages from here to the border are numbered in sequence. I call the base to ask how much further I can go without violating security regulations.

On the way back, I ask the driver to pass between the immense minarets of Herat. Giants visible from a long way away, some leaning like the Tower of Pisa. They've been stripped bare, and look like factory chimneys, but traces of the glossy tiles with which they used to be covered can still be seen. Fantastic. Something out of myth. Rising from the horizontal landscape of the city.

Problem
An unemployed Kuchi goes to the city and manages to wangle a day's work as a labourer. At the end of the day he gets paid 50,000 afghans, the equivalent of two dollars. He's spent 10,000 on getting to the city and he spends the same amount on getting back to the camp, so he still has 30,000 left.

The next day he goes back to Herat, but isn't as lucky as he was yesterday and can't find work. Transport – sharing a minibus with thirty others – still costs him 20,000 afghans. Of the money he earned on the first day he now has only 10,000 afghans in his pocket.

So the third day he decides not to go back to the city because if he's unlucky enough not to find work, he'll have spent another 20,000 afghans and be 10,000 down.

Question: was he right to stay in the camp or should he have risked it?

About ten kilometres west of Maslakh, we visit the village of Nawabat, where a community of Kuchis from the province of Farah settled in 1971 after a particularly bad drought. This is a good example of nomads who've become sedentary. At that time there were twenty families, now there are fifty. They have no title deeds to the land where they've built their houses. The young men graze their sheep on the nearby mountains, sleeping at most two nights away from home. At the market they exchange the wool for other products: sugar, oil, sweets. Milk and other dairy products are for domestic use. A certain amount of wool and cheese is given as charity to the poor in Maslakh camp, in accordance with the Koranic principle of zakat. They're certainly not thinking of migrating again – but if they had camels, they might consider the idea of resuming their nomadic life, why not? 'Life is unpredictable, it can always change,' says a little old man, who's had four-teen children in his life. Some work as labourers, repairing the road that leads to the Iranian border, others as farm hands during the wheat harvest. The older ones miss the nomadic life. Each family has on average five or six sheep. To start migrating again, they'd need, let's say, a couple of donkeys, three camels, and at least thirty sheep.

None of the children go to school (the nearest is two hours' walk). Only two people in the village can read.

A year-old sheep they sell for fifteen dollars, a lamb for ten.

The well-off families eat meat once a week, the poorer ones once a month. The staple food is poor-quality rice. They never eat vegetables.

24th July. The plane for Kabul was supposed to leave at ten, but it hasn't arrived. Another plane lands instead, carrying an American big shot, General McNeill. An orderly is there to welcome him with a line of very picturesque soldiers carrying the biggest sub-machine guns I've ever seen. They can barely wield them. Our plane seems to have been cancelled. There's no trace of it. It turns out it never left Kabul. One plane does appear on the runway, but it's going to Islamabad in Pakistan and doesn't have permission to land in Kabul. To calm the protests, the pilots say they'll try and ask for it during the flight. But the plane can only take ten passengers out of the eighteen on the list. Some of them claim to have absolute priority and say they must leave at all costs, even if it's by no means certain they'll be able to land in Kabul. Herat airport is too small to have a waiting room. Passengers have to sit on the ground. I lean against the low wall of the runway, in the sun, and read how the Romans took Veio, and a few pages later, the sack of Rome, but when I get to the episode of the geese of the Capitol, sweat drips onto the book. People run past towards the aircraft. I don't have my passport with me: it's at the Pakistani embassy in Kabul for the visa to be renewed. I don't have a diplomatic pass, either. If I landed in

Pakistan without papers I'd have my work cut out trying to prove I arrived by mistake. I try to stay calm and think of other things, but this mixture of anxiety and indifference produces a kind of hysterical emptiness. I can't move a muscle. And yet it's vital that I get on that plane. There's a crowd of people under the wings, and nobody's standing on ceremony. I'm the last passenger on the list to be called and put on the plane, all the names after mine have been crossed off, decimated. The other Italian has to stay behind, while I leave. I don't have long now, I murmur under my breath, I don't have long. So we travel through the clouds, not knowing where we're heading or where we'll land.

I have a lot of reports to write this afternoon. My final paper on the plight of the wretched Kuchis. Bullet points for specific initiatives to be taken. Under the flesh, the nerves. Under the nerves, the bone. I continue to bleed from top and bottom. Herat had a powerful effect on me: the light, the mosques, the tree-lined streets, the well-behaved crowds. Maybe the closeness to Persia. Maybe the dictatorship of Ismail Khan, financed by customs duties. The lorries pay between 200 and 1,000 dollars to cross the border. Plus all the cars newly arrived from Dubai. I read in an article by Ahmed Rashid (the author of *Taliban*) that Khan collects eighty million dollars a year in taxes on all goods, legal and illegal, crossing to and from Iran and Turkmenistan. At least some of the money is visibly reinvested in the city, which is orderly, clean, leafy.

Ismail Khan spent a year chained to a wall in a Taliban prison. This seems to have made him an even stricter and more devout Muslim.

We're landing. Where? In Kabul? As the plane loses altitude and we emerge from the clouds, we see the carcasses beside the runway.

Local colour
'A Kuchi caravan in motion is a beautiful sight. Big furry camels climb the rocky dunes followed by donkeys, horses, sheep, goats and fierce-looking sheepdogs. In the midst of their animals, the Kuchis walk proudly, tall and thin, valiant looking, often with rifles over their shoulders...' *(The Kabul Times, 23rd July)*

Humbug. I have to describe half a million people dying of starvation. That's not all: I have to suggest urgent counter-measures.

Dear Edoardo, the following is the translation of the three sentences. I am glad that you never have to use them. I hope that your experience in Afghanistan help you to earn a new perspective on life and on the human person who has to live it. In a few years I will be happy if I could see you in a different Afghanistan. Au revoir.

Mohammad

Dari
MAN BA MILALI MUTAHEED KAR MIKUNAM
MAN ADAMI KHUB ASTAM
RAHM KUNID MARA NA KUSHID

Pashto
ZA DA MULGARO MILATU SARA KAR KAWAM
ZA XA SARAI YEM
RAHM WAKREE MA MA WAZNEE

English
I WORK FOR THE UNITED NATIONS
I AM A GOOD MAN
PLEASE DO NOT KILL ME

I'm really not with it any more. I'm sick in the head. My farewell to Afghanistan (I realise now) will be arid, painful, congested. I can't breathe. I have to take gulps of air. I cry constantly. News from Kandahar: the Pearl of the South had a car accident and broke her arm. Chris was with her, and broke his pelvis and knees. It was just three days before he was due to go back to Switzerland to meet his son. I'm stunned by the news. They've been taken to hospital in Kandahar but a flight is being arranged to move them to Islamabad. Chris needs an operation, the kind of operation where if it goes wrong, you're crippled for life. The news is a real whack in the face. I feel a weight on my chest. I remember stagnant evenings in Kandahar talking to Chris. The Pearl vomiting. Me vomiting. The fan blades whirling round.

A message reaches me from Milan that my friend, the writer Ottiero Ottieri, is dead. And I'm here in Kabul. I cry in front of my computer. After a while a girl comes in from the next room, to find out what all the sobbing is about.

27th July. I'm going to Peshawar in Pakistan, to see the camps where a million Afghan refugees are still living. That's where the circle has to end, in the place where it all starts. I'll be going by car. No, I'm not going, the news comes like a bolt from the blue: the border with Pakistan has been closed because of clashes. It had to happen today of all days. I hand in my report on the plight of the Kuchis. I kiss it first. Let's hope it helps.

28th July. I'm not going. I'm going. No, too risky. If they close the border again, I'll be stuck in Jalalabad (a fucking stupid place in the tribal area) and won't get to Islamabad for the flight home. But to hell with it, I have to take the risk, I'm going. Wait for me, I run to the guest house to get my cases, I couldn't sleep so I did my packing during the night. I ask Waisuddin to drive me there immediately. My mouth is dry. I get back with my bags just in time to join the mission. I drink all through the journey. I feel dazed.

And at last I see what's behind those walls of rock that

I looked at from the encashment centre of Pul-i-Charkhi back in April, cut through by the mysterious road that leads to Pakistan. The bottleneck from which hundreds and thousands of lorries loaded with refugees have emerged: our people, the people I'm here for. *Was* here for.

There's a gorge... a track clambering up between the precipices... which sinks as it climbs...

I'm sorry, it's indescribable. All I can say is that there are two overturned lorries in the bottleneck between the mountains, near the wall of rock, not on the side where the ravine is.

Again, I feel a lump in my throat.

Sorubi, a good place for ambushes, ideal country for bandits (like Itri – Fra Diavolo's cove[14]). It's here that Maria Grazia Cutuli was killed. It's here that Commander Zardat unleashed Sag, the Dog.

'Go on, Dog, bite!' And Dog killed.

At last we meet up with the cars from the joint mission, which have arrived from Jalalabad to exchange passengers.

It's my last chance, there's still time to turn back if I stay in the car from Kabul. From this point, there's another four hours of dirt road, and then the dead end of Jalalabad if the border is closed.

Enough of this. I transfer my things to the other vehicle.

Last goodbyes to Sabur. In the car, trying to overcome the tension of parting with idle chatter, I told him I could see his first white hairs. He's a wise man now. He's thirty-three years old. We hug each other tight. He's crying behind his big sunglasses.

From here on, it's downhill all the way, down, down, down. Through incredible landscapes.

Next to me is an Englishwoman whose companion was killed in an ambush between Jalalabad and the Pakistani border. At that time they called them 'the Arabs', they didn't yet bear the political labels they have now. She'll go back to the scene of the killing tomorrow.

An hour later, a radio message informs us that the border with Pakistan has been reopened.

In Jalalabad, I swim in the dark sulphurous water of the pool, whose bottom is scraped. I rest on the edge. Only my eyes out of the water. I don't recognise Vicky, who's swimming towards me. It's almost night. You can feel the steam of India. The forests.

Driving to the border at Torkham, early in the morning. Again patches of desert. They confirm that the border is open. A car from Peshawar is already waiting for us. There'll be another exchange of passengers. They call us over the radio. Devastated villages, children sliding over the bodies of overturned tanks, goodbye to all that. No, goodbye is a word that has to be spoken or thought and I'm not thinking anything. I'm detaching myself like the backing from a sticker, at first it's hard to get hold of with your nails and then it comes off easily. There'll be work to do later, and I'll do it feverishly, like an automaton, but now I'm only a passenger, I have my suitcase with smuggled carpets inside. My mind empties. The border is pure chaos. The lorries wait for hours. Crowds gesticulating, but I hear nothing. I'm too exhausted to feel any emotion. While negotiations go on to cross the border and transfer to the Pakistani car, they offer me drinks, or rather they force drinks on me, so I drink, sweating through every pore: a cup of green tea, a Pepsi, a cup of Pakistani tea with milk, another cup of green tea, another Pepsi I can't finish. One of the border officials is keen for me to learn his name: Parah, it means 'spring'. Funny, for a man. Do you remember my name? Oh, yes. Parah. That's right. I sweat away my emotions. The hairpin bends of the Khyber Pass, (...all the armies that have tried to cross it... for hundreds and thousands of years... the trips to India...) which look like a picture postcard except for the lack of snow. I'd like to take a photo here, the last place from which the land of the Afghans can be seen, but the soldiers on top of the pass don't allow me to.

When I arrive in Peshawar about two, my escort can't believe that I really want to visit the refugee camps, but I do, I want to go straight there, without even having a cup of tea or a Pepsi.

UNHCR

The Office of the United Nations High Commissioner for Refugees (UNHCR) was established on 14th December 1950 by the United Nations General Assembly. The agency is mandated to lead and coordinate international action to protect refugees and resolve refugee problems worldwide. Its primary purpose is to safeguard the rights and wellbeing of refugees. It strives to ensure that everyone can exercise the right to seek asylum and find safe refuge in another state, with the option to return home voluntarily, integrate locally or to resettle in a third country. In more than five decades, the agency has helped an estimated 50 million people restart their lives. Today, a staff of around 5,000 people in more than 120 countries continues to help an estimated 19.8 million persons.

Notes

1. A reference to the novel *Zeno's Conscience* (1923) by Italo Svevo (Ettore Schmitz, 1861–1928), whose main protagonist, Zeno Cosini, is a hardcore nicotine addict who cannot quit smoking.

2. The story alluded to is included in the collection *Twenty-three Days in the City of Alba* (1952) by the Italian novelist Beppe Fenoglio (1922–1963).

3. The actor is not Alberto Sordi (1920–2003) but Ugo Tognazzi (1922–1990), in *Il federale* (The Federal Officer, 1961), a film directed by Luciano Salce (1922–1989).

4. Raf (Raffaele Riefoli, b. 1959) is a famous Italian pop singer and songwriter, Articolo 31 are a popular hip-hop band.

5. Title of a poem by Giacomo Leopardi (1798–1837).

6. Reference to the sonnet *Tanto gentile e tanto onesta pare* (My lady shows such gentle dignity) from *New Life* (c. 1290) by Dante Alighieri (1265–1321).

7. Pinocchio and Lucignolo are two characters from the children's novel *The Adventures of Pinocchio* (1883) by Carlo Collodi (Carlo Lorenzini, 1826–1890), which inspired a famous Disney cartoon movie.

8. Irpinia is a mountainous region in southern Italy (Campania district) which was hit by a major earthquake on 23rd November 1980. The reconstruction of the Irpinia villages after the earthquake was characterised by political bribes and bogus funding applications.

9. *Divorce Italian Style* (1961) and *Seduced and Abandoned* (1964) are two movies directed by Pietro Germi (1914–1974).

10. Ape ('Bee') is a small three-wheeled Piaggio vehicle very common in Italy. Viareggio, a riverside town in Tuscany, is the venue of a famous carnival.

11. 'I want to go home / where's my house?' From the song *Questa è la mia casa* (This is my house) by Jovanotti (Lorenzo Cherubini, b. 1966).

12. 'What keeps mankind alive', a ballad from *The Threepenny Opera* (1928), Act 2 finale, text by Bertolt Brecht (1898–1956), music by Kurt Weill (1900–1950).

13. Francesco De Gregori (b. 1951) is an Italian singer and songwriter.

14. Itri is a small town south of Rome, site of an impressive medieval castle and the birthplace of Michele Pezza (alias Fra Diavolo, or 'Brother Devil', 1771–1806), an infamous brigand who fought against the French army in southern Italy.